THE STORM SEASON

THE
STORM
SEASON

WILLIAM HAUPTMAN

BANTAM BOOKS

NEW YORK   TORONTO   LONDON   SYDNEY   AUCKLAND

THE STORM SEASON
A Bantam Book / February 1992

Grateful acknowledgment is made for permission to reprint the following:

Excerpt from "Roly Poly," written by Fred Rose. Copyright © 1946 renewed 1974 by Milene Music, Inc. (ASCAP) Used by permission/International Copyright Secured/All Rights Reserved.

Excerpt from "Bob Wills Is Still the King," written by Waylon Jennings. Copyright © 1974 Songs of Polygram International, Inc.

LIBRARY OF CONGRESS CATALOGING-IN-PUBLICATION DATA
Hauptman, William
The storm season / by William Hauptman.
p.   cm.
ISBN 0-553-08017-2
I. Title
PS3558.A758S76   1992
813'.54—dc20   91-23056
                                                               CIP

Published simultaneously in the United States and Canada

PRINTED IN THE UNITED STATES OF AMERICA

BVG   0   9   8   7   6   5   4   3   2   1

FOR MY BROTHER TOM

"In the dry places, men begin to dream."
—WRIGHT MORRIS, *The Works of Love*

This novel is a work of the imagination, and the characters are entirely fictional. At times, I have knowingly altered the terrain and recent history of North Texas. I would like to thank Gloria Loomis, Deborah Futter, Rob Weisbach, and above all my wife Marjorie for their assistance and encouragement.

SUNSHINE HILL

B y the time he was four, Burl knew his father was a little bad, and his mother very good. Burl took some pleasure in being both. With his mother, he went to Indian Heights Christian Church, while his father and his big brother Coy stayed at home and slept. The sermons were long, the air heavy with the smell of hymnals. Burl stared at his shoes, at the smooth polished pine of the pew in front of him, seeing faces in the blond grain. Hot tingles crept through his legs, but he sat as still as he could to please his mother.

With his father, he sometimes pissed outside in the backyard at night instead of going to the bathroom. His father said dogs and men got a certain pleasure out of it, and Burl could see, even at the age of four, that he was right. That was one of his favorite moments: pissing under the stars, while his father pointed out the Big Dipper. Another was looking at the Luger pistol his father had taken from a Nazi soldier. Then his father would tell him stories of when he'd gone to Europe to kick Adolf Hitler's butt. Burl, who had seen pictures of Adolf Hitler, liked to imagine his father kicking him around a boxing ring, while a crowd of soldiers cheered.

Before he learned how to unlock the gate, Burl couldn't leave the yard, and he spent his days playing in the cool dirt by the back step. Later, he was allowed to leave the yard, but not the block. At the end of the street was the Catholic cemetery, its gate topped with angels of black cast iron. Beyond that was the edge of Nortex, and beyond that, the rest of the world. Sometimes Burl stood on that corner and watched his big brother Coy disappear, when he went off to do whatever older boys did—play with matches, Burl supposed. The street was empty as a dry creekbed, but his mother had told him the moment he tried to cross it, a car would appear and run him down.

Burl's father, Willie Drennan, was an important man. Before Burl was born, he had found oil, and before that, he had played football for Nortex High, on a famous team sportswriters had called the Little Iron Men. He owned something called the Drennan Drilling Company. Sometimes he put on a suit and took Burl downtown, where he got a haircut at the Kemp Hotel barbershop, then went to see his friends, other important men who had offices in the Petroleum Building. Sometimes they stayed to see a movie and didn't come out until after dark. At night, downtown Nortex seemed important, too, as big and dark and dangerous as New York or Chicago.

But Burl didn't really know what his father did until the day his mother took him out to a roaring oil rig in a field. One of the men came walking toward the car, wearing a steel helmet and filthy coveralls. Not until he spoke did Burl recognize his father, moving with a strange, purposeful energy. He took Burl's hand, and they entered a pool of noise, so loud, so terrifying that Burl felt he had lost his body and was floating. At the top of the steel steps, he glimpsed the spinning drill pipe at the dangerous heart of things.

His father had his secrets, which he shared only with Burl. One of these secrets was his sadness. When Burl started Alamo Elementary, his father, who had so much money he didn't have to go to work, was sometimes waiting for him after school. Burl got in the car, and they drove out to the ruins of the old Magnolia Refinery, on Sunshine Hill.

Willie Drennan had been born there, in the year they drilled Magnolia Number One, and fifteen thousand men had come to Nortex, all hoping to get rich. Willie's mother was a Burkburnett girl, his father a driller from Houston who claimed to have fought in the Argonne. There were a dozen little boom towns springing up along the Red River, and they moved from one to another. They lived in Newtown, Stringtown, Petrolia, and Whizzbang—tent cities in a forest of wooden derricks, where a glass of clean drinking water cost ten cents. Willie's first memory was of a fire that burned for three days, destroying a good part of the Texas Wonder Pool. He thought the whole world was burning up.

Then Willie's father departed. Two years later, in 1920, he sent Willie's mother a postcard from Mexico City, saying he had remarried but hoped she would forgive him. He was thinking about heading down to South America. There were supposed to be some new fields opening up down there.

His mother took a job cooking at a café, and they lived in a tarpaper shack behind the Magnolia Refinery. In the fall, there were Blue Northers, and little jets of cold air came through the walls. In the spring, there were dust storms. The fine grit got into everything. Willie's mother tied a damp cloth around his face and wouldn't let him go outside. When he looked through the window he could see her at the well, pumping hard, the wind blowing her long hair. At night, she read to him by the light of a kerosene lamp. On the wall was a calendar with an illustration by Maxfield Parrish, which he stared at until he fell asleep—two children by a lake at sunrise, under a sky of liquid blue.

Willie grew up along with Nortex, played on the first football team to win a state championship. The month after he graduated from high school, his mother died of a heart attack and left him all alone in the world. He went on to do other things: became a tool-pusher, joined the army, fought in the Battle of the Bulge, and lost two toes to frostbite. Now Nortex was a big city, and the old wooden derricks had rotted where they stood. Only the storage tanks of the Old Magnolia Refinery were left, great rusted steel globes in a field of sunflowers.

But he still liked to go there and talk about his childhood, when he had found fossils along the Red River. "I wanted to be a geologist," he told Burl. "I might have, too, if the war hadn't come along. I saw myself going up to Alaska and making a big discovery. I thought it must look like the picture on the calendar—big lakes, golden mountains, the sky blue." It was hard for Burl to believe his father had ever been a boy. "No, it's true," his father insisted. "When I was your age, I used to sit right here and dream of getting out of this town someday."

Then he took another drink from the bottle he kept under the seat of the car. His medicine, he called it, and for a long time Burl thought that was what it was—some kind of cough syrup.

Burl started school. His teacher moved the hands of a cardboard clock, showing him how time fell into seconds, minutes, hours. The last hour before the bell rang, he noticed, was the longest of the day. He met a boy named Jed, and they explored the Catholic cemetery. At its center was a mound of cemented stones, topped with a blackened statue of Jesus on the Cross. The stones were hot and covered with scorpions, but they played there anyway.

At Christmas, the astronauts orbited the moon and read the Bible to people back on earth. Burl decided he was going to the moon himself someday. When they went downtown at night, he noticed how the moon seemed to follow them, rolling along between the lighted buildings. At night, downtown Nortex still seemed as big as New York or Chicago. But even then Burl had begun to wonder why more people didn't know about Nortex. Walter Cronkite had never once mentioned it on the national news.

One day Burl discovered he could read, found his eyes flowing effortlessly down the pages of a novel called *Tomorrow,* in one of his mother's *Reader's Digest Condensed Books.* He had opened it to look at a picture of a Russian plane with a big red star dropping an atomic bomb on an American City. The first thing he remembered seeing on television was an atomic bomb exploding. Something about the way the fireball expanded fascinated him. Then he read an article in the paper that said Nortex was number eight on Russia's Nuclear Hit List.

Fear overwhelmed him. For three days, he couldn't eat. There might be some warning, and there might not—that was the horrible thing about it. He sat on his bed, waiting for the flash that might come tomorrow, or a year from now, or the moment he fell asleep.

"You've got to get over this, son," his father said, when he finally confessed what was wrong. "Don't you want to be a little man?"

He did. But how, he asked them, could they not think of it every moment of the day?

"There's no sense in worrying about things you can't do anything about," his father said. "Think about good things instead, like how you're going to grow up and play football."

They were lying. He had noticed how quiet they got when they saw one explode, or heard the tone on the radio when there was a test of the Emergency Broadcasting Network. But in time he did manage to forget about it. He even became proud of the fact that there were Atlas missile silos just north of town, that the bombers at the air force base carried hydrogen bombs.

Burl found it harder to be good for his mother. He stole matches and, once, money from her purse to buy a comic book. Worst of all, he told her church made him sick to his stomach so he wouldn't have to go anymore. His father, who belonged to something called the Rosicrucian Society and believed in the theory of reincarnation, thought that was fine. "What difference does it make?" he said. "All preachers are fools."

This made his mother angry. When she was a little girl, she told Burl, she had learned there was a God, and he had a way of punishing people who did wrong.

Burl's mother had been born Doris Cade, on a farm ten miles north of Arapaho, Oklahoma. She had loved that farm and often told Burl stories about growing up there, like the time she found the little pink baby mice in the corncrib and brought them into the house on a napkin. But times were hard and her father was worried: the Depression, he said, was God's way of punishing this country for going off the gold standard and repealing Prohibition.

One morning Doris woke and saw a brown wall of dust rolling down on them. The sun blew out like a candle, and it stayed dark for three days. Her father compared it to the seven plagues of Egypt in the Book of Exodus. They held on for another year, but it was a dry summer and the corn burned up. They sold out and they moved to Arapaho, where he had a stroke and fell down dead on the floor of the hardware store.

Doris could never remember deciding to marry Willie, whom she met in Lawton when he was stationed at Fort Sill. At first, she didn't even like him. He was short and cocky, like Mickey Rooney, and he didn't seem to know his red hair stood up like the bristles of a toothbrush. But he was a good dancer, light on his feet. He was sent to California for six months and wrote her wonderful letters. He came back a sergeant, told her he was shipping out for Europe, and they were married the next day by a justice of the peace. "You made up your mind fast in those days," she told Burl.

Willie didn't want to go back to Nortex after the war, so they lived all over the Panhandle. They tried to have children but couldn't, and the doctor who examined Doris told her that her chances were next to nothing. But God could work miracles, too: when they were living in Benjamin, she found out she was pregnant with Coy. They moved back to Nortex, bought the house, and Willie went to work for his old high school buddy, George Staples.

Her father had told her Nortex was a sinful town, like Sodom and Gomorrah, but Doris found she loved it. Some of the wildcatters who made their fortunes in the Boom had stayed on and hired architects to build them homes as fine as any in Dallas or Houston around the Nortex Country Club. At Christmas, their lawns were covered with decorations, a Nortex tradition the papers called the Festival of Lights.

On Christmas Eve, Burl and his parents, along with everyone else in Nortex, drove out to see them. They joined the line of cars moving around Colonel Blake's home. Colonel Blake had more money than anyone else in Nortex, and more decorations. There was a Nativity, with the Star of Bethlehem shining down on the Baby Jesus on his crib, even a mechanical Santa bobbing up and down in the chimney, while loudspeakers played "It Came Upon a Midnight Clear."

"This is so lovely," Doris always said. "This is the most beautiful thing about Nortex."

Willie, who remembered shining Colonel Blake's shoes in the lobby of the Kemp Hotel, said, "Hell, honey. He's just trying to show us he's got more money than the rest of us."

"Don't say that," Doris said. "He does it for the poor children who don't have Christmas trees of their own."

"We're not children," Willie said. "And we're not poor."

Burl's mother loved his father, but she had no patience with his strange ideas. One morning, he told them he had left his body the night before and floated around the backyard at the end of a silver cord.

"Your father always wanted to fly," Doris told Burl when they were alone. "It broke his heart when he couldn't get into the air corps. When I was a little girl, I thought I could fly too. I was so sure of it, I closed my eyes and jumped out of the hayloft one day. It felt so wonderful, I thought I was really doing it, until I hit the ground." She smiled. "It's a wonder I wasn't killed."

It had been a lesson of sorts. A lot of her stories were lessons. Burl didn't tell her that he sometimes flew around the block at night, in his dreams.

Burl's father was making more money than ever. At the last game of the year, when the old football players were asked to come down on the field for the Pledge of Allegiance, his father got the biggest hand of all. He was so popular, some people were saying he should run for mayor.

But Burl sensed his father was troubled. They still went downtown sometimes, but now they went to the Denver Cafe & Domino Parlor, where they sat at the bar with the roughnecks. Burl ordered soda pop, and his father sipped a bourbon called Ancient Age.

"I used to come here when I was a boy," he told Burl, "to shine shoes and listen to the old cowboys tell stories. One of them, old Jake Slaughter, told me an interesting thing. A story I've never forgotten."

His father smiled at him. A dog slept in the shaft of sunlight falling through the big front window.

"After the Comanche surrendered," he said, "Jake made friends with an old brave called Talks In His Sleep. He told Jake there was a place out in the Medicine Mounds where you could have a vision of the story of the world. So one day they rode out there. On top of one of the mounds, there was a circle of stones. When it got dark, Talks In His Sleep built a fire and sang songs. Then Jake saw this country the way it was before the white man came. There were buffalo ten feet high, and giant armadillos, and up north he could see elephants with shaggy coats, like bears. He saw volcanoes spouting fire, and rivers of ice, and a lot more he couldn't even describe. And you know something? I found out later that's just the way this country was, back in the Ice Age."

It was the best story Burl had ever heard. "Let's go find that place," he said. "Maybe it's still there."

"I did once," his father said sadly. "Then I lost it again. But that's another story. I'll tell you that one when you get a little older."

At night, Burl woke and heard his parents shouting in the kitchen, arguing about money. It seemed like the more money he made, the sadder and angrier his father got. The whole world was changing. Burl thought this had something to do with the weather. His father said the atom bombs had made it worse.

That was also the year they started broadcasting tornado alerts. There were bulletins on television all day. Around three or four o'clock, big thunderheads boiled up in the west. Then it got dark as night, and they blew the siren atop the municipal water tower. Burl learned three tornadoes had struck Nortex before he was born. Two people on their block had storm shelters. Burl wanted to get one, too, but his father reminded him there was no sense in worrying about things you could do nothing about.

One night they watched a movie on television, *The Wizard of Oz*, which his father said he would like. The tornado slid toward the farmhouse like a vacuum cleaner hose, sucking it up into the blurred gray interior of the funnel. Dorothy looked out the window and saw a rooster float by, two men in a rowboat, then a woman on a bicycle who turned into a witch on a broom. Burl got sick to his stomach and, to his father's disappointment, had to go to his room and lie down.

When Burl's father wasn't fighting with their mother, he fought with Coy, who had refused to go out for football and was against the Vietnam War. Coy said if he got his draft notice, he would run off to Canada and smoke marijuana. Burl wondered if Coy was becoming a coward.

Sometimes, their father staged surprise inspections of their room. Burl stood at attention. Coy ignored their father: he lay on his bed, reading *Mad*.

"You think you're better than us," Willie said, holding a pair of Coy's Jockey shorts under his nose. "But to me you're just a slob who can't pick up his dirty underwear."

Anger filled the house like cigarette smoke, making Burl's eyes water. One night he woke to a terrifying blue-white flash of lightning and heard the sirens groan. He ran to the closet, where he sobbed in the dark for an hour until his parents talked him into coming out.

"Goddamnit," Willie said. "This is just like when you were afraid of the atomic bomb. Don't you want to be a little man?"

"I can't," Burl said, shameful fear scalding his throat.

His father wouldn't speak to him for three days. Burl heard him tell his mother if Coy didn't shape up, he was going to send him to military school. Burl was afraid he would do the same to him. He began having a nightmare in which he woke and found the house empty. A terrible silence lay upon everything, which was worse somehow than the silence of an empty house. Drawn to the front window, he looked through the blinds. At first he saw nothing, then a flash of lightning revealed the black pencil of a tornado coming right at him. He dreaded next spring, when another storm season would begin again.

WILLIAM HAUPTMAN

▼ ▼ ▼

As the years went by, Burl's fear of storms changed, became something like anticipation. In the spring, when the days grew longer and warmer, he studied the weather map in the paper, watching the cold fronts march toward them, waiting for the day when the forecast would be for scattered thunderstorms.

By the time he was in the third grade, Burl had discovered boredom. He was the smartest boy at Alamo Elementary and knew things his teacher didn't. He sat in the back of the classroom, so he could think his own thoughts. The hot spring days at the end of the year were the worst, so long he felt like he was walking in his sleep.

But on the days when there was a tornado alert, everything was different.

Burl stared out the classroom windows, watching the sky. Around two o'clock, bright little clouds appeared in the west, racing toward them. At three o'clock, Burl pedaled home on his bicycle as fast as he could and watched the bulletins on television. Then he got Jed and they went to the cemetery, where they played Exploring the Planet Mercury, a world so hot its surface ran with rivers of molten lead. On those days, it always seemed like the best game they had ever played.

And all the while the fast clouds kept going over, throwing the cemetery into shadow. When they did, a silence fell, in which Burl was aware of the sweat cooling on his forehead. The sunlight swept toward them, sharp as the blade of a knife, and they were drenched in heat and glare again.

Then Burl saw what he had known was coming all along—the blue wall of the cold front, rising in the west. Higher and higher it climbed, until it eclipsed the sun and the wind died. It was like night itself rolling down on the town. The whole world to the west faded off into pencil gray. Their parents called them home. More bulletins appeared on the television screen, and lightning flickered to the west. Grown-ups stood out on their porches, wondering how bad it would be. Every moment was important, and everyone was alert.

One afternoon when Burl was in the fourth grade, he stood in the backyard with his father, watching a long blue tube of cloud snaking over the western edge of town. "That looks like a funnel cloud," his father said. "Honey, come out here and take a look at this."

But Doris refused to leave the kitchen, where she was making supper. "Oh, honey," she said, "let's not look for trouble." Burl went to tell Coy, who was lying on his bed, reading *Stranger in a Strange Land.* "Who cares?" he said.

"Forget about Coy," Willie said. "He's nothing but a chicken-shit. Let's drive out and get a closer look at it. You'll come with me, won't you, son?"

Burl's stomach was tingling and he had to pee, but he got in the car and they drove out past the radio station. When they were under the storm, it looked different and the funnel could no longer be seen. His father got out and looked at the clouds, drinking from a half-pint. Then big hailstones began falling. "There goes the paint job," his father said, getting in the car and starting back. Burl thought the worst was over, but when he looked in the mirror he saw the funnel, on the ground now, blue as Scripto ink and right behind them.

"Shit," Willie said, and stepped on the gas. Burl couldn't take his eyes off the funnel: it seemed to pull them, like gravity. It jumped across the road behind them, smashing the Circle Liquor Store: for years, fragments of broken glass glittered there, along the side of the road. Willie pulled over, and they watched it go twisting off, over the mesquite. "Jesus Christ," he said, "did you ever see anything like that? You're all right, aren't you, son? You didn't think I was going to let it get this car, did you? I paid a lot of money for this car. But did you ever see anything like that big black sonofabitch?"

It wasn't the big one everyone had been expecting, but it was big enough—it went on to hit the air force base, where it did a million dollars' worth of damage. Burl and his father brought home a hailstone and cut it open. It was an agate, a fabulous geode from the sky, composed of concentric layers of milky ice. Burl went to sleep that night feeling like a bright light shone through his whole body. The tornado had come, just as he had known it would, but he had faced out his fear and stood his ground.

"You were a little man today," his father told him. It was the proudest day of Burl's life.

When they were thirteen, Jed got a joint from an older boy and they smoked it in the cemetery, where the tombstones hid them from the street. Burl stared at the clouds, at the pissants crawling through the brown cedar needles. His throat tingled, and a question seemed to hover over everything he saw.

When they were fourteen, Jed bought a red Yamaha guitar and a wah wah pedal. In six months, he taught himself how to play all those great Jimi Hendrix riffs. Burl learned the bass, but he could never play like Jed. When they were fifteen, they started their first group. Jed thought they should call themselves the Bizarros, after his favorite comic book character, but Burl, who was doing a science project on nuclear reactors, talked him into Uncontrolled Meltdown.

In September of their junior year, they played for a school assembly. Jed told the principal they were doing a medley of Monkees songs, then they got up there and kicked ass. The janitor had to cut the power off to get them offstage. They were in big demand after that. By the time they were seniors, they were the hottest group in Nortex. Burl had hair as long as a girl's, and he had made enough money to buy an old red Mustang, a real classic, from an airman. He was dating Nicky Staples, the best-looking girl in school. This angered his father, who had once worked for hers. But by then everything angered Burl's father.

The Drennan Drilling Company was in trouble. Willie spent less and less time on the job. One of his toolpushers—a young man he had hired because he was a Vietnam vet—lost a drill bit down a well, and they had to go on a fishing expedition to try to recover it. The insurance covered most of it, but by this time Willie's drinking had cost him his reputation, and it looked like he was going to go broke. He spent his days at home. Nothing had turned out as he had expected: America had lost the Vietnam War, and neither one of his sons had played football. Coy had burned his draft card, dropped out of college, lived on a commune in New Mexico, and was now back in Nortex managing a bar called the Town Pump.

The day after graduation, Uncontrolled Meltdown played in City Park. Three thousand people came. Girls were trying to get onstage and touch Burl, who was the best looking. But it was Jed who was the real leader of the group. When he played, Jed got this little smile on his face, and the harder he played, the bigger it got. If you were playing well, you got this sensation of intense happiness. It had nothing to do with anything you could name, you just felt better than you ever had in your whole life.

They played until after dark, which was fine with Burl, because the feeling was stronger at night. Then he and Nicky Staples drove out to Lake Caddo, where they smoked dope and made love for hours. Even then, he couldn't get stoned: you couldn't, when you were that way. You could smoke or drink all you wanted, but that good, clear feeling cut right through it.

Burl got up around noon. His mother was at the grocery store. His father, who hadn't gone to work for days, was sitting at the kitchen table reading *The Collected Works of William Shakespeare* and drinking Ancient Age. Anger shimmered in his eyes, like heat off a blacktop road.

Burl went down to Jed's, and they drove out to the old Magnolia Refinery. In the last year, he and Jed had sought out places on the edge of town where they could smoke dope and talk about the day when they got out of Nortex. Now it was almost here. They climbed the rusted steel steps to the top of one of the old storage tanks, and Jed fired up a joint.

"What'd you do last night?" Jed asked him.

"Just fucked around. What about you?"

"Tried to stay away from my parents," Jed said. His parents were Church of the Nazarene. "They're praying over me in shifts, but I think I've just about got them worn down."

Burl took a hit off the joint and stared off at the distant buildings. "This town," he said.

"It's like a black hole," Jed said. "I think the force of gravity is stronger. That's what pulls people back, like your brother." He lay back in the sun and closed his eyes. "Once we get down to Austin things are gonna be different."

They were going to be famous. Burl was sure of it. They would be discovered in Austin, cut a record, go on tour. They would be on the cover of *Rolling Stone*. The rest of his life would be spent in motion. He would never have to do anything but get that good feeling.

To the south, the buildings of downtown Nortex stood up on the prairie—dark silhouettes that seemed to collect the light. By now, Burl could see that the tallest of them, the Petroleum Building, was really only eleven stories high. At night, not a single window was lit. The last movie theater had closed and been torn down to make a parking lot five years ago. Burl had seen through everything: he knew now his father was no hero, but a drunk and a failure who had thrown away everything good in his life—just as he knew now that Nortex was a place of no importance where nothing ever happened, a town most people did not even know existed.

THE SANDS MOTEL

1

It rained the first week of April. The sky was full of fast, low clouds, and thunder woke him every morning in his room at the Sands Motel. He'd been living here for six months, ever since he had come back to Nortex and gone to work for the Fort Worth & Denver. The floor was concrete and the bathroom window was broken, but the rent was only fifty dollars a week, and Burl figured it would do until he found something better.

The Sands was owned by an Indian named Gupta and had a little sign out in front that said SPECIAL RATES FOR TRANSIENTS. Most of the tenants were from Vernon, Crowell, or Paducah. The little towns out in the Panhandle were dying out, and the factories in Nortex paid the highest wages around.

His next-door neighbors, Leroy and Tina, were from Electra. When he came back from work, he always found them sitting by the empty pool drinking Red Draws, beer mixed with tomato juice. "Hey, brother," Leroy would call out, "why don't you join us?"

They drank Red Draws while the sun went down, and watched bikers pull into the parking lot of a titty bar across the highway called the Rodeo Clown Saloon.

Leroy was pulling down unemployment and waiting for a job to open up at the fiberglass plant. The waiting was getting him down. "Man, if I could just get started," he said. "You don't have to join a union or know a goddamned thing. They put you right to work at fifteen dollars an hour."

When he made some money, Leroy was putting Tina through beauty college. Tina told Burl there was a real art to wrapping nails. She loved Nortex, thought it was a great town. "There was nothing to do in Electra," she said. "Sometimes I was so bored, I sat around and read the telephone book. But here you can always go out to the mall and walk around."

"Unstructured mall time," Leroy said. "It keeps you going."

When it got dark, Burl went back to his room. He had never thought he would be living at the Sands, with people like this—but after all, he was a working man now, just like Leroy.

He made supper on the hot plate, then plugged in his guitar. As he played, he thought about the night Carl Perkins had played the Broken Spoke in Austin, and he and Jed had talked their way onto the bus by knowing all the words to his songs. They had shared a bottle of Jack Daniels while the band loaded the instruments on. Carl Perkins's face was gray, but he looked young onstage, as if while you were playing you never aged. The bus had smelled like an ashtray, like this room, and at one point, Carl Perkins had looked at them and said, "What you smell is the smell of the road."

Burl played for two hours every night, pretending he was on the road, passing through a strange town on his way somewhere else.

More than anything else, Burl wanted to get along with the guys at work. But they didn't seem to like him. The only one he could talk to was John Arcement, a conductor on the Amarillo freight. When he got to work on Friday, John was sitting on the office porch, looking through some sort of catalog.

"What you got there?" Burl asked him.

John looked up. He had a long, lean face, white hair, and bright blue eyes.

"Prefabricated log cabins," he said.

He handed Burl the catalog. *American Lincoln Log Homes,* it said. They brought in the logs on a truck, and you put it together yourself. The deluxe model, with cathedral ceilings and a big front porch, cost twelve thousand dollars.

"That's what I'm going to be living in someday," John said.

John was a character, the other men said, a real philosopher. His father had been a gospel preacher, but John had lost his faith, dropped out of Bible college, and gone on a Search. He had hitchhiked around the country, joined the army, and read hundreds of books. It was impossible to guess his age, but Burl figured he was pushing forty.

"Yes sir," John said. "Someday I'm gonna quit this job and buy forty acres of land out near the Guadalupe Mountains. Then I'm gonna build me one of these log cabins, sit back, and let my river flow."

Burl thought it sounded like a pretty good idea—especially if you were living at the Sands Motel.

"I might do that myself someday," he said.

"You'll never quit," John said. "You'll be a railroading man forever."

John was always saying that. It was a joke, but Burl didn't think it was very funny.

"Not me," he said. "I'm only going to be doing this another year or so, then I'm going back to college."

"That's what I told myself when I signed on," John said. "Fourteen years ago."

He spat a stream of tobacco juice onto the hot cinders and walked away.

Joe Clebit, Burl's conductor, showed up. Burl was on the spareboard, working in the yard whenever he was needed, usually on a switching crew. They started putting together a freight, grabbing cars off different tracks and kicking them together. Clebit gave the orders. Burl and Leon, the other brakeman, threw switches and pulled coupler pins.

Burl liked the work itself. He had loved trains when he was a boy, and it was still exciting, working around those big diesel engines. It wasn't the hardest job in the world, but it was dangerous enough to keep you interested. Every year someone lost an arm or a leg, or fell between the train and got cut cleanly in two. Burl took some pleasure in its dangers. When he reached between two boxcars to pull a coupler pin, his groin tingled, and he could feel the heat coming off the great wheels, inches from his head. The top of the rail, polished by friction, had a bright, slippery surface that was always clean.

But at times there was nothing to do, and he found himself standing at the far end of the yard, picking up old tie nails and reading the date stamps. The sun was warm, and the ties gave off the smell of hot creosote. There were bits of pop bottles that had been out there decades, the glass turned violet by years of sunlight. His mind drifted, and he found himself wondering how he had ended up back here in Nortex.

The band had done pretty well at first, even played Armadillo World Headquarters a couple of times. Austin was the most beautiful town in Texas, and they might still be there if Jed hadn't taken too many mushrooms and ended up at the state hospital. Jed had been the heart and soul of Uncontrolled Meltdown. Burl tried to hold the group together, but one by one the others had given up and gone home.

Burl had stayed on, trying to make his grades. But somehow, he had lost his sense of time and started staying up all night and sleeping all day. This made it difficult to go to classes. At this point, he had begun having a nightmare: that he had forgotten to drop a course and had only three hours to study for the final in a subject he knew nothing about. Unfortunately, it finally came true. The day he got his grades, he threw his clothes in the back of the Mustang, dropped the apartment key in the mailbox, and drove back to Nortex. There was no place else to go.

His father had stopped drinking, but the falling price of oil had finally put him out of business. Money had become very important to him. Burl had promised he would pay back the money spent on his education, and his father had gotten him a job with the railroad through one of his friends in Alcoholics Anonymous. He was still so disappointed in Burl, they hardly spoke.

When I pay back that money, he thought, I'm getting out of this town for good. Just what he would do then wasn't clear. Building a log cabin sounded good. So did a lot of things.

"Watch your back," Leon said.

A boxcar drifted past, hot molecules of steel coming off its wheels.

"Your hair must have gotten in your eyes," Clebit said.

Burl had hair as long as a girl's. So did half the guys working for the railroad, but Clebit seemed determined to make a big thing out of it.

"I saw it," Burl said.

"Better get it cut pretty soon," Clebit said, "or we'll cut it off for you. We'll cut it off with a pair of rusty scissors."

Burl wondered when he would learn how to get along with these guys. He didn't really belong here, but that made it more important to be a good worker, to do a good job.

▼ ▼ ▼

At three o'clock, John Arcement and his crew came to pick up their train, carrying their bags. Burl wanted to talk to John and followed him as he walked the train, looking for uncoupled air hoses and loose brake riggings.

Carl Haney, the big blond brakeman, was waiting for them by the third car back from the engine. "Can you believe this sonofabitch?" he said.

A hobo lay sleeping across the knuckles of the couplers. He wore no shoes. When John shook him, the hobo rolled off the couplers and fell to the ballast.

"He's dead," Burl said.

"Dead drunk," John said.

He leaned close and shouted in the hobo's ear, "Where you headed, old-timer?"

"New Orleans," the hobo said, without opening his eyes.

"You're going in the wrong direction," John said. "This train's going to Amarillo."

"Then I'm going to Amarillo," the hobo said.

Haney laughed. John helped the hobo to his feet. "Don't you know better than to ride on those couplers?" he said. "You'll fall under the train and get yourself killed."

"I know my business," the hobo said. "I'm a railroading man myself." His pants were torn, his feet black as coal. "I worked for the Katy for forty years. Now she's gone. The Fort Worth & Denver took her over, and we lost our pension." He pulled a bottle of Night Train from his pocket. "Have a drink, boys," he said. "Have a drink on me."

"You can't ride on this train, old-timer," John said. "You're too drunk."

"What happened to our pension, boys?" the hobo said. "That's what I want to know. What happened to our pension?" The bottle slipped through his fingers, fell to the rail, and broke.

Haney was still laughing, but the hobo started to cry. John gave him five dollars. The last Burl saw of him, he was walking barefoot toward the thicket on the far side of the yard, stepping carefully over the hot cinders.

"You ever see anything like that?" Burl asked John as they walked back to the caboose.

"Most of these hobos are old railroading men," John said.

"Why is that?"

"No responsibility. It gets in your blood."

Burl couldn't figure out what John was saying. "Seems to me there's a lot of responsibility to this job."

John climbed onto the back porch of the caboose. "There's only two ways a train can go," he said. "Forward and backward. It ain't like you got to make a lot of decisions."

The train started with a boom as the couplers took up the slack, and John started rolling away from him.

"I don't get you," Burl said.

John smiled, his bright blue eyes practically disappearing. "That's why you'll be a railroading man forever."

On Saturday, there was a tornado watch. Burl called the yardmaster and found out he didn't have to work, so he drove downtown to the public library.

Since he had come back to Nortex, Burl had rediscovered his childhood interest in jet airplanes and nuclear weapons, the whole classified world of defense technology he thought of as the Big Secret. For two hours, he read *Aviation Week*. There had been incredible advances in electronic intelligence. Keyhole satellites could read the license plates of Russian vehicles from orbit and send back messages in real time.

But as the afternoon wore on, he kept thinking about what John Arcement had said about him being a railroading man forever. At five o'clock, when big yellowish-gray thunderheads were rolling up out of the southwest, Burl drove over to Coy's house in Faith Village.

Four years ago, when Coy was managing the Town Pump, he had married a girl named Margo. They wanted a home, so Coy had borrowed ten thousand dollars from their father for the down payment. Then the Town Pump folded. When their daughter Cyndi was born, there was a problem with her heart and they had to take her to Dallas for a pacemaker. She was all right now, but they had a lot of debts. Coy was selling Fords, and Margo was checking groceries at Safeway. He had never paid their father back. They hadn't spoken in almost two years.

Burl drove up Mockingbird, a street of almost identical white houses. People stood out on their porches staring at the sky. On the radio he heard there had been tornadoes in Jacksboro and Seymour. He parked in the driveway and pressed the doorbell.

Coy answered, a beer in his hand. In the last year, he had gained almost forty pounds. "What do you want?" he said.

"Just to talk."

Burl followed Coy back through the house. Margo had put a lot of effort into decorating it. There was a grandfather clock in the hall, a spinning wheel in the den. But it was still like every other house in Faith Village. It seemed dark to Burl, and it smelled of something like burnt matches. Maybe that was it, since both Coy and Margo smoked—the ashtrays were always full of butts—but to Burl it was the smell of anger and hopelessness. He felt sorry for them both, and sorriest of all for Cyndi, who was sitting on a white plastic training potty by the television.

Margo was in the kitchen, putting dinner in the microwave. "Would you like a drink?" she said hopefully, taking a bottle of vodka out of the refrigerator.

"A beer's fine," Burl said.

"Daddy," Cyndi said, "I want to watch *Little House*."

"Not now, sugar," Coy said, dropping into his leather recliner. "Daddy's watching his baseball game."

"Maybe you should turn on The Weather Service," Burl said,

meaning the Nortex channel that showed local radar. "There's a tornado watch out."

"I hope there is a tornado," Coy said, lighting a cigarette. "I hope one comes along and blows the whole goddamned town away."

His voice was flat and hard, exactly like their father's. It came to Burl that the older Coy got, the more he resembled him.

"How are you doing?" Burl asked him.

"I'm like that little boy who's spooning through a bucket of horseshit," Coy said. "I keep thinking there must be a pony in there somewhere."

"Things are that bad?"

"When the price of oil's down to fifteen dollars a barrel," Coy said, "people don't buy cars. They don't buy anything." He glared at Burl. "What's your problem?"

"I don't know," Burl said. "I guess I'm wondering if I'll ever get out of this town."

Coy laughed humorlessly. "You never should have come back here. I told you when you were a kid to get out of here, but you didn't listen to me. It's the worst town in Texas. Even the football teams aren't any good anymore. You should have stayed down there in Austin. I thought you were going to get famous."

"I don't care about being famous," Burl said. "It's a feeling I'm looking for." He leaned forward, suddenly sure he could explain it.

"Jed used to say there was this feeling of intense happiness you got when you were playing music. It's better than money, and I guess that's why musicians are willing to go through all manner of shit just to get it."

Coy stared at the television. "Jed went insane, didn't he?"

This was true. Burl had seen Jed just a couple of weeks ago, passing out handbills at the shopping mall. Jed had become a Jehovah's Witness, and he told Burl he was into loving the Lord with all his heart.

"Well, yeah," Burl said. "I guess he felt *too* happy. But what

I'm saying is, I don't care if I'm famous, just as long as I find something that gives me that *feeling* sometimes."

Coy was staring at him strangely. Burl was sure he understood.

"Well," Coy said, "welcome to the real world. Now you've got to work for a living, just like the rest of us."

He stood, went to the refrigerator, and got another beer. "I thought I was going to get out of here, too, but I'm not. Nobody does. You'll disappear here, and nobody'll ever hear from you again. You'll end up just like me, a Republican with a beer gut. Why do you think Dad hates me so much?"

There were many reasons, but Burl picked the one he thought Coy wanted to hear. "Because you didn't play football."

"That's not it," Coy said. "He hates me because Mom got pregnant with me and he came back here instead of going to Alaska. He wanted me to get stuck here too, and now that you've borrowed money from him, the same thing's going to happen to you. He'll never let you forget it."

"Daddy," Cyndi said, "I want to get up."

"Not until you've done your peepee," Coy said. "I've told you, you can't move until you've done your peepee."

He lit another cigarette. "Just don't buy a house," he said. "That's what I did, bought a nice house so I could forget I lived in Nortex. That was all I wanted: a house, a wife, and a kid who loved me."

"She would love you," Margo said from the kitchen, "if you didn't shout at her."

"Then I filled it with all this shitty furniture, to please my wife," Coy went on, waving his arms at the sofa covered with plastic, the spinning wheel, the grandfather clock. "I took a job I hated, but I still went broke paying for all this shit."

"Oh, stop feeling sorry for yourself," Margo said. "It's a lovely house. You haven't got any taste. It's a three-bedroom brick veneer, and it's worth thirty thousand on the market right now, if we can just hold on to it."

Burl looked out the window. It had gotten so dark, the streetlights had gone on. Coy and Margo were shouting at each other. They had forgotten he was there. Cyndi was staring at the wall, and all Burl could think of was how much Coy sounded like their father. "I don't care about that," he was saying. "I hate this house. It's destroyed my life. This house is a prison, and I'm paying for it."

The sirens groaned.

They looked at each other, then at the television screen, where the announcer had just appeared, looking scared. *We interrupt regular programming to bring you this special bulletin,* he said. *A tornado is on the ground near Memorial Stadium—*

The television popped and went off, at the same instant as the lights. Burl and Coy rushed down the hall to the front door.

It was like stepping into his old nightmare.

Greenish-black clouds pressed right down on the rooftops. Only to the west did a little light seep through, the same strange color as the glint of light at the bottom of a bottle of bourbon. Between them and the light was an immense funnel, black as factory smoke. The whole bottom of the storm twisted around it, like water going down a bathtub drain. It was no more than a mile away and headed straight at them, but they stared at it for an endless time until it lit from within with the coppery-green flash of exploding power lines.

"Let's get the hell out of here," Coy shouted.

They raced back inside, bouncing off walls in the darkness. Coy snatched up Cyndi off the potty and tossed her to Burl, then grabbed Margo, who was screaming like a girl in a horror movie. Back outside they went, knocking the screen door off its hinges. It had gotten darker, if possible, and big hailstones were falling. The tornado was so close, Burl could hear its high, humming roar, but he found himself thinking clearly. They had to take the Mustang: it was blocking the driveway. He threw Cyndi in the back seat and held the door open for Coy and Margo, fumbling in his pocket for the keys. He tried not to look at the funnel, but caught a glimpse of it as they shot backward out of the driveway—no more than a few blocks away now, rolling down on them and blotting out the last of the light.

He turned east on Fairway, but it was the only road out of Faith Village, and more and more cars were turning onto it, trying to get away like him. If he could get through the intersection of Fairway and Kemp, he could outrun it. Then he saw red brake lights ahead. Cars were stopping for the light, as if everything were normal. So did he.

The light was dying, and hailstones were bouncing off the roof. But when he looked at the Kentucky Fried Chicken, people were still standing in line. Across the road, in the parking lot of the mall, people were pointing at the sky. Nobody seemed that excited. A boy came walking toward them along the median, selling roses. When Burl looked in the mirror, the funnel was almost on top of them.

At that moment, Burl decided it was everyone for himself: the rules were suspended.

He pulled out of the line of cars and drove across the parking lot of the Kentucky Fried Chicken. He heard the oil pan clang on the curb. A Camaro was coming right at them, its horn blaring. Then he was through the intersection. He looked back and saw the mall disintegrate, the roof flying up, cars rolling across the parking lot like toys.

He drove on across town, doing seventy, eighty, passing other cars on the right. Coy and Margo and Cyndi were screaming, but all Burl felt was a strange weightless sensation of total concentration. He had always been a good driver: now all he had to do was drive as fast as he could. Their lives depended on it. In the mirror, he saw black dust and flying sparks. The tornado followed them all the way across town, until they got to the Central Expressway, where he hung a right. He got his best look at it then: three or four funnels, each one as big as an ordinary tornado, the whole thing wrapped up in a shroud of black dust. The last thing he saw in the mirror were some boxcars in the railroad yard, blowing away like cardboard. Each one of those boxcars weighed ten tons.

He took the long way around, behind Lake Caddo. When they were two blocks from the house, he stopped. Ahead, there was nothing. Nothing. As if a great steamroller had come along, crushing everything in its path. They got out and walked the rest of the way. Cyndi had stopped crying. They met a man with a bloody pillowcase wrapped around his face. To the west, where the storm was blowing away, Burl saw a rainbow against the blackness.

They had a hard time telling their house from the others. Margo finally spotted it by the furniture. It was scattered in the front yard, looking a little like a tag sale.

2

They finally drove to their parents' house in Indian Heights. There was no place else to go.

Willie was standing out in the front yard, looking at the clouds. "Dad," Coy said, when he got out of the car, "the house is gone. It's totally demolished. Nothing left of it."

"Oh, what the hell, son," Willie said, putting his arms around Coy. "What the hell."

Doris came out on the front porch. "Thank God you're alive," she said. They went in the front room and sat down on the sofa. They could hear what sounded like hundreds of sirens, headed toward Faith Village. "I lost my house," Margo kept sobbing. "I lost my house."

Burl was more worried about Cyndi. Her hands were cold as ice.

"Mom," he said. "We'd better get a blanket around Cyndi. I think she's in shock."

Doris got blankets for them all, but still Cyndi wouldn't say anything: just sucked her thumb and stared straight ahead, her eyes like nailheads. Finally Burl asked her why she wasn't talking, and she said, "Because we left my doll."

Everyone smiled.

"Why, I'm sure your doll's all right," Burl said. "We'll go back for her tomorrow."

"Do you promise?"

"I promise."

Everyone started talking at once, even laughing. It was getting dark. There was no electricity, so Doris lit the red Christmas candles and put them on the coffee table. Everyone seemed to feel good, Burl noticed. It had been the longest time since he had seen his parents show any sign of affection for each other, but now his father kept putting his arm around his mother and smiling.

"Where were you when it hit?" Margo asked them. "Did you see it?"

"We hid in the bathtub," his mother said. "Willie pulled a mattress over our heads."

His father lit a Winston. "It's the first time I've been able to get your mother in a bathtub with me in twenty years."

"Oh, honey," his mother said. But she was laughing delightedly. In fact, Burl couldn't help but notice, everyone felt better than they had in years.

Suddenly they were all hungry. His mother found some canned goods, and his father lit the hibachi and heated them in the backyard. Burl went out and stood with him for a while. The sun had gone down, and the horizon glowed like heated iron. A yellow crescent moon sank into the glow, brilliant Venus burning above it.

"You haven't said much, son," his father said.

"You should have seen it, Dad," Burl said. "It was the biggest thing I've ever seen."

His voice sounded funny, as if he were talking in his sleep.

"Just as long as you're all right," his father said, putting his arm around him.

For some reason Burl remembered the nights when his father had taken him downtown, when they'd walked the dark streets, Burl holding his hand, and his father had seemed tall and strong enough to hold off all the terrors of the world.

They ate at the dining-room table, by candlelight. Doris put out the good china, and Willie said the Blessing for the first time in twenty years. "Our Father," he said, "we thank Thee for Thy mercy which has kept us safe from harm." They ate corn and ham and lima beans. Then they sat in the front room, and Doris got out the shoebox full of family pictures. They passed around the old Kodachromes, and Willie told Margo how they'd gone to Turner Falls on their honeymoon. "We were just a couple of kids," he said, "but we sure were in love."

Helicopters were going over, the chop of their rotors shaking the house. Burl felt flat and sleepy. It was too much trouble to talk. Inside, his thoughts were going so fast, he couldn't grab onto them. Once he'd spent the day at Padre Island, and every time he closed his eyes that night, he'd seen waves rolling toward him. Now he saw the tornado: black dust and flying sparks.

Coy and Margo slept in the boys' old bedroom, Cyndi between them. Burl slept on the couch in the front room, but he could hear them talking through the open door. "It's like the night we brought her home from the hospital," Margo said. "I'd forgotten how happy we were then. But lately, it seems like we've been drifting apart."

"We're alive," Coy said. "That's the important thing. I love you, honey."

"And I love you."

Burl listened to the silence in the house, thinking how everyone was together tonight, their differences forgotten. For the first time in years, they were a family. But he still felt removed from it all. He stared at the candle on the coffee table, unable to sleep. There was something like a knot in his chest, getting tighter and tighter. He got up and went outside.

To the south, helicopters were circling Faith Village, their halogen searchlights stabbing down like knives. It was a fine night, cool and moist. He could smell grass and green pecan tree pollen. It was the finest time of the year, before the hellish summer heat set in. After a while, he felt his life come rushing back to him: he sat down on the grass and cried like a baby.

Then he sat there enjoying the night. The main thing the tornado had made him feel was small. Burl had never dreamed anything could be so big. He felt like the man in the movie *The Incredible Shrinking Man*, when he slipped through the screen and wandered off into endless blades of grass.

The next day, there was a dust storm, the wind coming around to the north and gusting up to forty miles per hour. The sky was orange, the sun a pale blue disc you could look at with the naked eye. It reminded Burl of the Viking photographs of the surface of Mars.

At noon, he took Coy and Margo to Faith Village to see what they could recover.

They drove back along Fairway, the road they'd taken the day before. The Kentucky Fried Chicken was gone. Streetlight poles were bent over like drinking straws. The pavement was gritty with fragments of broken glass.

There was a barricade across Mockingbird Lane. National Guardsmen stood around an armored personnel carrier, rifles slung over their shoulders. A sign on the barricade said:

WARNING
RESTRICTED AREA
LOOTERS WILL BE FIRED UPON

One of the guardsmen leaned through the window. "You folks live here?"

"We used to," Coy said.

"Got any proof you're a resident?"

Coy showed him his driver's license.

"All right," the guardsman said. "You folks go ahead. Just be sure you're out before dark."

He stepped back, threw them a little salute.

Beyond the corner, the ruins began, a great plain of broken lumber. The street had been cleared by a bulldozer. Burl drove along slowly until he came to their house.

There were a few other people walking around. Several were in bathrobes—he supposed that was all they had left—and one woman wore a pair of galoshes. She carried a shopping bag and stopped every so often to pick something up.

Coy and Margo started into the house, Coy holding Cyndi's hand. "Be careful you don't step on a nail," he told her.

Burl stayed there a moment, looking to the south. With the houses gone, he could see all the way to the smokestacks of the fiberglass plant, two miles away. The air smelled like a construction site. There was a drabness to the ruins he had not noticed yesterday. The only color was the fiberglass insulation blowing everywhere, pink as cotton candy. Trees were still standing, but they had been stripped of their leaves, giving the landscape a strange, wintry look. Burl had the feeling he'd seen it before somewhere, but couldn't place it.

He followed them into the house. Pale sunlight slanted through the rafters. Where was their roof? Somewhere in Oklahoma, he supposed.

Coy and Margo were in their bedroom, looking through the closets. Their clothes were covered with dirt and shingle dust, sprayed with red mud as if from a hose.

"Everything's so dirty," Margo said, starting to cry again. "Oh, we've lost everything."

"So did a lot of other people, honey."

Cyndi came walking up, holding her doll.

"So you found her," Burl said. "How is she?"

"She got cold last night," Cyndi said. "And she's hungry. She's going to have a tea party."

"That sounds like a good idea."

"Yeah," Coy said. "Why don't you get her out of here before she hurts herself."

They found the tea set and walked out in the front yard. Cyndi found a place where there was no broken glass and set out cups and saucers. Burl sat on the couch and lit a cigarette. He stared off over the ruins, wondering why they looked so familiar.

Then it came to him.

Hiroshima. Nagasaki. The soldiers in their camouflage uniforms. The smokestacks of the fiberglass plant. The people walking around, collecting their belongings.

Ever since he was a child, he had known there was going to be a nuclear war. He had dreamed of this day from the time he had read *Tomorrow* in one of his mother's *Reader's Digest Condensed Books*. Now it had finally come.

Maybe that was why he felt so calm. When the thing happened you feared the most, there was nothing left to fear. You could stop thinking ahead. He sat there in the sun, with no past, no future. Cyndi, he noticed, felt better too. She was already singing a little song to herself.

A man wearing a raincoat came walking up the street, his arms folded across his chest, a bloody bandage around his forehead. He looked at Burl. "Howdy, neighbor."

"Howdy," Burl said.

"People were killed around here," the man said suddenly.

"Were they?"

"Woman was killed on our block. Poor woman with diabetes who couldn't get out of bed. I seen her. Turned her into a pincushion. Splinters sticking out all over."

Burl shook his head. A big black crow landed in the leafless tree. They watched it for a while.

"You hear it?" the man said.

"Yeah," Burl said. "I heard it."

"Never heard anything like it. Supposed to sound like a freight train, they say. Or a jet airplane. Sounded more like a dynamo to me. I looked up when it tore the roof off my house," the man said. "Got a look inside of it."

"What did you see?"

"Blue light. There's light inside. It's just the color of fluorescent light. And it's made of rings."

"Rings?" Burl said, intensely interested.

"That's what it looked like. All these big rings turning. But you can't hear a sound when you're inside it," the man said. "Just your heart beating."

"You want to join us?" Burl said. "We're having a tea party."

"No, I figure I'd better be getting along. You folks be glad you're alive. People were killed around here."

He started off up the street, then stopped.

"Always knew it would happen," he said. "Always knew the big one would come along someday."

"So did I," Burl said.

He watched the man until he disappeared, thinking of what he had said.

Burl stared off over the ruins, at the strange low skyline under the blue sun. Crows called. A torn American flag flapped in the middle distance, its pole leaning at exactly the same angle as the flag on Mount Suribachi.

Ground Zero.

They were back at their parents' home when power was restored and the television came to life. The first thing they saw was the sober face of Dan Rather. "We bring you a special report," he said, "from Nortex, Texas, which was struck by a catastrophic tornado at six o'clock yesterday afternoon." There were helicopter shots of Faith Village, showing acres of demolished homes. "The entire city is completely cut off from the outside world. We have no figures on the number of dead or injured, but the damage path extends for miles." He praised their courage, the courage of the American people. Then Rather—who, Burl remembered, was a Texan—stared at the camera with the special sorrow he lent to bad news from home. "We'll have more on this story in the days to come."

Nortex had finally made the national news.

3

For weeks, Burl saw everything with new eyes. It was a time of wonders. Everything was interesting, even the paper. On the fourth day after the tornado, the *Nortex Daily Times* got out a special edition.

People who sheltered in their bathrooms had heard pipes rattling. Pipes had rattled all over the south side of Nortex as the tornado destroyed two thousand homes. Sixty-three people were known to be dead, but everyone thought there must be more. On the first night, police had shot and killed a man they thought was a looter when he refused to identify himself. He turned out to be an illegal alien who spoke no English.

Volunteers from the Church of Jesus Christ of the Latter-Day Saints arrived on the second day. The Mennonites had also come, bearded young men who refused to accept payment of any kind and had to be taken everywhere, since none of them knew how to drive a car. There were rumors of Unidentified Flying Objects on the third night.

Blades of grass had been blown into tree trunks. Jars of unopened baby food were found to have dirt and splinters of glass inside. A letter addressed to a woman in Ardmore, Oklahoma, had fallen into her front yard—blown from her sister's kitchen table in Nortex, a hundred miles away. Catfish had fallen in some parts of town, presumably sucked up from Lake Caddo. One had weighed almost fifty pounds.

Burl turned the page and read the rest of the paper. *Playboy* had been banned from local Seven-Elevens. The Cowboys for Christ were holding their second annual revival at the 4-H Club barn. Creationism would be taught next year in Nortex schools. The head of the science department at Nortex High thought it was a good idea. "After all," he was quoted as saying, "evolution is just a theory, which many scientists have stopped believing in."

The Federal Disaster Assistance Administration opened an office and started taking applications for loans at three and a half percent interest. Willie Nelson offered to give a benefit for the homeless. Vice President Bush was supposed to tour the ruins, but had to cancel at the last minute.

The city council formed a recovery committee. The chairman was Luther Babbs, a businessman who told his friends he felt Providence had personally selected him for the job. He coined a slogan, "Let's Roll Up Our Sleeves," that appeared on billboards all over town.

The air was full of hope. No one worried anymore about the price of oil or the closing of the Lone Star Refinery. Burl stopped wondering if he was ever going to get out of Nortex and start playing music again. Nortex was no longer invisible. For once, they were living at the center of the world. At night, they watched themselves on the national news and went to bed feeling the love and concern of the whole rest of the country pouring in.

And everyone liked one another. Everyone felt good. People expressed their innermost feelings to total strangers. They walked around in a state of wonder, accepting everything as it came.

Only John Arcement had not changed.

"It was an act of God," Carl Haney said one day when they were all standing around on the office porch, talking about the tornado. "That's all you can say about it."

"If it was an act of God," John said, "why did he spare Country Club?"

Burl smiled, but it was true: the tornado had destroyed almost a fourth of Nortex, but somehow it had left the great mansions of the oil millionaires untouched.

"We don't know the answer to that," Haney said.

"Well, maybe you should think about it."

Royce DeWitt, the engineer on John's train, laughed. "I guess the high rollers got all the luck, as usual."

"Either that," John said, "or God's trying to tell us something: he don't like working men." He stood up, looked at his watch. "Gentlemen," he said, "let's take out a train."

A fantastic hunger for women possessed him. At night he heard Tina and Leroy making love through the wall, the bedsprings shrilling louder and louder until Leroy gave a strange cry, like a calf. Sometimes his hunger for a woman, or at least a look at one, almost drove him across the highway to the Rodeo Clown Saloon, but the bikes parked out in front scared him off.

He settled for going to the video parlor on Kemp, where he played Pac Man and Battle Zone for hours. It was a good way to burn the energy off. He stood among crowds of adolescent boys, working the joystick, a cigarette smoldering on the console by the coin slot. Sometimes he spent twenty dollars a night, looking for the flashing lights, the kinetic thrill of a score.

On the way home, he sometimes drove past his old girlfriends' houses, wondering where they were now, wishing he could talk to them. He didn't just want sex, although sex would be great. What he really wanted was to get *close* to a woman, to share what they'd both been through. For the first time he saw nothing meant anything if you couldn't tell it to a woman. He wished he were in love.

Coy and his family lived with Burl's parents for a week. Then the Federal Disaster Assistance Administration brought in five hundred mobile homes and set them up all over town. The largest group, of fifty, was in the parking lot of the Safeway. Coy and his family got number forty-nine.

Burl went over to see them the day after they moved in. The trailer had a stove that ran off bottled gas and a chemical toilet. Margo served them a meal of hot dogs and potato chips, her face shining. Coy had not taken a drink since the day of the tornado, and he told Burl he thought he might just stop for good. There was none of the anger and hopelessness he had felt in their home in Faith Village. The trailer was clean, compact, functional: a little like a log cabin.

After dinner, Margo went to the Laundromat and Coy and Burl sat on the steps. The sun had gone down and the sky was a deep, clear blue, except for a rusty afterglow that clung like sediment to the horizon. A little society of the homeless had already formed. Cyndi played with other children on the jungle gym donated by the Kiwanis Club. Two shirtless young men tossed a Frisbee back and forth. Others stood in line at the glowing egg of the pay phone. A woman walking by with a baby on her arm said, "Hello, there," as if she'd known them her whole life.

"You know," Burl said, "this is pretty nice."

"Nice?" Coy said. "We're living like rednecks here."

"Margo seems pretty happy."

"That's because we got the insurance check for our house today," Coy said. "I talked to the construction people, and they say they can start rebuilding it next week."

Burl stared at Coy in disbelief.

"You're rebuilding your house?"

"That's right," Coy said. "I got twenty thousand from the insurance company, and I can borrow another ten thousand from the government, with thirty years to pay it back. It's too good a deal to turn down."

"I thought you hated your house."

Coy smiled. "Things look a lot different now. Do you know who I met over there in the Safeway the other day? Buddy McAlester. We hadn't spoken to each other in ten years, but the minute I saw him, it was just like old times again. I told him I'd lost my house, and he offered me a job at Prairie Savings & Loan. That's what I've been doing at the Ford agency anyway, looking over loan applications. It's a big chance for me."

"But you said your house was a prison."

"Margo needs it. And so does Cyndi." Coy put a hand on Burl's knee. "And you know something? I've learned I need them a lot more than they need me. You'll understand when you have a wife and kids of your own."

Burl looked away, wondering why he always found it so annoying when someone told him he'd understand someday, when he had children.

Margo came back with a bag of laundry. They watched Cyndi playing on the jungle gym. Coy told Margo the construction company said they could move the trailer onto the lot and live right there while they were rebuilding. She put her head on his shoulder. "I'm going to have my house back, just the way it was," she said. "Every single brick."

Coy smiled at Burl and said this was the best feeling he'd ever had in his life. "I'm starting over again," he said. "And this time, I feel strong enough to get it right."

Leroy got on at the fiberglass plant. The job was everything he had hoped for, but there were a lot of aliens working there—Mexicans, and even some boat people. He told Burl there was no way that fiberglass could get into your lungs, and anyway they gave you a chest X ray every six months, just to be sure. There had been some cases of tuberculosis. Leroy figured the boat people had brought it in. He worked ten hours a day, five days a week. Every other week, he worked all night. When he did, Leroy acted strangely. One morning Burl got up and saw Leroy sitting on the diving board with a beer in his hand, staring into the empty pool. Something in his eyes made Burl decide not to speak to him. A few mornings later, Burl found him sleeping on the cinderblock retaining wall around the parking lot.

Tina was pregnant. It was what they'd always wanted, but Leroy grew short-tempered. He was always arguing with Gupta about the rent. "You fucking Moslem," Burl heard him say once. "I ought to kick your ass back to Iran, where it belongs." He had long discussions with Burl about the need to get tough with those chicken Shi-ites.

Burl helped Leroy put new brake shoes on his ancient Camaro. In return, Leroy pressed something into his palm, which Burl recognized by touch: a little gold bottle with a hinged spoon on the cap. "Crystal meth," Leroy whispered to him. "Industrial strength."

Sometimes Burl spooned some into his nose and stayed up all night. He hated its burning, mineral stink, but it made him forget about women. He practiced the guitar or read his college astronomy textbook, which he'd kept even after he failed the course. Burl had once wanted to be an astronomer, and when he got high, he could understand the Big Bang, when the universe had cooled and split like a diamond into the forces of gravity and electromagnetism.

He had never been so alone, except for the time in Austin when he'd spent an hour in an isolation tank. Floating in darkness and warm salt water, he had hallucinated himself flying over warm, black ice at the speed of light. This was a little like that. He felt like he was voyaging off into space while he read about black holes, neutron stars, the first three minutes of the early universe.

On the first of May, he went over to his parents' for his father's birthday. He was looking forward to it, hoping he could get more of that family feeling they'd all had the night after the big tornado.

Coy and Margo couldn't be there—the roofers were coming to give them an estimate. Burl's mother had rented a projector, and after dinner they watched the old home movies. Burl enjoyed this more than his parents. There were scenes of an old jackknife rig spouting oil, of Willie in uniform lighting a Camel, of Doris driving the green Dodge they'd owned after the war. His mother never drove anymore, not unless she had to. But she had been a good driver then, and what was more, she had been beautiful, with shiny blond hair and nice legs. His parents fell silent watching this, as they did when they saw an atomic explosion.

"I wish Coy and Margo could have come," his mother said when the movies were over.

"They're putting their life back together," his father said. "And this time, I think he's really going to make something of himself." He looked at Burl. "How are you doing?"

"My conductor's giving me a hard time," Burl said.

"Are you standing up for yourself? You've got to look people in the eye, you know. You don't want them to think you're dishonest."

"It's not that. He thinks my hair's too long."

"Are you going to get it cut?"

"There's nothing in the rule book about it."

"You can't go through life with a chip on your shoulder," his father said. "You're going to get yourself fired."

Stand up for yourself, but not too much. Look people in the eye, but don't get fired. It made no sense. Or was his father trying to tell him something about getting along in the world, something that Burl, for some reason, could not understand?

"More coffee, honey?" his mother said.

"Not for me." His father lit a Winston with the battered Zippo he'd carried around since the Battle of the Bulge. "I've got to get up and go to work tomorrow."

Sometimes Burl thought how much his father had changed in the last four years. When he was drinking, his father had seemed like the angriest man in the world. Then he had stopped drinking, for reasons that were still mysterious to Burl. He had lost his money but regained his honor, becoming a leading member of Alcoholics Anonymous. Garland Moffit, an old friend and one of the Little Iron Men, had given him an office job, looking at core samples and reading mud logs. It wasn't much of a job, but he did it well. He never complained.

But sometimes Burl missed the old Willie, who had raged against God, the town of Nortex, and everyone in it. He had taken the big step, admitted he was powerless against alcohol, and sought the help of a Higher Power. But there had been a time when his father would not have admitted he was powerless against anything. And in those days he had shared his secrets with Burl, told him things he never told anyone else.

"Let's get out the telescope," Burl said.

"Oh, hell," his father said. "It's too much trouble."

"The air's real clear tonight. The moon's out."

"It's up in the attic," his father said. "I don't even know if I can find it."

"I'll help you," Burl said.

▼ ▼ ▼

One summer evening when Burl was four years old, the moon had risen, brown as breadcrust and seemingly magnified to three or four times its normal size. He had run in and told his father, who got out his deer rifle and laid it across the fender of the car, so they could look through the telescopic sight.

His father had pointed out the craters, the seas, and the terminator—the line between light and shadow, day and night. He told Burl it was thousands of miles away, but the astronauts were going there soon. When Burl asked him what for, he said, "Why, there might be gold, or diamonds, or uranium up there." He laughed. "There might even be oil." Burl's mother had told him everything lost on earth went to the moon, and up to that time he had pictured it as being covered with pencils, paper clips, and rubber bands.

On that night, Burl's interest in astronomy was born. Later, they had built the telescope, grinding the mirror themselves on a card table in the garage. It was a reflector, like the two-hundred-inch Hale Telescope on Mount Palomar that astronomers called the Big Eye. The mirror collected starlight like water in a dish. Now Burl shifted the telescope while his father pissed in the grass by the fence. He found the moon, a blinding blue-white disc, and waited for his pupils to contract so he could see. There they were, all the old features whose names he still remembered: the Sea of Rains, the Ocean of Storms, the Sea of Serenity.

His father peered through the eyepiece. "Beautiful," he said.

"I should have been an astronomer," Burl said.

"You could have been," his father said. "You've got a wonderful mind, and you could have been anything you wanted to be, if you'd just applied yourself. But you didn't. Now you're going to have to work for a living, just like I did."

"Dad," Burl said, "I'm too smart to spend the rest of my life working for the railroad."

"A friend of mine got you that job," his father said. "A good friend of mine in the program. He was doing you a favor. And I hope you're going to pay us back the money we spent on your education. I'm not rich anymore, you know." He sighed. "But hell, you'll probably give up on it, just like you gave up on the telescope."

After a hundred hours of grinding the mirror, Burl had lost interest. This no longer bothered him. He had learned in his astronomy class that telescope makers never finished grinding their mirrors. The perfect mirror was a mathematical abstraction. Anyway, it had won a blue ribbon in the science fair.

"It's still a good moon scope," he said. "We can see the rings of Saturn, and that's good enough for me. And we should be able to get a good look at Halley's comet in a couple of years."

"That's right," his father said softly. "I've been looking forward to it ever since my mother told me about it, when I was a little boy. She said it lit up the whole sky." He put his arm around Burl's shoulders and they stared up at the stars together.

"There's a lot of things up there they don't understand, aren't they?" he said after a while. "And here on earth too. How could the Egyptians have built the pyramids? And those giant figures on the Plain of Nazca. Did I show you that picture in *Chariots of the Gods*? How could a tribe of Stone Age Indians have done that? They must have had some help. You know who I'm talking about. They've been here from the beginning. I've seen their ships."

Burl's father believed in flying saucers. When Burl was a boy he had already seen several, and he would tell anyone about them who cared to listen, including the roughnecks at the Denver Cafe. To Burl, this had been proof of his father's intelligence. Burl believed in them, too, and was forever hoping to see one himself.

On New Year's Eve, when Burl was nine years old and his father was so popular people wanted him to run for mayor, Willie had gone down to Clay County to look at a well he was drilling. The Highway Patrol brought him back at daybreak. He had seen a flying saucer, he told Burl and his mother, and chased it all the way back to Nortex—he would have caught it, too, if they hadn't pulled him over and arrested him for drunken driving. But he was going to fight it all the way. "Oh, honey," Doris said, "why don't you just forget it?"

"Forget it?" Willie said. "I'm telling the air force. They'll want to know."

Willie not only notified the air force, he insisted on telling the Nortex paper, which printed an article the next day.

LOCAL OIL MAN SEES UFO

William Drennan, oil operator, was arrested by the state police at 3 AM on the morning of January 1, and charged with reckless driving, resisting arrest, and driving while intoxicated. Mr. Drennan claims he was following a flying saucer, which he sighted near Olney. The prominent local oilman says the air force is interested and is investigating the incident.

But when the investigator from Project Blue Book, a Sergeant Harold Otis, arrived, Burl could tell he wasn't all that bright. He chewed Black Jack gum, and it took him fifteen minutes to get his tape recorder working. When Willie had told his story, Sergeant Otis played it back and they sat listening to his father's speeded-up voice. "Sounds like chipmunks, doesn't it?" Sergeant Otis said.

Then Sergeant Otis stood up and said he had to be going. "Now wait a minute," Willie said. "The air force must know a hell of a lot more about this than they're letting on. Can't you tell me what these things are?"

"Sir," Sergeant Otis said, "the air force has given a lot of thought to that question. There is a theory they are Martians who have seen our atomic tests. But to do this, they would have had to watch us for years, and this would be pretty dull sport. We don't think of doing the same thing to them."

"We do," Burl said. "We've got a telescope."

Sergeant Otis ignored him. "In the opinion of the air force, they are optical illusions—sightings of Venus, for instance, which is a very bright star."

"Venus isn't a star," Burl said. "It's a planet. And it wasn't up that night. I looked in the astronomical tables. Dad couldn't have seen Venus."

"It can sometimes appear to be in motion—particularly if the observer is intoxicated, as you were, Mr. Drennan—and that is what I'm putting in my report."

Then Burl's father stood up and told Sergeant Otis that was the biggest load of horseshit he had ever heard. It ended with him chasing Sergeant Otis out the door. But for Burl, at that moment, everything fell apart. If Sergeant Otis was a fool, so was his father for expecting anyone to believe him. Suddenly he saw his father clearly: a former toolpusher who thought he was an expert on not only flying saucers, but reincarnation, astral projection, and the Lost Continent of Atlantis. In other words, a man who was out of his depth.

It was the beginning of his father's downfall. Abner Spell, the barber at the Kemp Hotel, became mayor instead—a man who was a Democrat or a Republican, whatever you wanted to hear, a man everyone liked. Burl had never completely forgiven his father. The telescope had gone into the attic, and Burl had decided flying saucers were really temperature inversions, ball lightning, flocks of migrating birds. He felt the same way now: he could no more believe in them than he could become a born-again Christian.

"I'm sorry, Dad," he said. "People made those figures. It was some kind of religious thing. It's got nothing to do with flying saucers. They don't exist."

"Well, you're a lot smarter than I am," Willie said. "And I should know. I sent you to college."

"I'll pay you that money back someday," Burl said. "That's a promise."

"Oh, hell," his father said tiredly, starting for the house. Halfway there, he stopped and turned back. "You know what your trouble is?" he said in his flat, hard toolpusher's voice. "You think you're too good for us. But someday you're going to learn a simple lesson: you can't walk through the cow lot without stepping in cowshit."

The back door slammed. Burl stayed for a while, looking up at the stars.

When his father had stopped drinking, he had given up his anger. That was one of the precepts of the Program: Stop getting angry at things you can do nothing about. But his anger had not really disappeared, only changed. It was a cold anger now, instead of a hot, but it still hurt.

4

He was alone in the house he'd grown up in. It was night. He didn't know how he'd gotten there, but he could tell the house was empty somehow. An airless silence lay over everything, and his hands and feet tingled with pins and needles. He walked into the front room, peered out through the blinds into the darkness. Then, in a flash of lightning, he saw a tornado coiling over the cast iron angels atop the cemetery gate.

Burl sat straight up in bed, his heart pounding. The sirens were blowing. He pulled on his jeans and ran out into the parking lot of the Sands.

A storm was moving in from the southwest. He could see nothing but the space between the bottom of the cloud and the ground, which was lit by continuous bolts of lightning—a long slot of incandescent air, sometimes blue, sometimes bourbon gold. He watched it, shuddering with cold and fear, until hailstones began falling. Then he ran back inside and turned on the television to The Weather Service.

The blue outline of the state of Texas floated in a black void. Nortex was surrounded by red echoes. *At five* AM, the meteorologist's recorded voice said, *a severe thunderstorm was moving into the Nortex area. Stay tuned to this station for further bulletins.*

The sirens stopped, but Burl watched for another fifteen minutes, smoking cigarette after cigarette, until he was sure there wasn't going to be another tornado.

It was too late to go back to sleep, so he took out the bottle of meth Leroy had given him and spooned some into his nose. He lay back down on the bed and waited for it to take hold. The ceiling bulb burned into his eyes.

He was losing it.

There had been that feeling of wonder right after the tornado, of being free but close to everyone. He had thought it would last forever. But it had been slipping away. For just how long he didn't know, but his life was starting to seem like a dead end again. That was why he'd started taking meth: it gave him something like that feeling of freedom. But it wasn't the same, and when he came down, he always felt worse than before.

In a while, the meth took hold. The first blue light of morning shone through the blinds. Birds sang, and he felt capable of anything, even going to work. But the little gold bottle was almost empty, and he knew when he got off work he'd want some more.

The storm season was now at its height, and there were sometimes two or three a week. The next afternoon he was standing in the yard when something in the air, or the light, or the time of day made him look to the west. Then he saw it: the nickel-gray dome of a big thunderhead, almost transparent at this distance, fifty or a hundred miles off.

By the time he got off work, its anvil top had spread out, and it was rolling down on Nortex like a moving mountain range. When he turned on the car radio, he learned there was a tornado watch, which he'd already known somehow, by the feeling of energy on the air. Instead of going home, he drove across the Red River Bridge to meet it.

This is insane, he thought. There's a tornado coming. Everybody's trying to get out of its way, and here I am out driving around trying to *find* it.

On the other side of the bridge, he saw a white government van with a Doppler radar antenna and NATIONAL SEVERE STORMS LABORATORY stenciled on the door. I must be in the right place, he thought. He drove another mile until he was right under the storm, where the air had that bourbon glow. He got out and watched, until a hailstone as big as a softball shattered on his hood. Then rain blotted everything from sight.

When he got back to Nortex, it was dark and the streets were flooded. He felt no need to take meth that night: there was too much energy flowing through his body. Still, when he lay down on the bed, he fell asleep within five minutes.

The next day, he went to the library and checked out every book on tornadoes he could find. While he was there, he read the paper. The Nortex Storm Spotters were having a meeting that night.

Nortex was proud of its Storm Spotters, volunteers who drove out to the edge of town to keep an eye on incoming storms. The paper called them "Good Neighbor Sams." Anyone interested was invited to attend. Burl decided to go.

The meeting was held in the study hall of Nortex High. Almost a hundred people showed up. Burl sat in the back of the room, at the desk he'd had his senior year. He found his initials, still inked into the old brown wood. The president of the Storm Spotters gave a little talk about doing their community a service. "We pray there will never be another tornado like the one this year," he said. "But if there is, our warnings can save countless lives." Burl felt a little uncomfortable. He wasn't really like these people: he had never prayed for anyone, and he wouldn't have minded seeing another tornado.

He found out he couldn't be a Spotter. You had to have your ham operator's license, and you had to be able to take a day off when storms came. Most of the Spotters were plumbers, carpenters, electricians. Burl worked for the railroad, and he never knew when he was going to be free. That damned job, he thought as he drove back to the Sands. It's really got me nailed down.

But he brought back a pamphlet called *Tornadoes: A Storm Spotter's Guide*. Inside, there was a diagram of a Great Plains Cumulonimbus, or Supercell.

The storms that produced tornadoes, he learned, were different. Supercells were much more powerful than ordinary thunderstorms. They spun along on the jet stream, like little hurricanes, and could travel for hundreds of miles. Supercells looked different too. They had distinct features—an anvil, a gust front, a precipitation shaft, a rainfree base—and the stronger the storm, the clearer these features got.

It was a discovery. Burl had always thought storms were formless, but now he saw they had shape, structure: an intricate architecture of air. He thumbtacked the diagram to the wall over the dresser, by the calendar. That was the storm he was looking for, the one he had to find.

Another cold front came through. Burl had some personal days off coming, and for three days, he chased thunderstorms.

In the mornings, he kept the television tuned to The Weather Service radar. Around three o'clock, the first faint blue echoes appeared, down near Seymour. A moment later, there were three tones, and a bulletin from The Weather Channel scrolled up on the screen: *Severe thunderstorms, and possibly tornadoes, are expected along and fifty miles either side of a line from Abilene, Texas, to Frederick, Oklahoma. This watch includes the Nortex area.*

Burl watched the echoes go from blue to red as the tops built above thirty thousand feet. When they were close enough, he got in the Mustang and drove out to meet them, usually on 82 or 287, the road atlas next to the gearshift and the radar detector on the dashboard.

He told no one he did this, except Coy.

"Chasing tornadoes?" Coy said. "What in the hell are you doing that for?"

They were standing in the front yard of Coy's house. The workmen had the walls up and were starting to lay bricks.

"I don't know," Burl said. "I just like it."

"Christ," Coy said. "Every time it thunders, Cyndi wakes up screaming, and all I can think of is getting out of that trailer. I hope I never see another tornado for the rest of my life. It sounds like you're trying to get yourself killed."

It wasn't that, Burl thought. He was trying to become part of the energy that filled the air before a storm, the energy he had noticed as a child that made every moment important, and everyone alert.

He saw no tornadoes, but some of the storms resembled the diagram in the *Spotter's Guide,* which he had learned to recognize from all angles. Tornadoes always appeared in the southwest corner of the cell, beneath the long, flat bottom of the storm the guide called the rain-free base. Burl recognized this as the place where the air glowed and the clouds pressed down his head, the place he felt compelled to go. To be there made him numb with terror, but his body seemed to need the fear. He came back feeling changed, but in what way he couldn't say.

▼ ▼ ▼

In one of his tornado books he found an account written by a man in Abilene, Texas, who, back in the fifties, had stared up into a tornado funnel.

> Hailstones were coming through the roof, and when I saw the corners of it lifting up, I knew it must be a tornado. Suddenly, I was thrown into the fireplace. The next thing I knew, my house disappeared. I heard nothing but a pounding in my ears. Looking up, I realized with a shock I was in the tornado itself. The interior of the funnel was a long tube, composed of rings. It sounds funny, but it reminded me of the throat of a hog I had seen after butchering. At the top was a blue, shimmering cloud. Then the edge touched my neighbor's house in passing, flicking it away like sparks from a grindstone.

He stared at the page until he felt a stinging and saw his cigarette had burned down to his fingers.

He remembered what the man wearing a raincoat had told him about the big tornado, the day they went back to his brother's house in Faith Village. *There's light inside. Blue light. And it's made of rings.*

For months, Burl had been looking forward to getting enough seniority to go into road freight, so he could take trains out of town. When the brakeman on John Arcement's freight booked off sick, the trainmaster told Burl he would replace him for one trip. Burl had never been to Amarillo. As he packed his bag the night before, he was as excited as a kid going to scout camp for the first time.

They left at eight. "Well, if it ain't my favorite brakeman," Carl Haney said when Burl showed up. "You know, you'd make a beautiful girl, if you only had tits."

Burl rode in the caboose with John. It was like going to sea in a little steel ship. The riveted walls were painted pale green, and light bulbs hung from the ceiling in wire cages. There were two bunks, a desk, a stove, and a chemical toilet. Burl sat up in the cupola, where he could see the train ahead. John sat at the desk, filling out wheel reports. On the wall above him was the conductor's valve, which John could use to throw the train into emergency stop. Railroading men called it going into the big hole.

Amarillo was two hundred and forty miles away. The trip took ten hours.

Beyond Vernon, the country opened up and there was nothing to see. Amarillo was on the Caprock, a thousand feet higher than Nortex. There was a slight grade all the way, and at times the train went so slowly, Burl had the illusion they were standing still while the prairie flowed by.

John spoke to him only once, when they crossed the Prairie Dog Fork of the Red River. "Keep your eyes open here."

"What for?"

"Lots of give in the rails. Track ain't been worked on here for a long time."

They got to Amarillo at sunset. The railroad kept rooms at a motel called the Canyon Courts. They could be called again in eight hours, but John said they probably wouldn't get another train until morning. He went right to sleep, still wearing his clothes, but Burl talked to Royce for a while.

Royce told Burl the worst thing about being an engineer was the accidents. People were always driving out in front of trains. Burl asked him if he'd ever killed anyone, and Royce said right away, without thinking, "Three men, and last year, a senile old woman and two little girls." Burl hadn't thought much of Royce, but he could tell he was really torn up about it. Then Royce went to sleep, and Burl, numb from the motion of the train, took a shower. He lay down on the bed and closed his eyes.

When he woke, his mouth tasted of tin, and for a while he

couldn't remember who or where he was. When he looked at his watch, he saw it was two in the morning. Haney was watching television and working his way through a couple of six-packs of Bud.

Haney said there was an Allsup's across the highway, so Burl walked over and bought a stick of beef jerky and a bottle of Big Red. He was still bothered by a feeling of not knowing exactly where he was. He leaned on a cyclone fence behind the motel and stared off into the darkness. There was a feedlot out there somewhere—he could smell cowshit. But all he could see was a distant line of blue lights.

He spent the rest of the night talking to Haney and watching television. Haney had a pit bulldog he'd named Arnold, after his favorite movie star, Arnold Schwarzenegger. He sometimes wrote letters to his favorite singer, Hank Williams, Jr., and had once gotten back an autographed photo. The satellite dish got a hundred channels, including Tokyo, but Haney preferred the one that showed nonstop pornographic movies.

"Kid," Haney asked him, around four in the morning, "have you ever seen a dick as big as mine?"

"I've never seen it," Burl said.

"Then I'll have to show it to you, won't I?" Haney said. "Why don't we step outside right now?"

"What would I want to do that for?"

"Because it's the biggest one you'll ever see on a white man."

"I don't want to see it," Burl said. "I don't care if it's so big it glows in the dark."

Burl thought Haney was joking. But Haney gave him a dirty look and said, "All right, asshole." They didn't speak for the rest of the night.

They pulled out at seven o'clock, hauling a hundred cars of coal to the power station at Oklaunion. Burl was sorry he hadn't gotten to see Amarillo in the daylight, but he could tell it was just like

Nortex—bigger and a little cooler, being closer to the Rockies, but basically the same town.

The sun was in his eyes most of the way. He could see now why Haney, who was the senior brakeman, rode up front. The air back in the caboose was full of coal dust, and it jolted from side to side with the motion of the train, making the chemical toilet slosh around.

They reached the power station at three o'clock. The smokestack, topped with flashing violet strobes, could be seen when they were still thirty miles away. The plant itself, an open structure of pipes and girders bigger than any building in Nortex, gave off a constant low roar. They bled off air, and Royce backed the train over the dumper, while Burl stood off to one side and watched. Bulldozers crawled over the surge pile, a black hill of coal. Burl stared off over the gray surface of the artificial lake where ash was dumped, stunned by the scale of things. After a while, a van drove up with another crew, which would take the train back to Amarillo. "Boys," John said, "we're dead."

The van took them forty miles back to Nortex, and Burl put his name on the bottom of the list. When they walked out in the parking lot, he asked John if he felt like a beer.

"I don't much like bars," John said. "Why don't you follow me home?"

"All right," Burl said. Nobody, as far as he knew, had ever been to John's house.

John lived on Austin Street, in one of the oldest parts of town. The house was bone gray, the paint completely worn off. There was a sofa on the front porch, swollen from years of being left out in the rain, and a rubber tire hanging by a rope from the pecan tree in the front yard. John said he'd left it there for the neighborhood kids to play on.

He'd lived here since he was twelve, he told Burl, when his

family moved here from Lawton. Now his parents were dead, and his twelve brothers and sisters were scattered all over the country. The front room was full of books, so many shelves of old paperbacks it looked like a secondhand bookstore. In the corner was a leatherbound family Bible on a reading stand, a magnifying glass on top of it. "Read this," John said, pulling a book off the shelf. "It's one of the best books ever written." It was called *Wild Animals I Have Known.*

John went to the kitchen, got them a couple of beers, and turned on the television. "Well," he said, "how do you like road freight?"

"Haney's got a problem," Burl said.

"There's one in every town," John said.

"One what?"

"A guy with a big dick. I guess that's all Haney's got, and that's why he's proud of it. Try to see it from his perspective. My father always said you never understood a man until you walked a mile in his shoes. He also said, I felt sorry for myself because I had no shoes, until I met a man who had no feet."

"What does that mean?"

"I'm not sure," John admitted.

Burl drank his beer. "It seems like a good job to me," he said. "There's nobody looking over your shoulder. And there's not many jobs where you can make so much doing so little."

"Oh, it used to be a good job," John said. "You could work when you wanted, and all the boys got along. Plenty of time to think, and I thought that was what I wanted to do."

"What happened?"

"It changed," John said, "like everything else. They work us too hard now. You go into road freight, you're in the rotating pool. That means you're only guaranteed eight hours off. Anytime after that, they can call you back to work. We used to be able to take twenty days off. Now we can only take two. When Royce killed those little girls, you know what they told him? You can take a day off, but it'll come out of your pocket. It's easy to see why some of the boys drink too much, like Haney. But you don't want to rat on a guy, not when his job's all he's got."

"I guess you're right," Burl said.

John took a little Baggie full of brown dope out of the desk. "Myself, I'm a pot-smoking man," he said. "You look to me like you might be a pot-smoking man yourself."

Burl did some thinking. They had to take a drug test once a year. Speed and alcohol were out of your system in twenty-four hours, but pot could be detected for thirty days. If you weren't careful, you could get in big trouble for a joint you'd smoked a month ago. But his next physical was almost a year away. He had plenty of time.

"Sure," he said.

John twisted one and they smoked it, watching Country Music Television.

"I do like trains, though," Burl said after a while. "And it's great to get out of town."

"Oh, there's no feeling in the world like getting on a train and pulling out," John said, "leaving all your troubles behind. It gives you the illusion of going someplace, forward motion. But you lose your most basic human freedom, the ability to think more than eight hours ahead. It turns you into a little child again," he said softly. "Pretty soon, you're like Railroad Bill in the old song, you got nothing to do but ride, ride, ride."

"Why have you stayed with it for so long?"

"I got a plan," John said. "I'm gonna build that log cabin. You don't. I can tell, because you've got the look."

"What look is that?"

"You look like you want somebody to tell you what to do. People like being told what to do," John said. "That's why I liked the army, even though I said I didn't. Railroad's the same way."

He got up and went into the kitchen. Burl noticed a picture on the wall, of John and two black guys in 'Nam. They had big grins on their faces and were holding on to each other like they were so tired or drunk they were about to fall down.

They smoked some more. Burl's headache went away and he felt a lot better. He looked at the catalog of American Lincoln Log Homes. Finest grade Southern yellow pine, it said. Guaranteed free of rot and insects. Free shingles supplied. He closed his eyes and let his thoughts drift. Waylon Jennings and Hank Williams, Jr., sang a song about whether the really great country musicians came from Texas or Oklahoma.

> When you cross that ole Red River, hoss,
> That name don't mean a thing.
> No matter who's in Austin,
> Bob Wills is still the king.

"One more year," Burl said.

"Next year or the year after that," John said. "That's what I keep telling myself. Then I'm gonna build my log cabin and live like Kit Carson in the Shining Mountains. That's what they used to call the Rockies, you know. Or maybe I'll find some ole ugly woman to marry me, and we'll sit out there on that front porch together."

John scratched a match with his thumbnail and lit the joint again.

"Meanwhile, I'll smoke pot," he said. "I'd rather be a pothead than a drunk any day. Pot gives you a little more room, a little more time. And you're always short of time when you're working for the railroad. You got all the time in the world, and never enough."

5

An article in the paper warned of unscrupulous "contractors," who accepted money to rebuild homes, then disappeared. The city council turned down Willie Nelson's offer of a free concert, saying they were afraid it would bring in a "bad element." Dan Rather did a couple of follow-ups on Nortex and the courage of the American people, but then they stopped hearing about themselves, just about the time the temperature started hitting a hundred every day.

Burl was leaving the video arcade one night when he saw a girl crossing the parking lot. She had honey hair and a look that said she had money, but it would be worth your ass to go for it. When she caught him staring at her, she smiled.

"Burl," she said. "I can't believe it's you."

It was his old high school girlfriend, Nicky Staples.

They talked for a while. She told him she'd quit Southern Methodist six months ago. She'd been studying drama, and her teachers told her she didn't have any talent. "But what are you doing in Nortex?" she said. "Are you going to be playing someplace?"

"It's a long story," he told her. "Can't we get together sometime?"

Nicky thought for a moment, then said, "All right. I'll meet you at Big Brother's on Saturday night, around nine o'clock."

She walked to a red Beamer, her heels clicking on the blacktop, and drove away.

Burl drove back to the Sands, feeling he had been delivered. All this time he'd been longing for a girl, and all this time Nicky had been here. It was fate, he decided. They were supposed to meet. By Thursday afternoon, it had begun to seem that this was the reason why he had come back to Nortex: to get back together with Nicky. To repeat the past, but do it better this time, get it right.

Big Brother's was a shitkicker place, a long sheet-iron shed with a bar at one end and a bandstand at the other. The walls were covered with old license plates and pictures of famous football teams. Burl was at the bar, working on his third beer, when she came up behind him. He had some of Leroy's meth in him, and his stomach was turning like a dynamo.

She'd done something to her hair. There was too much of it. She wore rhinestone earrings, a shiny blue top, jeans, and cowboy boots.

They smiled at each other.

"Let's get drunk," she said.

"Fine with me."

The bartender was right there. "What'll you have?"

"Tequila gold."

"The same," Burl said. "And bring me another beer."

Heads were turning all over the room. Some of these guys probably knew who Nicky was, but they would never have recognized her tonight.

"How do I look?" she asked him.

"Pure white trash."

"That's the idea."

The bartender brought them their shooters. Burl drank his down. It sank instantly to every part of his body, like heavy oil.

For a while they talked about their parents. Nicky told him her father had divorced her mother and married a flight attendant with Texas Air, who belonged to the LaRouche organization and the Church of Scientology.

"Now he's sick," she said. "They found a spot on his liver, and he's going to Dallas for chemotherapy."

Burl's father hated George Staples, but Burl liked him. George belonged to the Confederate Air Force and had always told Burl he was going to teach him to fly someday.

"That's too bad," Burl said. "Tell him I said hello."

He went to the jukebox, dropped in a quarter, and punched up Merle Haggard's "I Guess I'll Just Sit Here and Drink." He asked her to dance.

"I was hoping you'd say that."

Nicky kept her eyes on him while they danced. Other girls stared off into space, thinking about themselves. But Nicky looked right at you, smiling. She had a marvelous ass, and every cowboy in the room was staring at it.

There were two more shooters on the bar when they came back.

"Baby," she said, "just tell me one thing. What are you doing back in Nortex?"

He told her the whole story: how the group had broken up, how he had to go to work for the railroad to pay back his father.

"Well, I hope you don't give up your music," she said. "You had a real talent for it, Burl."

"It's a lot harder to make it than we thought," he said, feeling he was losing ground. "Anyway, it's the feeling that's important, and I can't get it without the group. Seems like the only way I can get it is to get close to a tornado."

"I'm not sure I know what you mean."

"I got real close to the big tornado. I think it did something to me. Didn't you notice how it made people feel better?"

She looked away. "Lots of people got killed."

"I know, but the ones who lived through it felt good. My brother and his wife were about to get a divorce, but it brought them back together again. It made people *feel* something, it made me feel so good, I've been going out and chasing thunderstorms, looking for another tornado. They scare the hell out of me, but they make me feel good, too, sort of like when I first fell in love with you."

Nicky turned her shooter this way and that. Little sparks of light ran around the rim, like ball bearings.

"Oh, baby," she said, "we should have gotten married, back in high school."

"You're drunk," he said.

But there were tears in her eyes.

"Remember how some kids used to do that? Run off to Oklahoma and get married? That's what we should have done. Daddy wouldn't have minded. He liked you. Oh, shit," she said. "I loved you so much. I still do."

She was kissing him, coming up off the stool somehow so her whole body was pressed against his. "Look at that," he heard someone say in a far corner of the room. He was so high, his ears were ringing.

"Let's get out of here," she whispered.

▼ ▼ ▼

They got in the Mustang. It smelled good, like cars did at night. "I'm so glad you still got this ole car," she said, taking a joint out of her purse. "Want some? This is supposed to be pretty good shit."

It had the dirt taste of good dope. At the first hit, memories strobed through him: of the first time he'd kissed her, of the night after graduation when they'd made love on a blanket out at the old Magnolia Refinery. He closed his eyes and smelled the night smell of Nortex: hot, dead grass.

"This is almost like being back in high school," she said. "When things were normal."

Burl didn't remember it that way. Nicky's life had never been normal. She had told him once she'd had her first abortion when she was thirteen. In high school she'd dated grown men, hadn't gotten interested in him until he was so popular other girls were following him around the halls.

"You got a boyfriend, Nicky?" he asked her.

"I've been seeing Jimbo Naylor, off and on," she admitted.

Burl knew Jimbo. He belonged to one of the richest families in town and was a good twenty years older than Nicky.

"He still got all that money?" It was all he could think of to say.

She inhaled, and he heard resin crackle. "Yeah," she said. "He's still got that money, but he's got to work hard to hold on to it right now. But you know what Jimbo says."

"What's that?"

" 'If it was easy, niggers'd do it.' "

He had forgotten she could be so crude. The cold suspicion crossed his mind that she was playing with him.

A police car passed slowly through the streetlight. Nicky spat in her palm and put out the joint.

"Let's go someplace," she said.

"Where?"

"Let's go out to the lake."

"Lake Caddo?"

"Why not? It'll be like old times."

He sure as hell couldn't see going back to the Sands Motel.

Lake Caddo was artificial, created by an earthen dam over Kiowa Creek. It was really just a big mud puddle sitting out there on the prairie. The water was the color of tomato juice, saturated with red Permian clay, and the shallows were full of snags and stumps, the bones of drowned mesquite trees.

Burl took the dirt road over the top of the dam and parked on the north shore. They got out. Hot gusts of wind were blowing out of the darkness, like there was a big fire out there somewhere you couldn't see. There weren't too many stars: maybe the moon was too bright. It hung overhead, slightly past full, white and hard as a broken plate.

They sat on the hood, sharing the last of the joint. Two little gas rigs floated in the lake a hundred yards out.

"Where'd those come from?" he said. "I don't remember those."

"They belong to Jimbo," she said. "He drilled 'em a couple of years ago, then when the price started going down, he capped 'em up."

Again cold suspicion ran through him. His blood felt like mercury.

"You been seeing a lot of Jimbo?"

"Anything wrong with that?"

"No," he said slowly. "Except he's old enough to be your father. But he's got more money."

"He's not that old," she said happily. "Get fucked."

It was the meth, he told himself. He was over the top and coming down, getting paranoid.

But she'd done it before. Played with him, then cut him loose when she was through. People didn't change.

"Bullshit," she said suddenly, sliding off the hood. "Let's go swimming."

"Not me," he said. "I'm ripped."

"Well, I'm going. Help me off with my boots."

She sat on the bumper, extending one leg, cowgirl style. He pulled one boot off while she planted the other in his ass. When he pulled off the second one, she gave him another kick that knocked him down.

Then she was taking off her jeans, top, everything.

"You're out of your mind," he said. "You're going to step on a snag. Or get tangled up in somebody's trotline."

She just laughed and went for the water. He turned on the headlights, illuminating her ass as she dove in, arms out in front of her. Burl pulled off his clothes as rapidly as he could, tiptoed through the smell of dead fish into the water. He stroked out, thinking of cottonmouths, fishhooks. "Goddamnit, Nicky," he shouted, "this is dangerous."

It was the meth that had gotten him into this, he thought. Meth, and Nicky's goddamned way of making you prove something to her before she would put out. He could still see her in the expanding cone of light, which got fainter the farther they got from shore, heading for the nearest rig. Once he got a mouthful of water, frightening him, before he caught up with her. The rig loomed over them, waves echoing off its underside like pistol shots. They climbed the rungs of a ladder and stepped onto the floor.

It was a world of steel and rust. He followed her, shivering from exposure and meth, to the little sheet-metal shed on the side of the rig. The lock was broken. She disappeared inside, came back out with an old blanket smelling of hydrocarbons. She's been here before, he thought. Nicky wrapped the blanket around them, and they stared up at the moon.

He touched one intricately creased nipple. "Why," she said, "I believe you're after my ass."

He had never made love to the same girl after so many years. They had both learned things from other people, and now they showed them to each other. It was exciting at first, but as it went on, he began to sense a hunger in her that was greater than his own. He felt she was hurrying him along, urging him to go faster. The meth had left him wasted, and somehow it was not as wonderful as it should have been. He finally went ahead, thinking that was what she wanted, and she came after him, digging her nails into his back, using the last, unconscious movements of his body to come herself.

He lay atop her, stoned out of his mind. A jet flew over. He wanted to do it again, but he fell asleep. "Look at that," she was saying when he woke up.

The moon was low, a slug of blurred gold, lit from below by an invisible source of light, which was of course the sun, on the other side of the earth.

"I don't want anything but this," he said.

He licked her all over. She tasted of clay. He felt her tongue on his cock, rough as a cat's. They swam back just before daybreak, when the air was getting blue. The battery had gone down and he had trouble starting his car. It didn't seem to matter now if they went to the Sands, so at Big Brother's, she got in her Beamer and followed him back.

He woke with a headache. She lay beside him with her mouth open. Burl got up and opened the blinds: light stabbed his eyes. It was a hot, bright day, and everyone but them was at work or school. He could feel it on the air somehow, a hum of distant activity. Nicky sat up, holding the sheet over her breasts. "Shit," she said. "What time is it?"

He looked at his watch. "Noon."

She got up, disappeared into the bathroom. "There's mold in the shower," she said.

"You didn't mind last night."

"I was stoned last night."

She came out, pulling on her jeans and top, not bothering with her underwear.

"When are we going to see each other again?" he asked her.

"Look, baby," she said. "I can't afford to do this all the time. Someone might see us."

"What's wrong with that?"

"What's wrong with that," she said, "is that Jimbo and I are getting married next month."

He stared at her. "You said last night you loved me."

"I do love you, baby. I'll always love you. But we're not in high school anymore. Things have changed." She went to the door. "Maybe we can see each other after the honeymoon. I'll let you know how it works out."

He turned away. "Forget it."

"Oh, stop trying to make me feel like this is my fault," she said crossly. "I felt sorry for you last night, if you want to know the truth. You're not playing music anymore, you're just working. You're not who you were. I don't understand you, baby," she said. "I'd love to get out of this town, and I don't know why you ever came back. There's nothing here."

Burl closed the blinds and fell back into something like sleep until four. When he got up again, he lit one of her cigarettes and was instantly sorry: he was sick to his stomach, his head was spinning. He was crashing from the meth, and the only thing to do was take some more. But when he turned on the light to look for the little gold bottle, the bulb burned out with a blue flash and the room went dark. He sat on the bed, feeling as if he weighed hundreds of tons. Nortex was a black hole, its gravity so strong that nothing, not even light, could escape.

He turned on the television to The Weather Service, and a

bulletin scrolled up on the screen: *Severe thunderstorms, with the possibility of tornadoes, are expected until 8 AM. This watch includes the Nortex area.* There was a big red echo just south of town.

He stared at it, thinking of blue light and steel rings.

The phone rang. It was the yardmaster, telling him he had to go to work.

"I'm taking a personal day off," Burl said, and hung up.

He drove out of town on the Amarillo highway. The storm, a textbook Supercell, hid the setting sun. The moment he passed the city limits sign, he felt better. Behind was confusion, ahead was clarity. Looking at the storm, he made out all the features in the *Spotter's Guide:* gust front, precipitation shaft, rainfree base.

He turned south on a little blacktop that would take him under the core. He was coming up on a wall of rain, black as outer space, when he passed a Storm Spotter in a pickup, who pulled in behind him and blinked his lights until Burl pulled over. "I wouldn't go down that road, son," he said. "We've got a report of a tornado on the ground up there."

"Appreciate it," Burl said, and watched the helpful smile fading from the Spotter's face as he pulled away.

Then he was in the rain, so heavy he had to turn on the headlights. It got darker, and big hailstones began hitting the roof, hard as bullets, sure sign of a tornado nearby. Burl heard himself laughing insanely. This is going to kill me, he thought. Then the rain stopped, and he was breaking out.

The rainfree base pressed down on his head, a room of clouds ten miles long and five hundred feet high. To the west, where a little light seeped in under the cell, he saw the funnel, a long black tube silhouetted against blue afterglow. He figured it was going to cross the road a mile ahead of him. Burl stepped on the gas, trying to get as close as possible, following the wet road that reflected the dying light like a ribbon of mercury.

There were levels to terror, and he was on the highest one,

where he had been once before, the one where you could think clearly. He pulled off the road when he was exactly as close as he could get and jumped out of the car. The tornado crossed the road a half-mile ahead of him. He heard its high humming roar, saw how the sucking mouth hovered just off the ground, like a flame hovering above the surface of a burning log, not quite touching it.

He had forgotten the telephone lines: the funnel took them with it. The shock rippled toward him. When it hit, the pole above him groaned and leaned and the transformer box spat blue balls of fire that bounced across the road. Burl threw himself back into the Mustang. The funnel disappeared into the darkness. Cold rain poured down, and he hid on the floor of the car, shuddering with terror.

In a little while, the rain stopped and he got out. Everything had changed. The storm had passed over, a few stars had appeared, and the world was a soft blue. He could smell the hot engine of the car and something like electricity. Then he looked up.

The storm towered over him, a sheer wall of marble sixty thousand feet high. He had to stare straight up to see the top, which was still in sunlight, a great ceiling of gold. As he watched, it faded to cream, to rose, to ice blue. The lower levels were lead gray. As it rolled away, the moon seemed to rise behind it. Suddenly, the whole storm was lit by one incredible flash of golden lightning. Burl held his breath, but heard nothing. Far to the south, another storm he had not noticed lit up, too, as if it were signaling this one.

He felt fortunate, sure of himself. He had seen another tornado, just as he had known he would. For a long time he stayed there, enjoying the stillness of the air. All its energy was spent. When he drove back to the Sands, his mind was clear. He could stick it out here for a while, make enough money to pay off his father, and then do whatever he wanted to do.

One more year, he promised himself, staring at the calendar thumbtacked to the wall. It stretched out ahead of him, like the clean, polished surface of the bright steel rail.

THE BOUNDARY

1

They were coming back from Amarillo on the first hot day of the year, pulling a hundred cars of coal. At Quanah they stopped to let the hotshot go by, and Burl walked across the highway to the little grocery store and bought some yellow cheese and crackers and a bottle of Big Red.

John met him on his way back to the caboose. "I want to show you something," he said.

"Can't it wait?" Burl said. "I want to drink my soda pop."

"No," John said. "You got to see this."

They walked along the train, their feet crunching on the ballast. John climbed the rungs to the top of a hopper car, and Burl followed him up. "What is it?" he said.

"Can't you smell it?"

Then Burl caught the odor of something dead—metallic and horribly sour, like the old tarnished spoons in his grandmother's silver cabinet. Protruding from the bed of coal was a hand.

"I guess it's a hobo," Burl said. "He was asleep and somehow this coal shifted and buried him."

He stared at the hand. The fingers were brown and stiff, the nails blue.

"No," John said. "I uncovered him a little. I don't think he's a hobo. His clothes are too good."

"What do you think, then?"

"Those coal towns are tough places," John said. "I think he crossed somebody, and they got even. They knew this coal was going to a power plant. That furnace burns at a thousand degrees. Good way to get rid of a body." He spat explosively. "Turn it to carbon in the blink of an eye."

Burl thought for a moment. "What are we going to do?"

"I say nothing." John looked at him. "I mean, this could be nothing but trouble."

"We haven't done anything."

"No," John said. "But first thing you know, we'll have to take a drug test. And I can't afford to pee into that little bottle." He spat again. "It troubles me, but I say we just forget we ever saw the poor sonofabitch and send him on down the line."

Burl decided John was right. They covered up the hand, and John closed his eyes and said a silent prayer. On their way back to the caboose, Burl threw his cheese and crackers into the weeds.

They rolled on through the long afternoon. At Chillecothe, Burl looked back and saw a thunderhead building behind them. Another year had gone by, and the first big cold front of the season was moving down across the Panhandle. If it pushed through, there would be storms in Nortex tonight.

Burl had been on the Amarillo run for almost a year now, and he was beginning to see what John meant about road freight. Sometimes he got home at four in the afternoon, sometimes at four in the morning. He smoked a joint, fell asleep, and woke full of a terrible uncertainty—for long moments, he couldn't remember who or where he was.

He was making plenty of money and had paid off some of his debt. But he no longer thought about getting out of Nortex and going back to school. In the last eight months, he had stopped thinking ahead. The motion of the train numbed him, until he felt he was drifting off into some kind of fog.

On the other hand, he had really learned to love this country out here. Burl had never known how big the Panhandle was, or how empty, until he started crossing it on a train. Out here, in Foard and Hardeman and Cottle counties, there was nothing but a great rolling plain of salt cedar. There were deer out here, and coyotes, and bobcats. There were plenty of rattlesnakes, too, and you had to be careful when you got out to throw a switch, because they liked to sleep close to the rails, for the heat. Just the other day, he and John had seen two big diamondbacks mating, gliding toward and away from each other like mirror images, a sight so strange it made his mouth go dry.

John had told him the Comanche believed this country belonged to none of the gods. They reasoned this from its savage weather, which they said drove men insane. Burl could believe it. It was out here, in the spring, that the Supercells were born. And one night last month, someone had taken a shot at him while he was riding up here in the cupola. The flash and the snap of the bullet going by had brought him up out of the fog for the first time in months.

Just before they got to Vernon, John climbed up in the cupola with him. They sat in silence for a while. "I've never seen a dead man before," Burl said.

"I seen plenty in 'Nam," John said. "Thing that always gets you is, there's something missing. They're like a stone or a piece of wood. You know they'll never move again."

Burl, who had told John about chasing tornadoes, pointed out the thunderhead behind them. "If you're gonna be doing it again this year," John said, "why don't you take me with you sometime? I'd like to get a closer look at one."

"All right," Burl said. "You can come with me."

John had become Burl's closest friend. He might not have a college degree, but he was the smartest guy Burl had ever known. John was an agnostic, but he could argue the Bible forward and backward. He'd been arguing with Carl Haney just last night, at the motel in Amarillo.

"Now this Rapture you're always talking about," he had asked Haney. "What is it, exactly? It sounds like some kind of sexual thing."

"You know what the Rapture is, John Arcement," Haney said. "It's when those of us who are saved go flying up to heaven, just before Armageddon. It's in the Book of Revelations."

"And you believe everything that's in the Bible?"

"Every word," Haney said.

"Then I guess you're in favor of incest."

Haney frowned. "Hell, no. That's one of the worst things you can do."

"But it says right here in Genesis," John said, pulling the Gideon Bible out of the dresser drawer, "that Cain and Abel took wives. If they were the sons of Adam and Eve, the first people in Creation, then where did they find 'em? There's no doubt about it," he said, thumping the cover. "They must have married their sisters."

Haney looked stunned. Royce, their engineer, laughed and said, "He's got you there, hoss."

"Damn you, John Arcement," Haney said. "Sometimes you sound like you're part of this conspiracy that's trying to stop our kids from saying their prayers in school."

"Who do you think's behind it?" John said.

"If you ask me," Haney said, "it's the Jews."

"Jesus was a Jew."

"Now you've gone too far," Haney said, and stomped off across the highway to buy another six-pack.

Later Burl and John had gone out behind the motel, where they stared off at the blue lights, which Burl had learned were the lights of Pantex, the final assembly point for all nuclear weapons in the United States arsenal. To the north, way up in the Panhandle, they could see flashes of lightning where the front was moving down.

"These damned fundamentalists," John said. "There's nothing more ridiculous than someone who believes in the literal truth of the Bible." He laughed. "Maybe if their fathers had been preachers, like mine, they'd know you can make the Bible say anything you please."

"There's sure a lot of them," Burl said. "When you turn on the television, it's all you see."

"Yeah, and it's not only the Christians," John said. "The Moslem fundamentalists are getting stronger too. The fundamentalist sects of every religion in the world are the fastest-growing."

"Why do you think that is?"

"Oh, I got that all figured out," John said. "The answer is simple. We're getting close to the end of the world."

Both Burl and John believed there was going to be a nuclear war someday. John thought it would start over religion. A Baptist president or a Moslem fanatic would push the button.

Burl thought it would start over power. He knew what had happened to Nortex when the oil had disappeared. The same thing would happen to the world. When there were too many people, and not enough gasoline and electricity, nations would get desperate. According to *Aviation Week*, they were making four warheads a day at Pantex right now.

▼   ▼   ▼

They reached the power station at six o'clock. Brown fumes simmered from the smokestack, indicating the presence of nitrogen dioxide. The fly ash was supposed to be scrubbed out, but Burl knew the plant was still putting out millions of cubic meters of carbon dioxide, the gas which would someday create a greenhouse effect in the earth's atmosphere.

"Look at that," John said. "I wouldn't like to work out here and have to breathe that shit every day."

"You probably do anyway," Burl pointed out. "The wind's blowing it toward Nortex."

They pulled into the shadow of the power station and bled off air. Burl and John got out of the caboose, and Royce started backing the train over the dumper. Burl could see the hopper car that held the body. He didn't want to think about it, and he looked the other way, at the power plant. From the first time he had seen the power plant, it had fascinated him. Somehow, it was a fitting addition to the landscape. Like Pantex, it belonged here.

"Man," John said. "I can't believe we're just gonna stand here and let this happen."

"You're right, though," Burl said. "We can't afford to get involved."

"No, but I don't much feel like watching it."

"Me neither."

John thumbed the send button of his radio. "Haney," he said, "Burl and I are gonna inspect the power plant. Give us a call if you need us."

Ten four, Haney said.

As Burl followed John into the power plant he entered a pool of noise so deafening, he lost all sense of his body and felt like he was floating. He remembered when he was a child and his father had taken him onto the drilling rig floor. Maybe that was when he had developed a fascination for places like this, a fascination with power. The plant seemed to be deserted. They walked through a long, empty room, under great cylinders in which the coal was ground to powder. The air was hot and dry and smelled of steel pushed to the limit, a smell he had noticed coming off the rails after a train had passed over them.

They found an elevator and rode up fourteen stories to a control room with windows all around. Four men wearing white shirts and ties sat at computer consoles. One, who had cropped gray hair and reminded Burl of a high school football coach, turned and looked at them.

"Mind if we take a look around?" John asked him.

"No," the man said pleasantly. "Just don't touch anything."

Through the windows on one side of the room, Burl could see the back of a turbine as big as a destroyer. The throbbing roar came up through the soles of his boots. He found it hard to believe only four men controlled all this. Men were almost unnecessary here.

"Quite an operation," John was saying.

"Yeah," the man said proudly, "we put seven hundred and fifty megawatts per hour on the grid. We send it all over West Texas. Oklahoma buys some too. Takes a lot of coal. Burns something like four hundred tons per hour. That's more than a hundred thousand tons a week. Gonna be keeping you boys busy for a long time."

Could there be that much coal in the world? But every time they came back from Amarillo, they hauled another trainload. Burl stepped to the windows on the other side, conscious of his dirty clothes in the clean room. Fourteen stories below, Royce was backing the train over the dumper. It looked like a toy. From this height he couldn't be sure, but he thought the car that held the body was just coming over the shaft.

John had joined him. Burl looked around, saw the men at the consoles were paying no attention.

"That the one?" he whispered.

John nodded.

Burl felt his stomach tighten. The hopper car opened, and a hundred tons of coal spilled into the shaft, a thick plume of dust hiding the car and anything else he might have seen.

▼ ▼ ▼

They took the elevator up three more stories and stepped out on a catwalk. To the west, the Medicine Mounds marched off. There, John had told him, Quanah Parker—the great chief of the Comanche—had gone to eat peyote and have visions. The storm hid the sun, but a bar of light shone through its scalloped top. Passing overhead, it seemed to bend, as if following the curve of the earth, until it vanished into the dusk rising in the east.

"I'm starting to hate this damned power plant," John said. "We're nothing but servants to it. It makes me feel like I'm one little ant in a whole long line, bringing it food."

The storm lit with a flash of lightning. There was power, too, Burl thought. A storm like that could generate the energy of an atomic bomb every three minutes.

"Better start building that log cabin," Burl told him. "You heard what that guy said. The way we're using energy, the shit's going to hit the fan pretty soon."

"I'm going to someday," John said.

"Best not to wait too long."

"We'll know when it's coming. There'll be signs beforehand."

Burl wondered if John wasn't more of a believer than he liked to pretend.

"You'll never do it," Burl said. "You'll be a railroading man forever." When John didn't reply, he said, "Anyway, it might not happen. Maybe people aren't that stupid."

John was staring off at the Medicine Mounds, where a black shaft of rain was falling, evaporating before it touched the ground.

"That's what the Indians thought," he said. "But their world ended too."

Burl had finally gotten out of the Sands Motel—found a duplex apartment, covered with gray asbestos siding, on the hill below the municipal water tower. It had four rooms, and he had bought more furniture at the Goodwill: a couch, a chair, and a chrome table with a yellow Formica top, which Burl liked because it was so ugly.

When he got back, he took a shower and lay down on the couch. The dead body had been like a bullet snapping by—one of those things that brought him up out of the fog, and for a while he could think. He had to do something with his life. The trouble was, he had no idea what, and it was hard to do anything when you could think no more than eight hours ahead. So they waited—Burl for some sign of what he should do with himself, John for some sign of the end of the world.

He woke to the sound of thunder and stepped outside. Violet lightning threw the water tower into silhouette.

Burl turned the television to The Weather Service. *At midnight*, the meteorologist said, in his flat, air controller's voice, *a line of severe thunderstorms was moving into the Nortex area. These storms may produce hail, damaging winds, and deadly lightning. Residents are advised to stay tuned to this channel for further advisories.*

His heart pounded. He took a couple of hits off a joint that flooded his brain with hot light. Then he got out his guitar for the first time in months and played while the storm rumbled in over Nortex, played until his fingers were sore and bleeding, not giving a shit what the neighbors thought.

2

That spring, the cold fronts came one after another. There were tornadoes in Abilene, Sherman, and Decatur. Burl got hailed on every time he drove out looking for a storm. He saw no tornadoes, but by the end of April, the Mustang was covered with dents and the paint had started to chip off.

Finding the right storm was not as easy as he had thought. Conditions had to be perfect. Burl watched the new weather channel on cable television, studying the satellite photos, trying to get a look at things on a larger scale. He could see the cold fronts coming days away—big lows, spinning down out of the Gulf of Alaska. As they got closer, they began pulling up moist air from the

Gulf of Mexico. Then the skies were full of fast, low clouds, and the days grew hotter and stickier. At night, there was a ring around the moon. Moisture covered North Texas like a bed of warm, thick oil.

Sometimes the fronts stopped out there in the Panhandle. The cold air lay alongside of the warm for hundreds of miles. Like oil and water, they refused to mix. Meteorologists called it a dry-line. Sometimes it stood still for two or three days, while the energy built up and Burl's excitement became almost unbearable. Then the jet stream dipped down, the front moved, and thunderstorms broke out all along the dryline.

Timing was all-important. He had to know when he could take a day off to see storms, when he could afford to go to Amarillo. Once he went to Amarillo, and storms broke out right after he left. Another time, he took a day off and spent eight hours staring at an empty radar screen. That night he got drunk and threw a beer bottle against the kitchen wall. I've got to have more information, he thought.

Burl bought a scanner at Wal-Mart and started listening to the Spotter net. The meteorologist in Fort Worth always called in and told them where the storms were going to be. It was a big help, but to get it he had to listen to the Spotters gossiping all day long, like housewives on the telephone.

I'm going to the hardware store, one would say.

Roger, what you looking for?

Gonna buy some finishing nails. Be off the air about fifteen minutes.

Roger, copy that.

He couldn't believe they were so removed from what was going on. Ten minutes later, the first one would call back. *Well, I got those nails. Guess I'll be heading out to Carrow's for breakfast.*

Roger, their hash browns are pretty good.

Burl was no longer sorry he couldn't be a Spotter. They were working men. They'd voted for Reagan, school prayer, the death penalty. They were Good Neighbor Sams, doing this because they felt they owed the community a service. He was doing this because he loved tornadoes.

Soon they were aware of him. *Here comes that red Mustang again,* he heard one say as he drove out to a storm near Windthorst. *Wonder who he thinks he is?*

In the year since the big tornado, Nortex had been completely rebuilt. There was a new mayor, Luther Babbs, former head of the recovery committee, and the one who had coined the slogan "Let's Roll Up Our Sleeves." He wore thick glasses, polyester shirts—with the sleeves rolled up—and combed his hair over his bald spot.

Babbs was remote, even prissy, but he could get emotional, especially on television. On the anniversary of the Big Tornado, Burl watched him dedicate a monument in Faith Park, where it had first touched down. The monument was a bronze tablet with a poem rumored to be written by Babbs himself:

> We dedicate this tablet
> Where the storm vented its rage,
> And left the name of Nortex
> Printed on the history page

"It is our duty," Babbs said, polishing his glasses and sniffing back a few tears, "to make this town bigger and better than ever, so that the dead will not have died in vain."

The night after that, Burl went over to Coy and Margo's for dinner. Except for the smell of fresh paint and new acrylic carpet, it looked exactly the same as before. Margo had even selected the same furniture. The tornado had pumped a lot of money into the economy, and Prairie Savings & Loan was expanding. Coy's boss, Buddy McAlester, was leasing a Learjet and had bought condos in La Jolla and Marina Del Rey.

Cyndi was having a little trouble.

She still had nightmares about tornadoes. A lot of kids were having them. Everyone in Nortex was suffering from tornado shock. An article in the paper said the patients at the state asylum were uncontrollable when there was a tornado watch. "I see them coming down the block," she told Burl. "They're just little ones, but there's no place to hide. And sometimes I dream my friends won't talk to me. I see them from the back, and when they turn around, they're not who I thought they were."

They had been sending her to a psychologist, Gayle Jo True, who had helped a lot of kids. "She told us we should get Cyndi to talk about her fears," Margo said. "Try to help her understand that God made tornadoes, but he also made good things too."

"He sure did," Coy said. "The tornado got me this job and bought us this house."

They told Burl they had rejoined the church. A lot of people had. It gave you a sense of belonging to something bigger than yourself.

After dinner they sat at the table and talked about the days after the tornado. No one could forget the constant sound of helicopters flying over. Everyone's clothes had been contaminated by particles of fiberglass and had to be washed in vinegar to get it out. Margo recalled how in that first month, the town had seemed full of strangers. "It still is," Coy said. The block looked just like it had before, but things were not quite the same. One of their neighbors had lost her husband and married one of the Mennonite volunteers. Someone had stolen Coy's tools out of the garage. Coy admitted he had bought a gun. As they talked on, Burl felt a chill descend on the room, and the night seemed to close around them.

Cyndi said nothing. She sat as close to the television as possible, watching her favorite program, *Little House on the Prairie*.

In the last week of April, conditions were perfect. He called John. "If you're still interested in chasing tornadoes, tomorrow looks like the best day of the year."

"I'll be over in the morning," John said.

John came over the next day at noon, bringing a bottle of Herradura tequila, *hecho en México,* and a Polaroid camera. He showed Burl the paper. There had been tornadoes in the Panhandle the night before. A mobile home park had been destroyed near Snyder.

"I don't see why you got to go out and chase tornadoes," he said. "Thing you should do is just live in a mobile home. They always head straight for 'em."

"I've thought about it."

"How does it look for today?"

"Couldn't be better," Burl said. "We're gonna have storms popping up all over around three o'clock. All we've got to do is find the right one."

"I hope so," John said. "I took a day off, you'd better find me a tornado."

Burl ate bacon and eggs while John read him the rest of the paper. The First Bank of Midland had folded, and Lone Star Drilling Company, the largest in Nortex, had filed Chapter Eleven. But everything would be all right, the editor said, if people had more faith in Ronald Reagan. And there was a good side to this: people were rediscovering their faith in the Lord. A record turnout had been recorded by the annual Easter pageant at the Holy City, up in the Wichita Mountains.

"When I was a kid, I played a part in that show," John said. "I was a little boy who brought a gift to the Baby Jesus. My father played John the Baptist." He sighed and closed the paper. "What do we do now?"

"There's nothing to do," Burl said, "but wait."

Burl went out on the front porch. His apartment was on the highest ground in Nortex, and he could see for miles to the north and west: this was the reason he had taken it. But the sky was cloudless, and after a while he came back inside, plugged in his Telecaster, and sat on the couch next to John, switching from The Weather Service to Country Music Television.

Things were sure going to hell here in North Texas. Even if he did quit the railroad, Burl knew he could never find another job, at least not here in Nortex. Coy might deny it, but the town was in trouble. Sometimes Burl had the feeling the whole world was in trouble. The trains were full of Mexicans now, heading north, looking for work. The week before he had dropped down into a gondola and found eight or ten of them, huddled together and staring at him with those sleepy Indian eyes. You were supposed to kick them off the train, but Burl had found himself giving them his lunch, and telling them, in his stumbling high school Spanish, how to get off before they reached the Amarillo yards.

At two o'clock, when he thought he could stand the waiting no longer, he switched to the Weather Service radar and saw the first faint blue echoes of a storm down near Seymour. "Here we go," he said. "Now we're going to get some action."

The echoes went from blue to red as the tops built above thirty thousand feet. The dispatcher told the Spotters to get ready to go out. From the back porch he could see the anvil spreading out to the west, glaring white in the sun.

John had fallen asleep on the couch. "Come on," Burl said, shaking him awake. "Let's go for it."

They headed out of town on 287. John hung his head out the window, his eyes closed and his mouth open, drinking in the air. Burl had to smile: he looked just like a dog.

The storm was headed to the northeast, toward Oklahoma. It was a good forty miles long, the anvil blowing out another fifty miles ahead of it on the jet. He could hear the Spotters talking on the scanner.

I'm sitting at Maybelle Corner, one said. *Man, it's sure getting dark over there to the west.*

Burl had learned to look for that darkness. The most intense cells seemed to radiate some kind of *black energy.*

Then they were under the anvil, in the shadow of the storm, and he could see it more clearly. At Electra, he turned off on 25 and drove south until they came to a little farm-to-market road that would take them under the core. He pulled off on the shoulder, and they got out. The storm was almost on top of them, and the air was dead still. A pumping jack nodded in the mesquite a mile away, its chugging diesel the only sound.

"I'm scared already," John said.

It was the silence that got to you: like watching a hundred-car coal train roll toward you, and hearing nothing.

"If there's a tornado, it's on the other side of that rain," Burl said. "There's nothing to worry about here except lightning."

John looked at him.

"I'm not joking," Burl said. "More people have been killed by lightning than tornadoes."

"I didn't think of it as a joke," John said. "Any way to tell where it's going to strike?"

"The highest thing around, or the biggest concentration of metal," he said. "Like that pumping jack." Or this car, he thought. He looked through his binoculars, trying to penetrate the blackness.

A couple of drops of rain fell. A moment later, a bolt of lightning hit the pumping jack.

Burl screamed and threw himself to the ground. At the blue-violet instant of the flash, he thought it had hit the car. The thunder was unbelievable, tons of falling stone.

John was smiling down at him. "Get in the car," he said, picking himself up.

"You were scared," John said as Burl fumbled for the keys. "You were scared shitless."

"That was nothing," Burl said. "Wait until one hits close enough so you can hear the plasma snap. Sounds just like grease on a hot stove."

The dispatcher was talking to the Spotters. *That storm has split into two cores,* he said. *We've got a hook echo in the cell to the north. That's the one we want you to concentrate on.*

I'm not getting any closer than I am right now, a Spotter said. *It's too hot for me.*

"Hear that?" Burl yelled. "A hook echo. That means a tornado." He started the car and pulled onto the road.

"What should I do?" John said.

"Get that camera ready. If we start hitting big hail, that means we're getting close to a tornado."

Just before they went into the rain, they passed one of the Spotters, sitting in a Toyota pickup with a whip antenna. Burl stepped on the gas and shot him the finger. A moment later, he heard him say, *There goes that damned red Mustang again.*

Then they were in the rain, so heavy he had to turn on the headlights. Hailstones began rattling on the roof. Soon they were big as golf balls. John took a big gulp of Herradura. Burl was laughing insanely, like he always did: he knew they could be driving right into the mouth of the funnel. Then he saw light ahead, and they were breaking out.

The rainfree base pressed right down on their heads. To the west a little light seeped in under the cell, but it was the dim orange of a sodium vapor lamp. To the north he made out a boiling confusion of clouds, right down on the ground. He took another little blacktop in that direction, and a moment later they passed an old Aeromotor windmill blown to the ground, and a herd of frightened cattle, shit dropping from under their tails. "It's right up in front of us," he yelled to John.

But now they had to catch it, and the storm was moving fast. They crossed the Red River on a little concrete bridge. On the other side, the pavement stopped. They were in Oklahoma now, and there was nothing between here and Lawton but dirt road, small farms, and abandoned Atlas missile silos.

"Find me a good road going north," he yelled, throwing John the road map.

The storm was getting out in front of them. A great shaft of sunlight poured down, and he saw more hailstones scattered everywhere, white as eggs in the sun. "Storm's heating up again," he said. "Get that camera ready!"

They met a biker on a big Harley chopper, and Burl wondered what he was doing out here. Then they topped a little rise, and he saw a figure ahead.

When they got a little closer, he saw it was a woman, walking right down the middle of the red clay road.

He slowed down so he wouldn't splash her. As he drove by, he got a glimpse of her: black hair, parted in the middle and plastered down by the rain. She wore a dirty white leather jacket that looked like she'd bought it at a thrift shop.

"Ain't you even going to stop?" she yelled.

He hit the brakes.

"We can't leave a woman in distress," John said. He looked back. "She's pretty good-looking too."

Burl looked in the mirror. She'd picked up a hailstone and was about to fling it. "Hey," he yelled, "you don't have to do that," and backed up.

"My ole man kicked me off his scoot," she said. "Do you think you could give me a ride to Lawton?"

"We're not going that way."

"Well then, give me a ride to a telephone. You can't leave me here." She had a big bump on her forehead, and her clothes were soaked.

"All right," he told her. "Get in."

She climbed in the back seat, and he stepped on the gas. "You have a fight with your ole man?" John asked, handing her the bottle of Herradura.

"We were going to Crowell to see his mother," she said. "We started fighting, and he told me to get my butt off. Then it started to hailing."

"Pretty inconsiderate."

She took a big pull from the bottle. "I thought I was going to get stoned to death, like some woman in the Bible."

"What's your name?" John asked her.

"Bebe Sanchez."

They jolted along the muddy road. She told John she was an Indian. Her ole man was a half-blood. He belonged to the Renegades, one of the roughest motorcycle gangs around. She leaned over the seat, breathing in his ear, and said, "You got the prettiest long hair. You look just like David Lee Roth."

"Burl here used to be a rock-and-roll star," John said. "Played rhythm guitar for Uncontrolled Meltdown."

"You're shitting me. Whatever happened to you guys?"

"We broke up," he said, turning onto another muddy road. "Stay on that map," he told John.

"What's your hurry?" she said.

"We're chasing a tornado."

She looked at John, then back at Burl. "Let me get this straight," she said. "You're chasing a tornado? What the hell for?"

"This is a spiritual quest," John said. "Ain't you never read Carlos Castaneda? We're looking for power, big medicine. Hoping to see Mescalito."

She took another pull from the bottle. "You're a couple of insane mothers, aren't you?" she said.

They came to a blacktop going north, and Burl stepped on the gas. For three or four miles he was doing eighty, then he saw a line of cottonwoods up ahead where there was a small town. He slowed down to go through the single traffic light, and she said, "There's a Seven-Eleven. They probably got a telephone."

"And I could use a couple of sticks of beef jerky," John said, "to keep me going."

"We're not stopping."

"Well, you're almost out of gas," John pointed out. "You're not going to be chasing any tornadoes on an empty tank."

Burl pulled off the road. "Now look," he said to John. "This is serious business. It's like an expedition. Now stay on that map, and *let's get our shit together*."

"I ain't seen no tornadoes yet," John said. "If you ask me, we should take it easy. It's my day off, and I ain't had any fun yet. Why don't we take her to Lawton? I grew up there, you know. I'd like to see some of the scenes of my youth. Maybe go up in the Wichita Mountains and take a look at the Holy City."

"Look at that," she said.

It was no more than five miles ahead of them, a long gray tube silhouetted against blue rain. It touched the ground, and big sparks shot up as it hit a power line.

"Jesus Christ," John said.

Then the rain closed in, and it was gone. Burl pulled back on the road and stepped on the gas, concentrating on driving as fast as he could.

He saw the grain elevator at Chattanooga, and a moment later, flashing red lights. There was a Highway Patrol car parked at the intersection. A mobile home down the street was torn apart, and pink fiberglass insulation was blowing everywhere. Burl pulled into the parking lot of a cafe, where several people were standing around. "You have a twister?" he said, jumping out.

"Sure did," one said. "Come through here five minutes ago, sounding just like a freight train."

When he turned back to the car, the windows were rolled up and the girl had disappeared. He looked around, but she was nowhere in sight. He knocked on the window, and John rolled it down. He was smoking a joint. "Where is she?" Burl asked him.

"In the café."

Burl went inside. Most of the people were standing at the windows. She was talking to the woman behind the cash register.

"I'm good," he heard her say. "I'm really good. I got clothes too. These aren't my good clothes. I got caught out in the rain."

"Honey, you'd have to talk to the manager," the woman said. "And I don't think he's gonna be in today."

"I've got lots of experience. I worked at the Ramada Inn in Oklahoma City. I can give you the name of the person there I worked for."

"You could come back tomorrow," the woman said, not looking at her. "But I don't think he's looking for anybody. There's three of us, and that's enough to take care of this place."

"Oh, all right, maybe I'll come back tomorrow." She turned around and saw Burl.

"What are you doing?" he asked her.

"Looking for a job. I just thought they might have a job."

She followed him out into the parking lot.

"Why are you looking for a job here, if you live in Lawton?"

"Well, we're not really living in Lawton. We're just sort of staying at his sister's right now. We're not really living anywhere."

"Look," he said. "Why don't you just stay here?" He found his billfold, took out a ten-dollar bill. "Here's some money. It's all I've got."

"But there's *nothing* here," she said.

"You can catch a bus or something."

"Look there." She pointed to the sign across the street that said LAWTON—30. "It's right down the road. Can't you just take me? My little baby's there."

She was wearing that stupid leather jacket, and her eyes had the same sleepy look as the Mexicans in the gondola. Furious, he held open the door for her, and she got in without a word of thanks.

A mile down the road he saw the white government vehicles of the Severe Storms Lab pulled off on the shoulder. One had a Doppler radar antenna turning on the roof. He pulled off behind them. "Who are these fellows?" John said.

Burl told him.

"You mean they're the big time?"

"That's right," Burl said. "*National Geographic Special* time."

They got out and walked up to a group of scientists and college kids. One of the kids glanced at Burl. It was like looking in a mirror: his hair was as long as Burl's, and the same color, but he wore glasses. "You can't get through," he said. "The power lines are down up ahead."

He turned back to the group. Burl moved a little closer, trying to hear what they were saying. "The Norman Doppler says it's got tops spiking up to sixty thousand feet," a scientist said. "And it's got the biggest mesocyclone the operator's ever seen."

"We've been following that storm," Burl said.

"Look, man," the kid said. "We're busy here. Why don't you take a walk or something?" He turned back to the others. One of them asked him something, and Burl heard him say, "Just a couple of shitkickers."

They walked back to the Mustang, Burl's face burning.

"Make you feel like stale beer, don't they?" John said.

"I've seen a few tornadoes. I've probably seen more than they have."

"Don't take it so hard." John put his hand on Burl's shoulder. "They're the big dogs here. They're the professionals. You're just a pup to them."

Burl slammed the door. Then, without knowing he was going to, he pulled around the vehicles and headed down the road. They were yelling at him, but he kept right on going. Ahead, he could see the toppled high-tension tower and the cables lying across the road, slithering around just like snakes trying to get close to a rail, for the heat.

"Whoa," John said.

"You're going to kill us!" she screamed.

"You wanted to go to Lawton," he said. "This is the road to Lawton."

John was trying to grab him. "I don't know if this is such a good idea."

"No, no," he said, laughing. "The tires'll insulate us. We'll be all right." Unless they touch the gas tank, he thought. If they did, there would be sparks, an explosion.

He felt his scalp prickle as they bumped over the cables, then they were in the clear and picking up speed. "Never again," John was saying. "Never again." She was laughing now, handing him the bottle of Herradura. He took a big gulp. They followed the storm for another thirty minutes. It was the best storm of the year, but it was moving too fast for them. On the radio he heard warnings for it farther and farther north, until finally even he had to admit they'd lost it. They passed some houses, came to a traffic light, then Burl looked ahead and saw neon signs and realized they were already in Lawton.

They went to a bar John knew of, the Missile Lounge, which he said had the best ribs in Oklahoma. She telephoned her sister and they sat in a booth, drinking Red Draws. The place was empty, except for two cowboys in the back shooting pool.

The waitress brought John his plate of ribs. John offered Burl some, but he wasn't hungry.

"You don't know what you're missing," John said.

Burl was watching the cowboys, thinking it was strange how the weather meant everything to him and nothing to them. To them it was just another rainy day, good for nothing but a game of pool.

She came back and sat down next to John. "How's your baby?" he asked her.

"She's all right. Look, if you boys are going on, I can hitch a ride from here. One of those cowboys'll probably take me."

"Let's have another beer first," Burl said. He looked at the waitress and held up three fingers.

"Want one of these?" John said, offering her a rib.

"I got to tell you something," she said. "When I was using the phone, I looked in the kitchen and saw an old colored woman standing barefoot on a pile of those ribs to get something off the shelf."

John looked at the rib. "Probably what gives 'em flavor," he said, and ate it anyway.

"Well, you're a couple of insane lunatics," she said. "But that was a lot of fun. Next time you decide to go chasing tornadoes, give me a call."

"Your ole man might not like it," John said.

"Screw him. He's nothing but trouble. I'm gonna get rid of him, he's got a drug problem."

"So do I," John said. "The railroad won't let me smoke pot. It's a clear violation of my Fourth Amendment rights."

"Well, I got nothing against pot. But he's on crystal meth. He drinks too much too."

"Alcohol's a worse addiction than dope," John said. "It's alcohol that really damages people's minds."

"They're all alcoholics in Russia."

A silence came in.

"Were you really in Uncontrolled Meltdown?" she said. "That was a great group. I thought you'd be on the cover of *Rolling Stone* by now."

"So did I," Burl admitted.

"Still a living legend in this part of the country, ain't you?" John said.

"More like ancient history."

Another silence came in. John got up and said, "Well, I guess I'll go test my knowledge." He went over to the Computer Trivia game on the bar and dropped in a quarter.

"You married?" she asked him.

He shook his head.

"I really love my ole man," she said. "But he's hard to live with. He used to work at Pantex, up in Amarillo, where they put together atomic bombs. Now he thinks he's radioactive." She drank her beer and smoothed back her hair. "He just can't seem to keep a job, and I can't seem to find one."

"We're all going to be on welfare," he said, "if Reagan gets his way."

"Hey," she said. "You want to see something funny?" She took a photo out of her purse and gave it to him. He had to look for a moment to figure it out. It had been taken at a carnival, in front of a big blown-up cardboard photo of Reagan smiling at you. She was on her knees in front of him, her hands on his hips, and it looked like she was giving Ronald Reagan a blow job.

"You'd better take a look at this," John called from the door. They stepped back out into the parking lot.

Everything had changed. The dryline had broken, and to the west there were three more storms under a common anvil. When Burl saw the one in the middle, silhouetted against the setting sun, an electric thrill shot through him: it had that *black energy*.

"Mean-looking bugger, ain't it?" John said.

It was right down the highway, and there was half an hour of daylight left. "That one's got my name on it," he said.

"I don't have to be at my sister's for a while yet," she said. "I'll go with you."

They headed down 82, a big four-lane, Burl doing seventy and eighty miles per hour. It was a race between them, the developing storm, and the light. As they got closer, they could see it concentrating: getting smaller, hotter, the base knife-sharp. Just when they needed a road to the north they found one—a park road, leading up into the Wichita Mountains, the little granite hills north of Lawton. "Watch you don't hit a buffalo," John said. The park was full of them. In the end, Burl found himself wishing he'd gotten out of the storm's way. It was dark as night on the ground, and they could see nothing but the tops of trees, tossing in the inflow. He stopped the car, and they got out. Just as they did, the setting sun broke through under the rainfree base, sending out a shaft of incandescent orange light.

"The Holy City," John cried. Burl saw three crosses on the stony hill in front of them, the buildings of Bethlehem and Jerusalem. The funnel dropped to the ground, connecting sky and earth, no more than a mile to the north. Then he heard the molecules singing in the roof of the car, and an instant later there was a violet flash as a bolt of lightning struck a tree a hundred yards away. He heard it snap as it broke up into beads of plasma, felt his hair stand on end, saw everything frozen forever, every stone and blade of grass, as her hand touched his.

3

The week after that, John talked Burl into going to the Mountain Man Rendezvous. For three days, members of the regional chapter of the North American Mountain Man Association gathered near Electra, to camp on the south bank of the Red River and shoot black-powder weapons. It was a warm, humid day, with isolated thunderstorms all over Texas and Oklahoma, none severe. The jet stream had moved up into Kansas, and Burl wondered if the season was over.

Bearded Mountain Men moved through the crowd of visitors, carrying rifles and wearing beaver hats. One had stretched a hide on a frame and was demonstrating the Oglala Sioux method of making brain-tanned buckskin. Dealers sold rifles, tomahawks, ball ammunition. For a while, Burl and John watched a shooting contest. There were three events: driving a tack, splitting a rifle ball on an ax blade, and snuffing out a candle. The noise of the old black-powder rifles was deafening, and Burl was getting a headache when he heard someone say, "Chase any more tornadoes lately?"

He turned around, and there was Bebe smiling at him, wearing a buckskin dress, and carrying her baby on her back in a cradleboard.

"Not lately," he said.

Her baby peered over her shoulder. She had little pointed black eyes, like appleseeds.

"This is Pearl," Bebe said.

"Hello, Pearl."

"So," John said, "you belong to this Mountain Man thing?"

"My ole man does."

"You're back together?" Burl said.

"Yeah," she said. "He'll be wondering where I am. Why don't we go back to our tepee, and I'll introduce you."

They followed her to a tepee in a grove of mesquite, the chopper parked beside it. Her ole man was working at a forge he'd set up, hammering a knife blade. His hair was long, tied up in back, and he wore a leather vest. He didn't look up, just kept hammering until the blade faded from white hot to dull red. He thrust it into a clay pot, and they heard the angry spit of bubbles.

"Chaney?" she said. "These are the guys I told you about. The ones who were chasing that tornado."

"Oh yeah?" he said, rubbing sweat off his forehead. He seemed unhappy to see them.

"You belong to the Renegades, don't you?" John said. "I might know some friends of yours."

John mentioned the names of some bikers who had worked for the railroad. Chaney seemed to relax a little. Burl decided he wasn't that dangerous. There was something soft about him, some kind of confusion in his eyes. But you could never tell about bikers.

"So you make your own knives," John said. "I admire people who can do things like that."

"This is a Bowie," Chaney said. "Real Mountain Men didn't carry them. It's made from the overload spring of a truck. It's not authentic, but I can sell it for a couple hundred dollars."

"You do good work."

"I made the tepee too. Shot the deer myself and cleaned the hide. See that stitching? It's tendon. We try to do everything right here."

"Wasn't the original Bowie knife made from a meteorite?" Burl asked him.

Chaney gave Burl a contemptuous look. "That was just some bullshit they came up with for a movie."

A boy about ten had appeared in the doorway of the tepee and stared at them. His face was thin, his black hair straight as rain. Burl smiled at him, but got no reaction. The blade rang as Chaney hammered it again, turning it over and over. Finally he thrust it into the pot again and said, "Why don't we sit in the tepee and have a smoke?"

Blades of sunlight fell through the hole at the top of the tepee. It smelled faintly, sickeningly of burnt cow chips. Two black-powder rifles leaned against one of the poles. "Jason," Chaney said, "the pipe." The boy gave him a clay pipe. Chaney filled it with tobacco and produced a pint of Old Crow. "It's close enough to what they drank to be authentic," he said.

"Tennessee whiskey," John said. "Always appropriate."

Chaney told them he was a Cherokee. John said he was one quarter Cherokee and half Coonass. They talked about the long war between the Comanche and the Texas Rangers. A lot of history had taken place right around here, John said, and they didn't even teach it in school anymore. For instance, there was the beautiful story of Cynthia Anne Parker, a settler's daughter, who was kidnapped as a little girl and later married Chief Nocona. She bore him a son, Quanah, the last great chief of the Comanche and one of the founders of the Native American Church. "They made a movie about that," John said, *The Searchers.* But they got it all wrong. For one thing, they made it in Arizona. I guess they thought Texas didn't look good enough. Then they made John Wayne the hero, instead of the Indians. The Rangers finally brought Cynthia back, all right, but in real life she died of a broken heart. And there's not a thing in it about peyote."

"The white captives never wanted to come back," Chaney said. "Not the kids, anyway. They knew it was a better way of life."

The sun was going down, and the tepee getting dark. The boy was listening closely. Bebe combed Pearl's hair, humming a little song to herself.

"I try to keep the old ways. That's what holds our family together. I can go for a few modern things, like motorcycles, but I try to stay traditional. I'd rather have a horse, but they're not practical. I haven't paid my income tax in three years," Chaney said. "I refuse to support the white man's government."

"Now, I really admire that," John said. "But what happens if you need a loan or something?"

Chaney laughed. "I've got my own ways of getting money."

Burl decided Chaney might be a little more dangerous than he'd thought.

"My son doesn't go to school. You don't learn anything but bullshit in there anyway. I can teach him everything he needs to know. He'll grow up in a different world anyway. The white man's poisoning this one."

"You worked at Pantex, didn't you?" Burl said.

Chaney looked at him.

"What of it?" he said.

"Nothing," Burl said, glancing at Bebe. "She told me you did, that's all."

"You know what they do in there?" Chaney asked him.

He did, but he wanted to see if Chaney knew. "Something top secret."

"They assemble nuclear weapons," Chaney said. "I'm not supposed to talk about it, or they'll throw my ass in prison." He laughed. "But I don't give a shit. That's how I got sick, working there. I've been contaminated by plutonium."

"How'd that happen?" John said.

Chaney picked up one of his knives, spat on the blade, and sharpened it on a whetstone.

"There's all kinds of shit that goes on in there," he said. "There's a dump where they bury the wreckage from Broken Arrows—that's what they call it when a plane carrying a bomb crashes. But mostly they assemble warheads. They do it in these big underground chambers called Gravel Gerties. The ceiling's got a layer of gravel over it. The idea is, if there's an explosion, the ceiling falls in and traps the plutonium particles. There was an explosion right after I started working there that killed two guys."

"You mean an atomic bomb exploded?" John said.

"No," Chaney said. "Nuclear weapons are set off with plastic explosive. It looks like putty, and it's real tricky to work with. You've got to cut the charges to fit on a bronze lathe, because bronze doesn't strike sparks. I cleaned the lathes."

"You were down in there?" Burl said.

Chaney glared at him. "I've seen the bombs, asshole. Want to know what they look like? The missile warheads are these black cones. The gravity bombs are silver tubes. They're a lot smaller than you'd think. The hydrogen bombs are full of plastic foam. It's saturated with some kind of chemical. There's a long rod down the middle. Sometimes they call it the uranium log, and sometimes they call it the spark plug."

"Yeah, go on," Burl said, getting excited. This guy had really been there, seen the Big Secret.

"After a while," Chaney said, "this guy I worked with got leukemia. I started getting headaches. Some of my hair fell out. I shit blood. When I raised hell, they fired me. I took it to the union, I took it to a protest group, but nobody would help me."

"If that ain't a hell of a thing," John said.

"The guy I worked with died three years ago," Chaney said. "I might not live forever."

He tested the knife blade with his thumb, gave it to the boy.

"But I try not to feel sorry for myself," he said. "That solves nothing."

The silence went on for a long time, so long, the baby started crying softly.

"Indian babies don't cry," Chaney said, looking at Burl.

"Why not?" Burl said, not sure what he was getting at.

"If they do, you just do this until they stop."

Chaney reached out and pinched the baby's nose. Her mouth opened and closed: she couldn't breathe. When he let go, she stared silently with her little appleseed eyes.

"See?" he said. "She's learning."

Burl stood up. "I'm going to get some air."

"Me, too," Bebe said.

"If you've got to piss," Chaney said, "don't do it by the tepee. Go down by the river."

When they were outside, Burl said, "I just felt like a walk."

"So did I," she said.

The visitors had gone, and the Mountain Men had withdrawn into their tents. Bebe took his hand and led him down through the mesquites. He heard running water ahead. They stepped out on a sandbar and walked across it to the river. The moon, white and full, hung over the cottonwoods like a bone button. A Comanche moon.

"Your ole man's had some hard luck," Burl said.

"He's full of bullshit," she said bitterly.

"But he worked there, didn't he?"

"Sure, he worked there," she said. "And that guy died. But I think he made the rest of it up. Those protest people didn't think he was really sick. They wouldn't have anything to do with him. And I'm thinking they were right."

She took off her moccasins and put her feet in the water.

"He's not really a Cherokee, either. Oh, I guess he's one-eighth or something, like everybody else in Oklahoma. He's always writing letters to the council, trying to get on the rolls. He thinks they'll give him some land. Same thing with Pantex. The guy who died got a million dollars. All I know is, he's never been the same since he worked there. You never know if he's telling the truth or not."

Burl thought about this.

"He takes too much meth," she said. "I loved him, but that's why we're out here playing cowboys and Indians—he's trying to get off meth. But he'll just start taking it again."

"Might be a good thing," Burl said finally. "If he was telling the truth, your kids could be contaminated too."

"They're not his kids," she said. "Neither one of them is his."

"Whose are they?"

"Other guys."

Burl didn't know what to say. The river flowed by, a red broth of twigs and foam. The moon was bright enough to see colors, as it was on only two or three nights a year.

4

Three nights later, he came back from Amarillo and found Bebe sitting on his front porch, the baby asleep on her shoulder. The boy was sitting beside her, one of the neighborhood cats in his lap.

"I can't handle Chaney anymore," she said. "I had to get clean out of Lawton. Think I could stay here a couple of days until I get my shit together?"

"How'd you get here?"

"Rode the bus," she said. "I looked up your address in the phone book. This woman in the coffee shop told us where it was, then we walked."

The bus station was three miles away.

"Come on in," he said.

He unlocked the front door, turned on the lights. She wore her leather jacket, a black top, and sandals. The boy carried a cardboard box tied up with string. When he asked her what was in it, she said, "Our things." She hadn't had time to pack a suitcase, she said. They'd had to leave in a hurry.

Burl heated up a pot of pinto beans. Jason watched a Spanish-language kung fu movie. "I won't be any trouble," Bebe told him. "I'll be going down to Houston in a couple of days. I've got a girlfriend there."

She nursed the baby, sitting at the kitchen table, while Burl and Jason watched television. She had gotten herself done up to please him, he thought. She wore lipstick and red nail polish. Her hair was pretty when it was brushed: black as a crow's wing, full of little blue highlights.

"You take the bedroom," he told her. "I'll sleep on the couch."

He woke at three in the morning, to the sound of thunder. The sycamores were tossing in the wind. He turned on the radar. It was just a little convective thunderstorm, going by to the north. He heard her go to the bathroom and blow her nose, figured she must be crying. Poor woman, he thought. She's got a lot of troubles. He thought she might come to him, but he heard her go back to the bedroom, and then he fell back to sleep.

When he woke again, his groin tingling, she was sitting at the foot of the sofa.

"What's the matter?" he said, his lips thick with sleep.

"It's going to storm," she said. "I can't sleep."

"It's just a little thunder and lightning."

"I guess it don't scare you?"

"No."

Lightning flashed. He got a glimpse of her: she seemed to be wearing only her top.

"Does Chaney know where you are?" he asked her.

"He doesn't care," she said. "He told me go on, maybe you'll learn how to take care of yourself."

Thunder rumbled. Big drops of rain began hitting the sidewalk.

"Could I ask you a favor?" she said.

"What's that?"

"Could you just hold me for a while?"

"Sure."

She lay beside him, and he felt her warm breath on his neck. She was all smells, in the dark. Her hair smelled like a cat's, but clean. Here we go, he thought.

More lightning. He counted to eight, heard thunder rumble.

"You're so nice to me," she said. "You're such a nice boy."

"I'm not a boy," he said.

"Yes you are," she said. "You're like a nice college boy."

He kissed her eyelids, her lips. Her breath smelled of tobacco and blood.

She shuddered violently. "Oh, Bebe," she said to herself. "What are you doing?"

"We don't have to do anything," he said.

Her hand slid under the waist of his Jockey shorts. "No, I've been thinking about it ever since I met you."

When he entered her, she was sticky, slightly rough. She breathed on his face, and again he inhaled that hot, bloody odor. Then he knew what it was: she was having her period. Burl liked making love to girls who were having their period. He had noticed they liked it, too, if they knew it was all right with you. Her hands were cool on his back. They moved together in the dark, until he thought he heard a noise coming from the bedroom.

"I wouldn't want Jason to hear us."

"He's asleep."

But she groaned loudly when she came. It was funny: she was the toughest girl he'd ever made love to, but she seemed the most innocent. She shook the whole time, as if she were frightened to death, like the first girls he'd done it with, back in junior high school.

The next day he got called up for another turn. He gave her the key, gave her ten dollars, and told her to go out and get herself and the kids something to eat.

As they rode up to Amarillo, he told John he had a house guest.

"I thought she liked me better," John said. "But if that's how she feels, I'm not gonna hold it against you. You needed a woman more than me anyway."

Her ole man was a troublesome factor, Burl admitted. "You think he's dangerous?"

"He hasn't paid his income tax for three years," John said. "You can figure he ain't planning to die in bed."

Burl decided not to worry about it. He felt good. Smelled her on his body all day long. Nothing could get him down.

He half expected to go home and find the apartment cleaned out, but she'd ironed his shirts and had dinner on the table. The food was shit, though. Hamburger Helper.

"Get Jason," he said.

"Where we going?"

"To get something decent to eat."

They went to Luby's, the cafeteria a couple of blocks from his house. But he'd forgotten it was Sunday. Everybody in Nortex went there after church, and they had to stand in line. She'd put on red eye shadow and some kind of strong perfume. The Baptists and Methodists were staring holes in them. Burl felt a profound hatred for them and their fat blond kids. He forced Bebe and the boy to order chicken-fried steaks with mashed potatoes and corn on the cob, watched until they'd eaten every bite.

When they went home, Pearl took a nap, and Jason went out in the backyard. She made Burl take off his clothes, and they got in the bathtub and smoked some pot she had. Burl hadn't been in a bathtub with a woman for a long time. The tub wasn't really big enough, but you could always find a way to fit if you liked each other.

She leaned back, smiling at him. Put her foot in his groin and worked her toes.

"When I was a kid," she said, "I was always taking baths. The kids gave me a hard time about being darker than them. I thought I was dirty. That's how I found out I was an Indian."

"You didn't know?"

"My parents were white," she said. "They adopted me when I was three. The Baptist church had this program. I thought I was white, too, and they wouldn't tell me. They thought they were doing me a favor. But then the kids kept giving me a hard time, so one day they finally sat me down and told me."

She took a hit off the joint, gave it to him.

"The only kid who would play with me was this girl. She was a mongoloid or something. Her eyes went off in different directions. But she was friendly. I hated the white kids, and pretty soon I hated my stepfather, too, the old sonofabitch."

"Why?"

She laughed. "You don't want to know."

It was the best pot he'd smoked in a while. He stared at the window shade, glowing with sunlight from the other side. The window was open, and it would move and stop. Move and stop.

"Weren't you interested in your background?" he said. "Didn't you ever want to see other Indians?"

"Oh, yeah," she said. "I used to be able to speak Kiowa. They sent me to Indian school when I was seven, and I could speak it for a while. The teacher gave me a record of Indians speaking Kiowa. I used to listen to it at night with the lights off. I had it for a long time. Then I lost it."

"What about your real mother?"

"They told me she tried to kill me," Bebe said. "They told me she put me out in the cold one night, so she could fuck this guy. But I don't blame her." She took the joint from him, had another hit. "She did what she had to do, you know?"

"Don't you ever want to talk to her?"

"I wrote her a letter last year. I got the address from the church. She lives in Chickasha. It came back saying there was, you know, no one at that address. But I know she's alive."

"How?"

"I talked to her. I got the number from information, and I called and she said hello. I know it was her. I could just tell. But when she did, I got scared and hung up."

She gave him a shy smile.

"That's too bad," he said.

Bebe leaned forward, put her lips on his neck. Every time the shade moved, the bathroom filled with gold radiance. He could hear birds singing outside.

"What's wrong?" she said.

"Is something wrong?"

"What are you crying for?"

"I don't know," he told her. "I feel fine."

But tears were running down his face. Everything turned to a gold blur.

I've been working too hard, he thought. He couldn't tell if he was happy or sad. When you felt them strongly, they were almost the same thing. They got into bed, made love, and fell asleep. He slept deeper than he had for a long time. Kept trying to wake up and sliding back into a deeper sleep where he didn't even know his name.

As often as she told him the story of her life, he could never get the facts straight.

Jason had been born while she was in reform school, or some kind of school for ethnic problem children in Houston, where they sent her after she got busted for shoplifting when she was eighteen. His father was an Apache, who she'd never seen again. The school was a real strange place where the Mexican girls tattooed tears in the corners of their eyes for every year they'd been there. Sad Eyes, they were called.

When she came out, she went back to Lawton, where she'd gotten hooked up with Chaney. He was working for Pantex, and he took them back to Amarillo, where they lived for two years, the longest they'd ever stayed in one place.

Pearl's father was a protester, the only one who had believed Chaney's story. He had gone over the fence at Pantex, been arrested for trespassing on government property, and was now in a federal prison in Colorado. "Does Chaney know?" he asked her.

"Oh, yeah," she said. "Chaney wanted me to sleep with him. It was his idea. David was a beautiful dude."

He was a devout Christian, and when they'd eaten dinner the night before, she'd thought of the Last Supper. They'd seen him once more, in jail, after he got sentenced. He sat on the other side of a thick glass window and spoke to them over the phone. He was sick, because he had some kind of stomach trouble and jail food was bad for him—he'd done six months after he went over the fence at Rocky Flats, and almost died. Chaney promised him he'd take care of the baby like it was his own.

Then they went to Oklahoma City, where Pearl was born while Chaney was in jail for throwing a rock through a liquor store window.

"Poor Chaney," she said. "We tried to have a kid, but he just couldn't. The doctor said he didn't have enough of those little tadpole things to make a baby. He thinks it's because he's radioactive."

Bebe didn't use birth control pills, she thought they gave you cancer. And the coil made you sterile. She'd tried a diaphragm once, but it felt like shoving a rubber doorknob up yourself. "So you don't use anything?" he asked her.

She shook her head.

"What if I got you pregnant?"

"I don't think it's gonna happen," she said.

"Why not?"

"I just got a feeling."

He bought a package of condoms, furious at her for taking such a chance.

"How can you live this way?" he said. "You think that was the right thing for you? Having those other guys' babies, and then just letting them take a walk?"

"I loved 'em," she said.

But he couldn't stay angry at her. She lived for love, expecting nothing. Each time they made love was like the first. Naked, she was shy, covering her breasts if she had caught him looking at them. When he touched her, she closed her eyes. Then she shuddered and sobbed, as if a gust of wind were blowing through her.

In another week it was clear she wasn't going on to Houston, at least not right away.

They settled into a routine. She always had food in the house when he came home. His shirts were always ironed. Sometimes they went to a movie.

The sex went on being good, and sometimes Pearl cried for him, held up her little hands when he came in, wanting to be picked up. He found himself doing things a father would do and enjoying them, like stopping off at the Seven-Eleven on the way home and buying Pampers.

When she'd been there two weeks, he asked her why she didn't look for a job here in Nortex.

"I couldn't leave my kids alone," she said. "I worked when

Chaney was out of work, but that was because he was at home and could take care of 'em."

"Maybe you could get Pearl into day care."

Oh, no, she said. She was afraid of those places. "They found out the day-care center in Oklahoma City was run by a bunch of child molesters. The cops found Polaroid pictures of them doing all sorts of dirty things."

He said he didn't think they were all like that.

"It's all you hear about," she said. "A lot more of that shit goes on than you think. I know what I'm talking about."

There was something like that in her past, he thought. He remembered her hatred of her stepfather.

"Well, if you're going to stay here, you should think about getting Jason in school."

"He doesn't go to school."

"He doesn't?"

"He went the first three grades in Amarillo, then Chaney took him out. It was a good thing too."

It took a while to get the whole story.

When Jason was eight, he started giving the teacher trouble at school. One day he stole some matches and started a fire. The school nurse diagnosed him as hyperactive and said they'd have to put him on Ritalin to control him. "She said that about every boy who gave them trouble," Bebe said. "Just the boys, none of the girls. She had three other little boys in his class on that Ritalin, and it's some kind of speed. Chaney said no way was he gonna let that bitch put our kid on drugs, so he took him out. And Jason's fine now," she said. "He doesn't know how to read, but he does just fine. He learns everything he needs to know from television."

"But he's got to learn how to read," Burl said. "How's he going to get along in this world?"

"Maybe he can get a job taking care of animals," she said. "He loves animals. He had a pet hummingbird in Lawton that would fly through the window and sit on his shoulder."

I've got to help these people, he thought. She had seemed so tough, so resolute when he'd seen her walking down that road. Now he knew she was frightened of everything, and the more he talked to her, the more he understood she had a right to be.

Jason: his name didn't seem to fit him. A Jason should be blond, Burl thought. He had that hair like black rain, and there was a silence around him Burl was afraid to violate. When he wasn't watching television, he sat under the tree in the backyard for hours, throwing grains of dirt down the ant lion cones. Then Burl would look out the window and he would be gone.

He did like animals. He never played with the other kids on the block, but he knew every cat and dog. He drew sketches of horses that Burl thought were pretty good. But he had also stolen a battery from the Seven-Eleven the first week. Burl discovered he had a whole collection of stolen batteries.

One morning he disappeared and Burl found him blocks away, standing on the corner of Kemp and watching the cars streaming by. "Where's everybody going?" he said.

"It's Monday," Burl told him. "Everybody's going to work."

As they walked back, Jason said, "Are we on Mondays through Fridays, or just weekends?"

Burl asked him what he meant.

"Like the people on the soaps, or the people on the specials?"

Burl didn't know what to say. It was something to think about.

Jason knew who Madonna was, but not Jimmy Carter. He thought New York was just north of Oklahoma City. Once he told Burl human beings ran by electricity. Burl wondered if that was why he'd stolen the batteries. He thought the Masters of the Universe were historical characters.

The third week, Burl was watching *The World at War* when

Jason came in and switched channels to MTV, just like he owned the set.

"Hey," Burl said, switching it back.

Jason punched him in the stomach.

Burl held his arms. Jason kicked and screamed. "I'll kill you, you faggot!" He was so strong that for a moment Burl thought he was going to break loose.

"That the best you can do?" Burl said.

Jason fell on the floor and kicked for a while, then stopped. "I'm gonna get a shotgun," he said, "and blow your head off some night while you're asleep."

"Now listen," Burl said. "You've got to stop watching this shit all the time. You've got to learn how to read."

"What for?"

"So you can learn something worth knowing," Burl said. "So you can learn to think for yourself. You don't know anything." He pointed to the screen. Adolf Hitler was making a speech at Nuremburg, a giant swastika behind him.

"Do you know who he is?" Burl said. "Do you know anything besides He-Man and She-Rah?"

"Sure," Jason said. "That's Adolf Hitler. He tried to take over the world."

"That's right," Burl said. "And what happened to him?"

"He got beat."

"By who?"

"John Lennon."

Burl went to the bookshelf and got down *Wild Animals I Have Known*. He opened it, showed Jason the sketches of pawprints and feathers and the phases of the moon. "Don't you wish you could read this?" he said. "There's some great stories in here. This one's about Lobo, a big wolf they tried to catch for years. This one's about a horse they called the Pacing Mustang. They're about great animals, animal heroes. The guy who wrote it did the drawings."

Jason stared at a sketch of Silvertip the crow, and the notes on crow speech.

"Don't you ever wish you were an animal?" Burl said. "Dream you were one? Do you think they can talk to each other? You'd better believe they can. They have their own language."

Jason said nothing, gave no sign of hearing, but there was a deepening of his silence.

They sat down in the backyard, under the cedar. Burl opened the book. "Now follow my finger," he said, and began reading:

> "Currumpaw is a vast ranch in Northern New Mexico. It is a land of rich pastures and teeming flocks and herds, a land of rolling mesas and precious running waters that at length unite in the Currumpaw River, from which the whole region is named. And the king whose despotic power was felt over its entire extent was an old gray wolf." ¨

He read Jason a story every day. John had been right: It was one of the best books Burl had ever read. The author told you everything that animals knew, and they knew a lot. Wolves could scent out any trap humans set for them. Partridges lived by the phases of the moon. Crows could count up to thirty, and they collected seashells and pebbles.

But it was also good because it was honest. The life of every wild animal ended in tragedy. Lobo, the King of the Currumpaw, died of a broken heart when his mate Blanca was killed. The Pacing Mustang was captured, but hurled himself off a cliff. Molly Cottontail, trying to lure the fox away from her son Raggylug, swam a frozen lake until her soft brown eyes closed in death. Saddest of all was Redruff the partridge. He was murdered by the owl one night in November, which was the moon of solitude, madness, and grapes, and his rainbow feathers blew away on the winter wind.

A few days later, Burl found Jason copying the drawings, lying on the floor of the front room. He watched him for a while, then went into the bedroom. Pearl was asleep on the bed, and Bebe was smoking a cigarette and rubbing cornstarch on her back.

"Bebe?" he said.

She didn't look up. "What is it, honey?"

"Nothing," he said. "I just wanted to say . . . you can stay here as long as you like."

5

There was one more day, at the end of May, when conditions were perfect. Burl felt he was destined to see another tornado. He and John took another day off and drove out to Foard County to look for storms on the dryline.

They waited in Copper Breaks State Park, south of the Medicine Mounds. He parked in a little campground and listened to the scanner. They were out of range of the Spotter net, but he could hear the Oklahoma thunderstorm forecast.

John lay on a picnic table, his cap over his eyes. It was so still out there, Burl could hear his heart beat.

"I wonder why the dryline always forms right around here," he said. "I wonder what's so special about this place?"

There was something about the feel of this country, the way it opened up and the salt cedar started growing. The soil was dark red, almost purple, and when it rained the ponds were a harsh, glittering violet. To the north were the Quartz Mountains, which his father had told him were remnants of the Ancestral Rockies, the oldest mountains in North America.

"Rainfall," John said.

"How's that?"

"This is just about where the one hundredth meridian runs. Maybe that's got something to do with it."

"What's the one hundredth meridian?" Burl said.

"East of it, the country gets more than twenty inches of rain per year," John said. "West of it, it gets less. The old geographers used to call it the beginning of the Great American Desert."

Then Burl remembered the map in his third-grade classroom at Alamo Elementary. Most of the United States was green, but there was a huge pink area called the Great American Desert. Nortex was right on the edge of it. After that, whenever Burl looked out the classroom windows, he thought he could detect a faint pink glow on the western horizon. It was one of the first times he'd had a strong sense of where he lived: on a border, a boundary, the edge of another kind of world.

At three o'clock, the dryline broke. Burl could see storms building to the north and south for a hundred miles. As the anvil of the nearest one spread over them, he felt at the center of a field of energy, in the presence of a great atmospheric event.

They followed the storms north that day, up into Oklahoma. The radio was broadcasting one warning after another. *There is a tornado near Hollis,* the announcer said. *There is a tornado on the ground near Frederick.* They passed through Frederick fifteen minutes later and fell in behind a Storms Lab vehicle, a van from the Lawton television station, and several carloads of teenagers following the storm.

"This is getting to be a popular sport," John said.

"Too popular," Burl said. The teenagers in front of them were drinking beer and blowing the horn like they were on their way to a football game.

At Hobart he turned left, toward a cell that looked more promising. Near Lone Wolf, they drove under the biggest rainfree base Burl had ever seen.

They bumped along a dirt road, leaving the sunlit world behind. Every living thing—birds, cattle, people—had disappeared, probably into shelter. The farmhouses looked haunted. Burl felt they were crossing the land of the dead, where things glowed with their own gray light. This, he thought, was the light that had shone on the Cretaceous extinction, when a comet had hit the earth, filling the atmosphere with ash, and the dinosaurs had died.

Suddenly the clouds tore open, sunlight poured down, and the wind gusted up to sixty miles per hour. In a field to the north of them, Burl saw something so strange, it filled him with terror: two ghostly funnels, pink against the black rain, moved toward each other, merged, and danced away again. They looked exactly like the two rattlesnakes he and John had seen mating. For one terrible moment, the storm seemed *intelligent*.

Then Burl realized what he was seeing—the funnels were not really merging, just rotating around each other. He drove north, trying to catch them, but they disappeared into the rain. Just then they saw a little yellow Toyota parked by the side of the road, and a man standing next to it whom Burl recognized as legendary tornado chaser Dale Webster.

Burl had read about Webster in an article in *Popular Science*. From it, he had learned there were a number of free-lance tornado chasers who didn't work for the Severe Storms Lab. Some were meteorologists. Others, like Burl, were just people who liked tornadoes. The article gave some of their CB call signs—the Cyclone Kid, the Watasha Brothers, Sam Buffalo Calf.

But Webster was considered the best. He had studied meteorology, but had given it up to become the minister of his late father's church in the small Nebraska town where he had been born. He still chased tornadoes, though. The Severe Storms Lab knew him well—he always got there before they did. The article said he had seen over a hundred tornadoes and sometimes drove a thousand miles to find a dryline.

He had thinning hair and wore glasses that looked like he'd bought them off the counter at Woolworth's. Burl introduced himself and said they were doing the same thing he was—chasing tornadoes.

"Are you a meteorology student?" Webster asked him.

"No," Burl said. "I'm just a free-lancer."

"Where did you come from?"

"Nortex."

"That's a long way," Webster said. "But you found the right storm. Of course you can almost always find tornadoes here this time of year. It's the greatest country in the world for them." He looked up and down the road. "I thought the Storms Lab would be here, but I guess they didn't make it. They missed an interesting sight." He held out his hand. "Well," he said, "I should be going. I've got to drive back to Nebraska and prepare a sermon tonight."

"Why don't you let me buy you a cup of coffee first?" Burl said.

They went to the Dairy Queen in Cordell and took a table by the window. The sky had cleared, and the sun was going down. The storm was moving away to the northwest, a white tower taller than any mountain on earth. John ordered a Belt Buster. Burl was too excited to eat.

Burl soon realized that Webster knew more about tornadoes than anyone on earth. Sometimes he sounded like a meteorologist, and sometimes like a minister. When Burl asked him why he chased tornadoes, he said, "To me, God has scattered a number of clear pictures through nature, and tornadoes are one of them."

"But how have you found so many?"

"I have my own system," he said. "Most meteorologists can't understand it. You have to take a number of factors into account. After a while you develop a feeling for it. Certain patterns appear, points of convergence."

The factors, he told them, were almost infinite. The atmosphere was in constant change. That was why meteorology was like no other science. "The atmosphere is a mirror," he said. "It reflects not only conditions on land, but the temperature and circulation of the ocean currents. When you study the atmosphere, you study everything."

Burl had a thousand questions he wanted to ask Webster. "Have you ever heard of the rings?" he said.

He told him about the man he had met after the Nortex tornado and what the man had seen when he looked up into the funnel.

"Oh, yes," Webster said, his face breaking into a smile. "The blue light and the rings. I've heard that a number of times. The blue light could be static electricity, or even the sky. Some people think the funnel goes all the way to the top of the storm. The rings are the most interesting part. If you want a scientific explanation, the higher the energy of a storm, the more coherent its structure. The interior of the funnel might be very highly structured—a very clear picture—if you lived long enough to see it."

They looked at each other and laughed—the same laugh Burl had heard himself give when hailstones started hitting the roof of the car, or when he almost got struck by a bolt of lightning.

John spoke for the first time.

"Well," he said, "I don't know you, but I know Burl, and it seems to me that's the point for you boys—to get as close to these damned things as possible."

"The point is to get a clear look," Webster said.

"You sure it ain't to get the hell scared out of you?"

"Clarity," Webster said, "is always a little frightening."

"But you do try to get close."

"Close enough to see, but not close enough to be in danger."

"Just tell me," John said. "What's the closest you've ever gotten?"

Webster tore open a package of nondairy creamer, his hands trembling slightly.

"Within a mile," he said. "Let's just say it was a moment of startling clarity."

When they went outside, night had fallen. The storm was now a hundred miles away, but they could still see it, lit from within by complicated discharges of lightning.

"Lord," John said. "What's that?"

Burl made out a rippling curtain of ice-green light, hanging in the sky above the storm. The stars shone faintly through it. "The aurora borealis," Webster said. "The northern lights. I heard it was reported in Denver last night. It's very unusual to see it this far south, especially this time of year. But this has been an active year for sunspots."

They stared at it in silent wonder.

"You know," Webster said to Burl, "you might consider becoming a meteorologist. You seem to have a feeling for severe weather."

"I do," Burl said. "I have from the time I was a kid. But you've got to take a lot of math, don't you?"

Webster took off his glasses and polished them on his shirt.

"A whole different kind of person is being called to meteorology now," he said. "They're nothing like the people who went into it a few years ago. Something is changing in our society or our atmosphere, I'm not sure which. I was one of the first who heard The Call. I never became a practical meteorologist—my ideas are a little too original—but it might be the right thing for you. If the atmosphere is changing, we're going to need a different kind of meteorologist to interpret the changes. Someone with an understanding of change and things on a larger scale. The most important factor might be a childhood interest."

Burl looked away. He liked Webster, but thought he sounded like a Christian youth counselor.

The northern lights now looked like a shower of red arrows pouring down from the zenith. "There's another factor for you," Webster said. "The correspondence between the weather and the sunspot cycle, solar radiation. The sun is a variable star, and the atmosphere varies along with it. The atmosphere mirrors everything. One might almost say it was the mirror of God, the nimbus or glory of His creation."

He shook Burl's hand and wished him good luck, then got in his little yellow Toyota and drove off.

"Now that was a very interesting man," John said as they started back to Nortex. "It would be a pleasure to hear one of his sermons."

"I think you just did," Burl said.

"He's got some original ideas."

"He's too intense for me."

John rolled a cigarette. "When you told me you were chasing tornadoes, I thought you were a little intense yourself. But one thing I've learned today, there's all sorts of people into this. I don't know if it's a new science or a new religion, but you're a fool if you don't make it your life."

"How do you mean?"

"Go back to school, like he was saying. You got the brains for it, and you ain't got a goddamned better thing to do." He scratched a match with his thumbnail. "Or maybe you'd rather be a railroading man forever."

As he drove on, Burl thought about what Webster had said about tornadoes being clear pictures scattered through nature. It was true when he looked at his past, tornadoes were among his clearest memories—something he feared and loved, something that had always seemed to change his life. Maybe they were also his future as well, the sign he had been looking for all along.

He stopped for gas in Hobart. When they went in to pay, Burl saw that the woman watching the little television by the register had some kind of hideous deformity, maybe skin cancer. Her head looked like vegetable matter, a purple cauliflower. He forced himself to look at her, but even then he didn't see anything: he couldn't find her eyes.

"Do you think we'll have any more storms tonight?" she said in a muffled voice.

"No, ma'am," he said.

"Oh, I hope not," she said, giving him his change. "I just hate those storms."

He walked back to the car, so disoriented he could say nothing for five minutes. "Jesus," John finally muttered. "That poor woman looked like the Elephant Man."

There was a clear picture for you, Burl thought. A clear picture of another kind. He thought it must mean something, but what, he didn't know. When they got back to Nortex, there was a message from his mother saying to call the hospital.

THE TELESCOPE

1

He drove down to the hospital. The lobby was deserted. The woman at the desk told him his father was on the second floor. He found Coy and his mother in the little waiting room by the nurse's station.

"What happened?" he asked them.

"Your father was sick all day," his mother said. "He had an upset stomach, and it just got worse and worse until he was doubled over. The doctor thought it was appendicitis, but when he operated, he found a tumor."

"It's cancer," Coy said.

Burl sat down. "How serious?"

"The doctor told us he got what he could," Coy said. "But it had already spread. He kept saying how sorry he was."

It seemed to Burl he had known the moment he found the message from his mother—had known for months now. Things suddenly fell into place. His father had lost a lot of weight in the last year. He had complained of stomach trouble, of not being able to get warm.

"But he said your father can have this chemotherapy," his mother said. "And it's helped a lot of people."

Burl put his arm around his mother's shoulders. "Sure, Mom," he said. "He'll be all right."

Coy took their mother home and Burl went to his father's room, where he sat by the bed, studying his father's sleeping face. There was a hollow look Burl associated with people who had cancer. Yes, his father had it—his eyes were sunken, and his cheekbones almost broke the skin. He must have had it for almost a year now.

Burl watched his father's chest rise and fall, sometimes sleeping himself. At daybreak, a blade of sunlight fell across the bed, turning his father's hair the color of iron oxide. It came to Burl that his father had beautiful hair, and it was wonderful that he had never lost it. It was really his handsomest feature.

When Willie came home from the hospital two weeks later, he was in good spirits. There was a long incision across his stomach, held together by plastic staples. The doctor had told him he should get on his feet, so every morning he walked. Then he went to his room and took a long nap. For dinner, he had beef broth. The doctor had told him he should stick to soft foods for a while.

"Your father's so much better," his mother told him when Burl went over to see them. "He's out walking right now. I think everything's going to be all right."

"Did the doctor tell you that?"

"To tell you the truth, I haven't talked to the doctor for a while," she said. "He's pretty hard to get hold of."

Burl went home and called Coy. "What the hell is going on?" he said.

"How do you mean?"

"I just talked to Mom. She thinks Dad's going to be all right. What did the doctor tell you, anyway?"

"That he can't begin chemotherapy until his incision heals, but he's not in any immediate danger."

"He's got cancer, doesn't he? I think he's going to die."

There was a long silence. Coy cleared his throat and said, "Look, Mom can only take so much. And maybe the doctor knows something we don't."

"He might," Burl said. "We don't know a damned thing."

Burl's mother told him two other people on the block had cancer. Lum, who lived across the street, had just had a lung removed, and the neighbor across the alley had cancer of the prostate. Everyone in Nortex seemed to be getting it. His mother thought it might be something in the water.

One morning in July, Burl joined his father and they walked to the neighborhood hobby shop. It was a hot, cloudless day. The cicadas sang, and the gutters were full of green pecan tree pollen. At the hobby shop, they stared at a brass model of a locomotive in a glass case.

"Now that's a beautiful kit," his father said. "Complete in every detail. When I was a boy, the Fort Worth & Denver had a locomotive just like that."

"Why don't you buy it?" Burl said.

"Oh, I don't have time to put it together right now."

As they left, the owner said, "See anything you need?"

"Not today," Willie said. "We were just looking."

"Dad," Burl asked him on the way back, "what did the doctor tell you?"

"About what?"

"About your illness."

"Oh, don't worry about that, son. Everything's going to be all right."

"Dad," Burl said, "I think this could be pretty serious."

"Hell yes, it's serious," his father said. "I don't know how I got this cancer. I must have let a negative thought get hold of me. But I beat drinking, and maybe I can beat this too."

"How?" Burl asked him.

"By concentrating on positive thoughts," his father said. "If I concentrate hard enough, I might not even need that chemotherapy. I might be able to will this cancer right out of my system."

Burl didn't know what to say. Willie moved ahead, stooped over his incision, moving so fast, so purposefully, that Burl could hardly keep up with him.

On the way back they met Lum, who was watering his lawn. He and Burl's father had never gotten along, but now they glared at each other with obvious dislike. People with cancer hate each other, Burl thought.

"How you doing, Lum?" his father said.

"Not so hot," Lum said, lighting a Camel. "They took one lung out, you know."

"You still smoking?"

"Doesn't seem to make a hell of a lot of difference now."

"Well, your lawn's looking good," his father said. "It'll look even better if we get some rain."

They walked on toward the house.

"He looks terrible," his father whispered. "They say the poor sonofabitch has only got six weeks to live."

Burl called the doctor several times and left messages but got no response.

"I can't understand why the doctor won't call me back," Burl said to his mother one day, while his father was taking his walk.

"If he thinks we need to know something," she said, "he'll tell us."

Burl stared out the kitchen window at the dying backyard grass. He couldn't understand his mother's need to know nothing. Perhaps it had something to do with this town, or the intense heat in which memory seemed to evaporate. A thermal high had settled in over the Panhandle, and the temperature had started hitting a hundred every day.

"Maybe we should take him to Dallas," he said. "See another doctor, get a second opinion."

"Your father likes this doctor," his mother said. "What good would that do? Everything will be all right, if we just take it one day at a time, like they say in the Program."

Suddenly Burl wondered if his father, for all his talk of getting better, might be thinking of something else. He went to his father's bedroom. In the corner was a cabinet, atop it a little gold sphinx his father had brought back from the King Tut exhibition in Dallas. In the bottom drawer was the Luger.

He pressed a button, and the clip fell out. It was empty. He searched the drawer, but could find no shells.

Burl sat on the bed, feeling relief, but also a strange disappointment. His father had already faced death as a soldier—won a medal for bravery. Now that the moment was here, Burl had expected great things of him. He had thought his father would be a hero. But all his father had done was deny it. Lum, with his nicotine-stained fingers and leaden, honest stare, was beginning to seem like the hero to Burl.

He went back to the kitchen. "It doesn't make sense," he said. "You don't just get cancer, walk out of the hospital, and forget it."

"You're being too negative," his mother said. On the television, Ronald and Nancy Reagan were getting into a helicopter. The president turned to the crowd and waved. "The doctor told me your father's got the same kind of cancer the president had, and he's completely cured."

▼ ▼ ▼

So Burl went home and tried to stop thinking about his father. He spent his next day off with Bebe and the kids. All things considered, it was probably better to follow his mother's advice and forget about the future—take it one day at a time, as they said in the Program.

One night John came over for dinner, and Bebe cooked chicken and dumplings. The dumplings were rock-hard, the chicken bloody along the bone. She smoked a cigarette while they ate. "Sorry," she said. "I guess I'm not much of a cook."

"No," John said. "It was real fine." While she did the dishes, they went out in the backyard. John had brought his clubs, and Burl watched him practice his golf swing. The sun went down behind the water tower, and Jason caught lightning bugs in a Mason jar.

"Well," John said finally, "I can see you and this woman have a serious thing going. You might even have a future together. I'd better teach her how to cook."

John started giving Bebe lessons. One night a week, he came over and they cooked a meal together. They made pork chops, fried apples, three-bean salad, and sweet potato pie. He showed Bebe how to make buttermilk biscuits and grind her own chili powder. Bebe liked John and took no offense. Before long, he allowed as how she was turning out some pretty good meals.

After Jason and Pearl had been put to bed, they all sat together on the sofa, smoked a joint, and watched television. John tried to come on Thursdays so he could watch *Lifestyles of the Rich and Famous*, which was, right now, his favorite program. He wouldn't allow anyone to talk during it, but he kept up a running commentary. Robin Leach took them through the home of Marylou Cornelius Vanderbilt Whitney at Saratoga. "Railroad money," John observed. Next, Robin talked to Joan Collins, who John said was the real First Lady of the land. "High-energy Joan keeps up a schedule that would tire Alexis," Robin said. They watched her getting in and out of limousines, going to parties. Then a picture of her without makeup flashed onscreen. They stared at it in silence. "Makes you think, doesn't it?" John said.

The last personality was Wink Martindale, master of ceremonies of *High Rollers*. "Really scraping the bottom of the barrel tonight," John said. Wink had led a long and interesting life, going from one game show to another. "For Wink," Robin said, "the joker is always wild!" The segment ended with Wink and his wife renewing their wedding vows by the pool of their home in Palm Springs. Barry White sang "Endless Love."

"I haven't seen him in a long time," Burl said. "He's still got a lot of energy, doesn't he?"

"He's probably on crack," John said.

The show, as always, closed with Robin Leach shouting, "And remember—if there's one thing better than making money, it's *spending* it."

"Amen," John said, turning off the television. "Now that's what I call educational programming. You can really learn a lot from it."

"Like what?" Bebe said.

"That rich people are the lowest form of human life," John said, and went home.

Then Burl and Bebe made love, while Pearl snored softly in her crib across the room. Bebe's motherhood excited him: whenever he watched Pearl nursing, he hardened, wanting to drink from the same source. Now he did, lingering on her nipples, sucking at them like a child. Her milk was almost gone, but sometimes he got a drop or two. At first, he had used the condoms, but he had never worn them before, and he discovered he hated them. Lately, he had started going without. It was dangerous, but there was something thrilling about it he could not resist. His sensitivity had increased until he was sure he could tell when she was ripe by a certain lushness, a sensation of heat and a smell like grass sap. On nights when she was safe, he came at once, Bebe meeting him as he burst with a long, melting sigh of pleasure. When she wasn't, he held back until he could stand it no longer, then pulled out and spilled, covering her belly with sticky pearls.

Then they lay in the warm ice of the moonlight. He kissed her poor brown toes, and they told each other all their secrets. He had been so in love with his second-grade teacher, he had cried when she got married. She had told other kids Elvis was her real daddy. Her children were favored: Jason was so pretty, all the nurses had fought over who would give him his bottle and almost wouldn't let her take him home from the hospital.

"We've got a good thing going, don't we?" he asked her.

"We don't belong together, though."

"Sure we do," he said. "Know what I'm going to do? Build us a log cabin. It's something John's always talking about. He wants to build his in the mountains, but I'm going to build us one out in Hardeman County, on the dryline. We'll cook on a wood stove, and Jason can have a horse, and in the spring we'll sit out on the front porch and wait for tornadoes to come along. Don't you think we could be happy, living like that?"

"Yeah," she said. "But you're going back to college, and you're going to be a weatherman. I can see you right now, giving the forecast."

He laughed.

"Why not? You're good-looking enough. And you already know all about it."

He put his lips to her ear. "I love you," he whispered.

"Don't say that."

"Why not?"

"You don't mean it," she said sadly. "You think you do, but you don't."

"But I do," he told her, certain he was telling the truth.

2

The year before, three women had applied for jobs with the railroad. Their applications had been ignored, but a few months later they'd come back with a lawyer from the American Civil Liberties Union, who threatened to file a sexual discrimination suit. The work came down they were going to be hired.

There had been long bull sessions about it in the motel. When the railroad had started hiring black men, fifteen years ago, John had been their biggest supporter. Now he supported the women. "Hell, Royce," he said, "the job ain't that hard, or you wouldn't be getting so fat. And I'd rather work with a woman than Haney any day." Haney said he wouldn't trust a woman to get the job done—

trust was a big thing at the railroad. She wouldn't be able to pull her weight.

The women had started to work in February. One of them, Charlotte Blue, was black. For months, it was all anybody talked about. Burl couldn't see what the big deal was. You could hardly tell she was a woman when she wore her bib overalls, which was all the time, even in the heat. She was supposed to be hard to get along with—some people said she wouldn't even give them the time of day.

One night in early August she deadheaded back from Amarillo with them. Burl offered her coffee, but she refused. They rode along in silence. Every so often he looked up from a book he was reading on nuclear weapons and found her looking at him.

Finally she said, "You got pretty hair. Don't I remember when you were a singer?" He said she probably did. "You like black music?" she asked him. "You like Lionel Ritchie?" Burl told her he preferred Sam Cooke.

She kept putting him down, getting blacker and blacker. Finally she said, "You ever slept with a black woman?"

"No."

"You ever think you'd like to?"

"Sure," he admitted.

She laughed. "I thought so." She looked at John, who was sitting at the conductor's desk. "What about you?" she said.

John looked at Burl. "You mean have I ever done it, or have I ever thought about it?"

"I mean you ever done it?"

"No," John said, smiling at Burl. "And I have absolutely no interest in doing so."

She slapped her leg and laughed. "Don't you know a black woman's a thousand times better than a white woman? Everybody knows that."

John looked at her. "That's a lot of nonsense," he said.

Then she lost her temper. She told John all black people were better at sex than white people. They knew how to move their hips.

"You take a white boy," she said. "He don't know how to move his hips."

"Well," John said, rolling a cigarette, "that just makes me sad."

"Why?" she demanded.

"Obviously you never slept with a white man who knew what he was doing. The fact is, most white people are superior at sex."

Burl had to bite his lip to keep from laughing. The story went everywhere in a day or so. Haney congratulated John for putting her in her place. Said he wished he'd been there so he could have heard it.

A week later, John showed up at Burl's apartment one night with Charlotte Blue. It took Burl a moment to recognize her. She was wearing cutoffs, a tight pink top, and big gold earrings. John looked different too: his hair was greased back, and he had on a Hawaiian shirt he wore sometimes, when he was in a good mood. "You know Charlotte here," he said, smiling. "We just thought we'd drop by. Brought a bottle of good wine."

Bebe came out of the bedroom. Burl introduced them. John asked if they had a corkscrew. Bebe found some clean glasses, and they opened the bottle of Almadén pink Chablis.

"This is good," Bebe said. "It's nice to be drinking something besides beer for a change."

"We thought maybe you folks would be interested in going out to dinner," John said.

They went to the Casa Mañana, the old Mexican restaurant downtown that had been there as long as anyone could remember. Charlotte was polite as could be—didn't give Burl any of that hostile black bullshit. When he mentioned this, she said, "Oh, I'm not at work now. Work's different—I got to put up a front." She told Bebe she had a boy herself, Akeem. They lived in the public housing project, down by the yard. Charlotte had gone to the

University of Houston on an athletic scholarship, where she ran the mile. Then she had gotten pregnant with Akeem and dropped out. She was working for the railroad to make enough money to start a business of her own.

After dinner, they went back to the apartment and had a drink of Herradura. Burl was alone with John in the kitchen for a moment, and he said, "What's going on?"

"Nothing," John said, staring into the sink. "I'm not sure what you're talking about."

Burl started to go back to the front room.

"Oh," John said, grinning. "But you know what she was talking about that night? Her theory?"

Burl nodded.

"She might have had something there."

Pretty soon, John started driving Charlotte to work in her car, an old gold Ford Torino convertible. She sat next to him, and he drove with one hand, the other around her shoulders. Kissed her while everyone stood on the office porch and watched.

"Ugh," Haney said, turning away in disgust. One night up in Amarillo he said, "I don't see how you can do that, John."

"When it comes to love," John said, "I'm color-blind."

Haney said she was after his money. John was known to have a lot of money in the bank.

"I didn't know you were prejudiced, Haney," John said seriously. "You told me you thought Charlie Pride was a hell of a good singer."

They started going out to dinner a lot. People stared at them, but John pretended not to notice. Once, they went to the public pool at City Park. Charlotte wore a two-piece and got a lot of stares there too. John wore a little bikini no bigger than a jockstrap. He was so thin, all his ribs showed, but he had a little potbelly Charlotte said was cute.

Burl liked Charlotte: there was a whole different woman under all that arrogance he'd never even suspected was there. She and Bebe started spending time together. She brought over Akeem, and he and Jason skateboarded in the storm drain a few blocks away. Charlotte was good for Bebe, he thought. One day he heard them talking in the kitchen when he'd just come back from Amarillo, and they thought he was asleep. "You got to get yourself a job that pays good money," Charlotte said, "so you can take care of yourself and those kids."

"Yeah," Bebe said. "But I never graduated from high school. I only got as far as the tenth grade."

"Why don't you go to the Rehab Center?" Charlotte said. She told Bebe her sister had gone there and gotten her high school diploma. Now she was working as a ticket agent for Texas Air.

"How much did it cost?" Bebe said.

"It's *free,* girl."

"But that's welfare."

Charlotte laughed. "So what? A woman with two kids needs all the help she can get."

"That's just it. I don't know what I'd do with my kids."

"You could put your little girl in daycare," Charlotte said. "And that boy of yours should be in school."

"I've heard stories about those daycare centers." She told Charlotte some of them.

"Girl," Charlotte said, "that's a lot of nonsense. Akeem was in daycare from the time he was two, and not one bad thing ever happened to him."

When Charlotte left, Bebe said, "You know, black people aren't so bad. Chaney was always talking about how stupid they were. But Charlotte's a good person. She loves her boy, and when she dresses up, she looks real fine."

"She does," Burl agreed.

"And she's smart," Bebe said. "I think she might be smarter than me."

"You're smart," Burl said, putting his arms around her.

"Chaney was always telling me I couldn't do anything. But we never stayed anyplace except Amarillo more than six months. If I'm going to be here for a while, maybe I could try this Rehab Center she was talking about."

"I told you you could stay as long as you want."

"It doesn't seem like that Rehab Center is something I could do," Bebe said. "But I'm going to think about it. I really am."

Haney started singing a song when he saw John coming, an old rhyme Burl remembered from grade school.

> Down across the railroad tracks, where nobody goes
> Lives a little nigger girl without any clothes. . . .

John just looked at him and smiled.

"I don't know if I want to work with you anymore," Haney said.

"We're thinking about having children," John told him. "She says I do it like a black man."

In the motel, John drove Haney insane with long monologues. John had hung out with black guys in basic and 'Nam. They drove all the APCs because they were better drivers than the white guys. Black people had a lot of abilities white society didn't recognize. The Egyptians had really been Nubians. All you had to do was look at their lips. There had been great civilizations in Africa while Europe was still in the Dark Ages. Throughout history, they'd been held back. "But things are changing," John said. "I think there's a good chance the next President of the United States will be Jesse Jackson. He's already got my vote."

Haney groaned and rushed from the room.

Burl and John went in on a smoker, made from a fifteen-gallon drum, and John cooked spare ribs in the backyard. After they put the kids to bed, they sat in the aluminum chairs Burl had bought from Wal-Mart, and John delivered endless lectures. Since he'd met Charlotte, his interests had shifted from religion to politics.

"We got to get out from under Grandma," he said—that was what John called Reagan, Grandma. He said Reagan reminded him of his grandmother in Lawton, who wore false teeth and dyed her hair and always said the Lord would provide. "He's fucking the country instead of his wife. And it's the working man who's really suffering. Somehow, Grandma's got him fooled into thinking it's all his fault. For instance, you ask a working man what he thinks the number-one problem of this country is, and he won't say he can't make any money. He'll say it's the disintegration of the family."

"But that is a problem," Bebe said. "The woman next door works, and her kids are home all day long, and they're always in trouble. I don't mean you, Charlotte, you're different, but it's just not good for kids to be away from their mothers."

"Why, sure she's working," John said. "She's got to. That's the only way people can keep their heads above water anymore, for both husband and wife to work. But the poor working man goes right on thinking it's his problem, that he's done something wrong. And Grandma's against daycare, because he's so dumb, he thinks women are working because they *want* to."

"You know he's right, girl," Charlotte said.

"But you women are gonna change all that," John said, taking out a joint. "Once you're out of the house and thinking for yourself, you're gonna set your husbands straight. Then all the working men and women of this country are gonna vote in Jesse, and that beautiful black man is going to turn this country around."

But John had never voted. If you vote, he'd told Burl once,

you got to do jury duty, and only assholes do that. Still, Burl was glad John had found Charlotte, and that they made each other so happy. They smoked the joint, and John got out his golf clubs and started driving balls at the water tower. Every so often, they heard one hit. Then John started trying to hit the streetlight on the corner. Soon golf balls were bouncing off roofs all over the block. Burl was laughing helplessly, and the girls hid in the house, but John kept right on blasting those little white pills through the halo of glare around the streetlight until the cops showed up and said, "You boys professional golfers?"

"It's all in your mind, ain't it?" John said.

"Well, you'd better knock it off," the cop said, "or you'll finish your game in jail."

John and Charlotte went home, and Burl and Bebe lay in bed together. "I called this Rehab Center," she said. "They told me to come over and see a counselor."

"Good," Burl said.

"Trouble is, if I stay here, I'm not far enough away from Chaney. He can find me if he really wants to."

"You let me worry about Chaney."

She touched his face. "You don't mean that," she said. "But it's nice to hear you say it."

3

The Rehab Center sent Bebe to a diagnostic counselor. He gave her a series of tests that showed she had a learning disability. It wasn't neurological, just an inability to grasp abstract concepts, but it qualified her for state help. The next week she started classes, five days a week, from eight to three. Charlotte helped her find a daycare center for Pearl that took toddlers.

Jason enrolled in the third grade at Alamo Elementary. The first day, Burl walked him there and introduced him to his teacher. Alamo Elementary smelled exactly as it had when Burl was a boy: of pencil shavings, crayons, and the compound they polished the floors with. It won't be so hard for him, Burl thought. He's small for his age and he's new, so he won't suffer that terrible shame of being a grade behind.

The end of August came, and Willie's incision refused to heal. Chemotherapy had been postponed indefinitely. He took his walks in the evening, when the sun had gone down, then went to bed early and slept twelve hours. His bedroom had a bitter odor, like carbon, that scared Burl: the odor of sickness.

One evening a week, Burl joined him. He wanted to hear the old stories, the old lessons, tried to get his father to talk about the Battle of the Bulge, the Little Iron Men, the Texas Wonder Pool. But his father wasn't interested. "Oh, hell, son," he said. "That was so long ago, I can't even remember it now."

He moved ahead of Burl in the dusk, walking as fast as he could, staying stubbornly in the present.

At night, Bebe studied grammar, basic math, and human biology. Burl read his astronomy textbook at the kitchen table. Now he read not about the beginning of the universe, but the end. There was a black hole at the center of the galaxy, slowly devouring it. At the end of time, the universe would be consumed by black holes, or scatter into nothingness, each star growing cold until it died the heat death.

The last week of August, Lum died. Willie refused to go to the funeral. One night Doris told Burl that Willie had taken the Luger to a gunsmith, gotten it cleaned and oiled. They waited, as they always waited this time of year, for the heat to break, for the first blue norther.

The only thing that excited Willie was the approach of Halley's comet. An article in *Time* called it "The Show of the Century." It would be visible in late November, and again in early April. Willie wanted to make sure the telescope was in working order, so one night, they took it out in the backyard to try it out.

They stared at Jupiter, a slightly flattened orange gem, the sparks of its satellites floating on either side. "The largest planet in the solar system," Willie said, "and the most beautiful." Then Burl turned the telescope on the Andromeda galaxy, a great wheel of cold blue fire. "With all those billions of stars," Willie said, "there must be millions with planets that have life."

"I don't know, Dad," Burl said. "There may not be anybody else out there."

Recently, Burl had read an article in *Scientific American* on the search for extraterrestrial intelligence. In ten years of listening, the radio telescopes had heard nothing. The universe was strangely silent. Even Carl Sagan had given up hope.

"Why do you say that?" Willie asked him.

"The universe may be a more dangerous place than they used to think," Burl said. "They're saying now that comets hit the earth every billion years or so. That's what killed the dinosaurs, you know. Then you need water for life, and the earth is the only planet in the solar system that's been able to keep enough moisture in its atmosphere. The other planets are all too hot or too cold, too big or too small."

"That can't be true," Willie said. "That would mean if life ended here, it would disappear forever."

He seemed so troubled, Burl was sorry he had brought it up. "Don't worry, Dad," he said. "There's life out there somewhere. You're the one who's always saying you've seen their ships."

"You're goddamned right I have," Willie said. "I know you don't believe me, but I'm not the only one. They're here, I'm telling you, and they're real."

Burl didn't want to hear about flying saucers, but they were among the old stories, and he forced himself to listen. Willie told him again about the chrome ball he'd seen spinning over the prairie near Odessa, the red light that hovered over their car one night when they were parked out on the Caprock. But the closest he had ever gotten was the one he had seen in Clay County on New Year's Eve.

Willie didn't really know why he'd gone down there that night. He was drilling a well and told himself he needed to look at the log. But on the way back, he stopped off at Number One, where he'd first found oil. There was nothing there anymore but a pumping jack and a storage tank. When he got out of his car, he stepped on a cow pie, so he sat down on the steps of the tank and took out his pocketknife to clean it off. "Then a searchlight shone on me," he said. "I looked up, and there was this little flying saucer. I had the idea it was waiting for me."

It was the first time Burl remembered hearing this. "What do you mean?"

"I mean you always know you're going to see them before you do," his father said. "It scares the hell out of you. And here's another thing: it's always dead still around them. Even out in the country you can always hear some sound, you know. Like the sound of your body. But it was so still, it was like when you walk away from a rig and can't hear anything for fifteen minutes. So still, it was like there was no air. You talk about scared. I was never that scared, not even in Europe! But I wanted to see it, too, and when I thought that, it came closer."

"What did it look like?"

"Hot," his father said. "About like a red-hot stove ring. It made me feel funny to look at it, like I couldn't think straight. The searchlight shone right in my eyes. I can't tell you what color it was, but it went right through me, hot and cold at once, like touching dry ice."

His father shook himself, and Burl felt a chill go through his own body.

"Then it took off down the road," he said, "and I started chasing the sonofabitch! It seemed like we got back to Nortex in no time at all. And here's the strangest thing: it followed this road I'd never seen before. What's more, I've never been able to find it since. To tell the truth, I don't know if I was following it, or if it was leading me, but I'd never been as close as I was that night, and I kept thinking, if I could just catch it, I'd be the man who solved the mystery of the flying saucers!"

His father fell silent. "You know what happened," he said, after a while. "The Highway Patrol pulled me over and found a bottle in the car. They had to stop me in front of the state hospital, and then they woke up a doctor who asked me all sorts of fool questions, like did I love my mother and did I pull my pud?" He shook his head. "I never should have told the papers. That's something you'll learn as you get older, son: There's a time to keep your mouth shut."

Yes, Burl thought, you should have kept your mouth shut. But tonight, he couldn't be angry. For one thing, when he really listened, it was hard to believe his father hadn't seen *something*. For another, when he thought of his father chasing the flying saucer down the road, it wasn't all that different from him chasing a tornado.

"I'd like to believe it, Dad," Burl said. He put his arm around his father's shoulders for the first time in months. They were shockingly thin.

"Thanks for listening. It does me good to tell it."

"What do you think they want with us?"

"I think they're saving the earth. The first atomic bomb started some kind of cancer in the atmosphere, and they're saving it. Maybe they come from the future. Or another dimension."

"I've heard that," Burl said.

Burl went home and read his astronomy textbook. He wanted to believe in flying saucers, but the stars were so far apart, it took hundreds of years for light to travel from one to another, and nothing could travel faster than light. His father's theory about them coming from the future—now that was interesting, but it was also impossible. You might be able to go into the future by passing through a black hole, but never into the past—and that, of course, was the only place worth going.

Burl closed the book and went out on the back porch. It was

a hot night, dust and dead sycamore leaves blowing down the streets. He smoked a cigarette and stared at the red beacon light atop the water tower. The truth was, he wasn't interested in life on other planets. What he was interested in was life after death. Did his father have a soul, and what would happen to it when he died? Everyone else had already decided. His father believed he would be reborn into countless other lives, his mother believed he would be with the Lord in the City of Heaven, which she had once described as being full of shining buildings bigger than any in Dallas or Houston.

Only Burl had not made up his mind. His religion had always been astronomy, the telescope—Burl believed in light. It made him uncomfortable to think about these things. He had avoided thinking about them most of his life. But for the first time since he was six years old and stopped going to Indian Heights Christian Church, Burl had to know.

The last week of September, Willie began having stomach pains. Burl was in Amarillo when his mother called him and told him the doctor had performed another operation.

When Burl got home the next morning, he went straight to the doctor's office and told the secretary he wanted to see him. "He's got appointments all day," she said. "He might not be able to see you at all."

"That's all right," Burl said, sitting on the couch. "I'll wait."

In ten minutes, the doctor appeared. "I'm Doctor Young," he said pleasantly. "And you must be Willie Drennan's son." He wore a green surgical gown and red python-skin cowboy boots. Burl followed him into his office. On the wall was a diploma from Brigham Young University and a large acrylic painting of Conan the Barbarian, sitting on a throne of bloody skulls.

"Now then," the doctor said, sitting behind his desk. "What can I do for you?"

"I want to know what's going to happen to my father."

"Your father has a very aggressive cancer," the doctor said. "I don't know if I can describe what I saw when I opened him up, but it was as if someone had poured Elmer's glue all over his lower intestine. Chemotherapy might have helped, but at this point it will probably only prolong his discomfort."

"How long does he have?"

"Of course I can't make a prediction, but I would say he's got three months to live, probably less. Death will come from starvation and the total collapse of all life-support systems."

Burl's mind was empty, except for a picture of yellowish-white Elmer's glue pouring from a bottle. He wondered why the doctor had not told them before. Well, it made no difference now. "Thanks for being honest," he said. He couldn't take his eyes off the painting.

"That's an original," Dr. Young said. "I'm something of an art collector. It was done by the fellow who paints the covers of the Conan books. They're my favorite works of literature. Did you see the movie?"

Burl told him he had.

"Arnold Schwarzenegger was pretty good," the doctor said, "but I'll tell you, he just can't measure up to the original."

Burl drove to the hospital, where he found Doris and Coy in the waiting room. She stood up, and Burl put his arms around her. "It looks like your father might not be getting over this thing after all," she said.

"No, Mom," Burl said, "it looks like he might not."

As they walked to his father's room, he said, "Mom, I'd like Dad to meet Bebe."

"He's too sick right now," she said.

"When he gets a little better then," he said. "I'd like you to meet her too."

"Oh, I don't think that would be a very good idea," his mother said. "She's not family."

She went into his father's room. Burl turned to Coy. "I've seen the doctor," he said. "I think we should talk. Why don't you and Margo come over for dinner?"

"All right," Coy said. "What about Saturday night?"

Bebe bought a tablecloth, flowers, and a black dress. The temperature was in the low eighties, and the first cold front of the season was moving in. At seven o'clock, a cell appeared on the radar near Vernon. Storms were rare this time of year—but tornadoes had been known to happen in September. Burl watched it towering up against a sunset, a great blue dome. In another hour, it had collapsed. There was no upper-level support, no jet stream.

Coy showed up at eight. "We lost our sitter," he said. "Margo had to stay with Cyndi."

He was so clearly lying Burl felt his face burn. When he looked around to see if Bebe had heard, she had already disappeared into the kitchen.

"Honey," he said, "come out here and meet my brother."

They had catfish for dinner. Coy picked at his, carefully removing the bones. Bebe had smoked pot: her eyes were red, and she forgot a cigarette that burned a hole in the tablecloth. Halfway through the meal, Jason came in and said the neighborhood dogs had left a dead rat on the front porch. Burl had to go out with a dustpan and throw it in the trash.

After dinner, Bebe put Pearl to bed, then said she was so tired that if nobody minded, she thought she'd go to sleep herself. Burl and Coy sat out in the backyard. Coy chewed Maalox tablets. "Stomach trouble," he explained. "I've been working too hard."

Burl nodded, staring at the water tower, its belly glowing green in the streetlights.

"Well," Coy said, "it looks like the old man's not going to make it."

"Two or three months. That's what the doctor said. He should have told him before."

WILLIAM HAUPTMAN

"Dad's known all along," Coy said.

Lightning flashed to the east. Burl stood up and walked to the fence to get a better look.

"Then why is he pretending it's not happening?" he said. "Isn't there someplace he wants to go, something important he wants to do? They're both hiding from it, and every moment's important now. That's why I want him to meet Bebe. But Mom says she's not family."

Coy chewed another Maalox tablet. "Where'd you meet this girl?"

"I met her in Oklahoma, while I was chasing a tornado."

"Christ," Coy said. "You're still doing that?"

"I like storms. I've always liked them. I've been thinking about going back to school next year and studying meteorology. What do you think?"

"I think you'd better concentrate on getting your shit together. You're making a lot of money working for the railroad, and there are guys in this town with college degrees who are cleaning toilets right now. You know," Coy said, "I used to be just like you. I didn't want to grow up. I thought nobody loved me. Look at this place you live in. Can't you do any better than this? I mean, you've got rats here. And this girl's already got two kids. I think Mom's just wondering what in the hell you're doing with yourself, and to tell you the truth, so am I."

Burl stared off at the lightning, feeling a hot surge of anger. "I like Bebe," he said. "She's been through a lot of hard times."

"What is she, a Mexican?"

"No," Burl said. "She's a Kiowa Indian."

"I'm sure she's a wonderful person and she really cares for you. But if you ask me, you'd better concentrate on getting your shit together, instead of opening a home for battered women."

By now, the lightning was continuous, bolts of cloud-to-ground that turned the night sky daylight blue.

"It looks like it might storm after all," Burl said. "You feel like going home?"

"No," Coy said. "Margo and I had a fight."

"Then why don't we drive out and get a closer look at it?"

Coy laughed. "Sure," he said. "Why not? Maybe you can show me a tornado."

Before they left, Coy got a bottle of Jack Daniels from under the seat of his car. As they drove south out of town, the digital clock on Prairie Savings & Loan said 12:00 AM. Burl had never chased a storm at night before, and he found it almost impossible to figure out the structure: the lightning was blinding, and with each flash he seemed to see a different storm. At Scotland, he turned east on a little blacktop he had never gone down before, heading toward a big white rain shaft.

"Christ," Coy said. "This is like something Dad would do."

Burl laughed. "You're right."

"I should spend more time with him. What does he talk to you about?"

"Last week we talked about flying saucers."

Coy took a drink. "Remember when he wrote that letter to the paper, saying he'd seen one? It ruined my whole senior year. Dad could have been a big man in this town, if he hadn't gotten into that *Twilight Zone* shit."

"Maybe he really did see something," Burl said. "Have you ever thought of that?"

"No," Coy said. "I used to think about the mysteries of the universe, but now I think about money. It's the only thing that makes sense. I hated Dad for holding that money I borrowed over my head, but he was trying to teach me a lesson, and he was right. Dad had a lot of money once," he said. "I don't know why it didn't make him happier."

"I don't care about it all that much."

"I know," Coy said, "but you'd better start. If the price of oil doesn't go up, this town's going to be in a hell of a mess pretty soon." He took another drink. "But I'm doing all right. In another month, I'll have Dad paid off. Then I'm going on a vacation."

"Where?"

"Buddy's taking Margo and me to Hawaii. He knows this place on the big island where a helicopter drops you off, and you can run around without any clothes on for a week."

They hit the rain. The drops were cold, the sign of a storm with a high top. Sparks of rain and hail flew toward the headlights, like a movie special effect of flying through a star cluster at the speed of light. Lightning hit no more than a mile away. The bolt seemed to be on the ground for two or three seconds, leaving a burning image on his closed eyes.

"Slow down," Coy yelled. "What are you getting us into?"

"Maybe trouble," Burl said, laughing.

He stepped on the gas. There was some pleasure in terrifying his brother.

Then they were through the rain, and Burl pulled off the road. Lightning flashed all around them, but he heard no thunder: they were in the dead spot under the rainfree base. Burl got out of the car and looked around. Live oaks leaned over the road. The countryside, lit by flashes of lightning, looked like no part of the county he had ever seen before. Burl thought of the strange road down which his father had chased the flying saucer. He saw a hill ahead that couldn't possibly be there, and waited for another flash.

"I get the feeling we shouldn't be here," Coy said.

"No," Burl said. "We're in the right place."

It was a Supercell. He knew it by the temperature of the rain, the silent intensity of the lightning, and most of all by the feeling of pent-up energy about to be released. He ran a hand through his hair, heard it crackle like a cat's.

"What's going to happen to Dad?" he asked Coy.

"What do you mean?"

"When he dies."

Coy laughed nervously. "Why are we talking about this right now?"

"You believe in God, don't you?" Burl said. "You're the one who joined the church. You must have thought about it."

The next flash showed Burl what he had been looking for: a long, pale tube of cloud, hanging over the fields to their left, that tapered down to a little coil of vapor.

"Look," Coy said stubbornly. "My beliefs are my own business. Anyway, it's not something you can talk about. When you get older, you think about it, but you don't talk about it. Your kid wants to believe, so you tell her you do, too, and later you find out maybe you mean it. You stop thinking about it, that's what I'm saying, and you feel a lot better."

"I can't stop thinking about it," Burl said. "I want to know what's going to happen to Dad."

Then Burl heard something so strange, his heart stopped: a long, thin cry that seemed to come out of the earth. A moment later, it was answered by other cries, and Burl realized he was hearing coyotes. Every coyote in the county must be howling at the storm.

"Holy hell," Coy said. He groaned and threw up into the ditch. Burl looked the other way.

"Oh, Lord," Coy said. "Dad's going to die, and Mom can't take care of herself. What are we going to do?"

Watch him die, Burl thought. There was nothing else they could do. It would be painful beyond all imagining, but in some way he needed to see it. At the exact moment when his father left his life—he might not learn if his father had a soul or not, but at least he would learn something, one way or the other.

4

When Willie came home from the hospital, he was angrier than he had been since his drinking days. He spent most of his time in his room and hardly spoke to them. Now he had two open incisions, stapled together, but incredibly, he was up and walking in three days.

"He just won't talk about it," Burl's mother said. They were talking in the kitchen while Willie took his afternoon nap. "I mentioned something yesterday about making sure his will was in order, and he walked out of the room. And there's something else. He's talking about taking our savings and flying to Canada. There's supposed to be someone there who's got a cure for it. What if he spends all our money?"

"I'll talk to him, Mom," Burl promised.

The next morning, Burl walked with his father to the hobby shop. On the way back, Willie mentioned the doctor in Canada. He said he'd heard about him from a friend in the Program. "He thinks he's got a cure for the damned stuff," Willie said. "He gives you drugs you can't get in the United States, and shoots you full of gold, and somehow that stops the cancer."

"Dad," Burl said, "I don't believe in those cures."

Willie turned on him. "That's easy for you to say. You don't have the damned stuff! Well, you can give up on me if you like. It's just like you! But I've gotten everything in my life by fighting, and I'm not going to quit now."

Burl couldn't face his father and turned away. Willie walked on, and Burl followed him home, troubled by a feeling that he finally identified as anger. He was as angry at his father as his father was at him. If he chose the pistol, Burl thought, if he took that way out, I could understand it. Why does he keep on denying it?

When they got home, Doris had to clean Willie's incision with hydrogen peroxide. Burl left the house: he couldn't stand to hear his father's cries of pain.

Two days later, on the way up to Amarillo, they met the first blue norther of the season, a low, leaden wall of cloud that hit with a gritty blast of wind. It sleeted all over the Panhandle that night, the earliest ice storm anyone could remember. The next day, they rolled back across the glittering prairie. The mesquite trees were so coated with ice, they looked like coral. John built a fire in the caboose stove, but the cupola was still cold. When they started up the grade west of Vernon, Royce had to dump sand on the tracks so the wheels could get a purchase.

They got in long after dark. Burl called and told his father they would go walking the next morning, but he overslept. When he got to the house, at noon, his father had been gone for an hour, and his mother was frantic.

"I begged him not to go," she said. "What if he falls down on these slippery sidewalks?"

Just then, Willie came through the door, his face pale with cold and effort.

"Oh, honey, honey, *honey*," Doris scolded him. "I was out of my mind with worry. How can you do these things to me?"

"Goddamnit," Willie shouted, tears of rage in his eyes. "Can't I even go for a walk if I want to? Do you have to treat me like a child?"

He went into his room and slammed the door. Doris sat at the kitchen table. "I can't take any more," she said. "I have taken all I can stand."

At that moment, Burl knew he couldn't either. He went to his father's room and knocked on the door.

"Come in," Willie said. He lay on the bed, staring at the ceiling.

"I'm sorry I missed our walk. Let's go for a drive instead."

"No," Willie said. "Your mother worries about me too much. She thinks I'm a child. I'll just stay right here."

"We've got to talk," Burl said, helping him to his feet.

They got in the Mustang and drove north out of town, on the Central Expressway. Willie said nothing when they turned off on Red River Road and bumped along over the ruts to the Magnolia Refinery. Burl helped him out of the car, and they walked through dead sunflowers toward the old storage tanks. The sleet had melted, but the muddy ground was frozen hard as plaster under their feet.

Willie sat on a crumbling foundation. The old pumping jacks clanked and nodded, the chug of their diesels coming to them clearly on the cold, still air. "I don't know why we had to come all the way out here," he said.

"You used to bring me here when I was a little boy. You told me all about it. The discovery well was right over there, wasn't it?" Burl prompted.

Willie nodded, staring at some large black crows that had landed and were eating sunflower seeds. "On that little rise. Sunshine Hill, they called it. Those wells over there have been producing since the beginning. Something like ten thousand people lived right here, in tents."

"And your parents spent their wedding night right around here, isn't that right?"

"Somewhere around here," Willie said absently, as if it were a thing of no importance. "But I don't know why in the hell you want to talk about this. It's ancient history."

Burl's eyes filled with tears. "Because you're going to die," he said.

Willie glared at him with a look of such hatred that for a moment Burl thought he was going to hit him.

"All right," he cried. "I fought this cancer as long as I could, but it looks like it's beat me. There's no reason to go to Canada. I thought about blowing my brains out—that's why I got the gun cleaned—but then I thought about what it would do to your mother. So I guess I'll go out in the hospital. I'm going to die! There, I've said it! I hope it makes you happy!"

His voice rang off the storage tank, and the crows scattered away.

"I'm sorry," Burl said.

"I wish I could leave you more," Willie said after a while. "I did find that oil down in Clay County. I know you boys never stopped to think about it, but you had just about everything you wanted when you were growing up. I might have made a million dollars if I hadn't let the bottle get hold of me."

"It doesn't matter."

"No, I should have started sooner. Time was always running out on me. I worked for three years to save enough money for college, and just when I got ready to go, the war came along. And it took so much out of my life."

Now, as his father talked, Burl felt all his anger leave him. There was nothing more to be said, and he just sat there, letting the sound of his father's voice flow through him and seeing the things around him very clearly: the pebbles in the yellowed concrete foundation, a rusted cable lying in the grass, the crystals of frost on the red clay at their feet. Later, he remembered them as well as anything his father said to him.

"Nothing happens for years, then everything happens at once. I thought when I joined the army I'd get to see a little of this world, but they sent me to Lawton, not forty miles away, and I spent a year there sitting on my butt. Of course I met your mother there, so it wasn't all wasted. Then two days after we were married, I got on a troop train to Fort Dix, and a week after that they put us on the boat. I didn't take a damned thing but *The Collected Works of William Shakespeare.* I didn't really think I'd read it, but do you know something?" His father smiled at him. "It turned out to be the best book I'd ever read.

"The day we landed in France, we heard about the Battle of the Bulge and headed for Bastogne. Five days later I got lost in a snowstorm, and the next thing I knew, I was in a rifle company, fighting for my life. I was lucky. I only lost two toes—they turned blue, then black, then fell off one day when I was taking off my socks. By that time, it was all over. In another month, I was back at Fort Sill."

He shook his head. "Some nights, I'd lie awake doing arithmetic: I'd lost two toes and four years out of my life, and had nothing to show for it but a Bronze Star and a Luger I got from a kraut I caught taking a crap. I was twenty-six years old and married to a woman I hardly knew—your mother and I were still strangers to each other, son. It takes time for a couple to understand each other's needs." He glared at Burl. "Or it used to. I guess now you just jump into bed right away, but it was different then."

"I don't know, Dad," Burl said.

His father stared off at the sunflowers. The crows had come back and were eating sunflower seeds again.

"It's funny," he said. "Time is everything, but you don't notice it, except now and then. I didn't want to come back here at all, then I ended up working for George for ten years. It's easy to go along, forgetting you've got something to do in this world, thinking you'll stay the same, like the people in the funny papers." He laughed. "I was thinking that just the other day. Here I am, almost finished. Blondie isn't a day older, and the same old shit's still going on in Gasoline Alley."

"What changed it for you?" Burl asked him.

"One day George said to me, 'Willie, can you tell me what's on your mind in five minutes? My time is important.' And I thought, mine is too. Ten years I've been working for this sonof-abitch, and he hasn't made me his partner yet. So I told him off and walked out. I didn't know what I was going to do, but I had the idea there was this little shallow pool down in Clay County. The next day I drove down there. There was this little hill west of the acreage, the moment I saw it, I remembered this story an old cowboy had told me about a mysterious place where you could see the story of the world."

"You told me about that once, at the Denver Cafe."

Willie smiled. "Did I, now?" he said. "Well, that's what I was thinking about. And when I saw that hill, it was like time stopped. I didn't see the story of the world, but I saw the story of my life. It was like dreaming with my eyes open, and it all came right around to that spot. It was a cold day, about like today. I looked around, and I thought: this is where I'm going to make my money.

"The Indians, who knew a hell of a lot more about this than the preachers do, would have called it a true dream. The rest was easy. I went to Big Jim Naylor, he loaned me some money, and I leased the jackknife rig from George. For months, people stopped me on the street and congratulated me. But I'd already known it was going to happen."

Willie laughed, staring off over the mesquite at an orange gas flare. Burl could hear its faint sputter.

"I don't know how the drinking got hold of me," Willie said after a while. "We had plenty of money, and I tried to tell your mother what I needed was time—time to think about all the mysteries, like the dream that told me I was going to find oil, and other things. Sometimes, when I was drinking, I almost had it figured out. My head was full of light, and my thoughts were like something Shakespeare wrote."

He shook his head. "Before I knew it, I was living from drink to drink, and I never did get it figured out."

"You had the dream. That's the important thing."

"Yes," Willie said. "But I forgot the first one hadn't come out of a bottle. Lord knows I'd like a drink right now." He looked at Burl. "Don't you ever start."

"No, sir," Burl said. "I won't."

"Good."

Willie stood painfully, shoved his hands in his pockets. "There's something I want you to promise me."

"What's that?"

"Take good care of your mother. I don't know what she's going to do without me."

"I promise."

Willie nodded. "I'm glad we got this out of the way." He stared off at the downtown buildings. "This goddamned town," he said. "I never thought I'd die ten miles from where I was born. I never even got to Paris. My father was there, during the first war—at least, that's what he told my mother. But I spent the war up to my ass in snow, and then they shipped me back to the States." He shook his head. "You know," he said to Burl, "maybe you should get out of this town."

"I still owe you money," Burl said.

"It doesn't seem so important now," Willie said. "It's no place for a young man to spend his life. It's dying now, and so am I."

Burl looked up at the sky. A little daylight moon hung up there, so pale it was almost invisible.

"Where do you think you'll go, Dad?" he said.

"West," his father said. "That's what they used to say in the army when someone got hit. When I get there—well, they say you go into the light and meet everybody you've ever known. Your mother, your people."

His voice broke. Burl looked away.

"If I get there, and there's any way to tell you, I'll let you know." He put his hand on Burl's arm. "There's only one thing I'm afraid of—the pain. I don't know if I can stand the pain."

Burl heard the fear in his father's voice and shuddered.

"You'll do fine, Dad," he said.

As he helped his father to the car, the silence was broken only by the clank of the pumping jacks. The old ones, still producing after sixty years.

5

Now, as October passed, Burl found himself wondering all the time about love. Was it really the strongest force on earth? Could a man and a woman love each other their whole lives, or was that just an illusion? His parents still weren't getting along. Burl had thought his father's approaching death would make them love each other as never before, make every moment important. But not even death could do that. Maybe it wasn't close enough yet.

It seemed impossible for men and women to be happy together. Terrible things seemed to happen to people when they were married—like Haney, for instance, who was getting a divorce.

Nobody knew the details, but Haney had started drinking more when they were at the motel in Amarillo. "Stay up with me," he had said to Burl once. "I feel like talking tonight." Burl said he had to get some sleep. Later, he heard Haney talking through the wall. He seemed to be talking to himself.

Burl dreaded the idea of hearing Haney's troubles, but one night when he had nothing better to do, he found himself hearing the whole story while they watched porno movies and drank beer.

"Let me tell you, kid," Haney said, "you're lucky you aren't married. You'd think a guy as well hung as me wouldn't have any trouble, but when you're working road freight, you're never at home, and when a woman's alone, she's gonna start fooling around. You take my wife."

Haney popped the top off another beer.

"I never knew a woman I couldn't satisfy, but last year my wife and I started having trouble in bed. It was the same time this woman moved in next door. She called herself Sapphira and said she belonged to the order of wicca, which meant she was a witch and could cast spells. Then my wife told me she was afraid of getting pregnant and wanted me to get a vasectomy. I just hated the idea, but damned if she didn't talk me into it. Sure you don't want another beer?"

"No, thanks," Burl said.

"Then last month, she told me she and Sapphira were lovers, lesbian sisters. She had a whole new outlook on life and wanted a divorce. So I went a little apeshit," Haney said. "I broke out some windows and threw her clothes outside and set fire to 'em. She told the judge, and he put a restraining order on me, so now I can't even see my own son. Can you believe that shit?"

"Not hardly," Burl said.

"He calls me sometimes and cries. They won't let him play football because they say it's a violent sport. They're going to Dallas next month to get a lesbian preacher to marry 'em, and this summer they're going to Colorado for the gathering of the Rainbow Family, which is nothing but a bunch of old hippies. Worst of all," Haney said, "Sapphira put some kind of spell on me so I'm impotent. It's either that or the vasectomy, but something took the lead out of my pencil."

Haney sighed. "Well, that's my sad story. It all happened because I didn't stay home enough. Now I ain't got a home. I'm living in the back of my pickup with my dog Arnold. Good thing I bought a shell. I'm writing a song about impotence. I'm going to give it to Hank Williams, Jr."

"Maybe we'd better get some sleep," Burl said.

"When I was a kid," Haney said, "I thought with my dick I had it made. I called it John, after John Dillinger. He had a big one, too, you know. It's in the Smithsonian, along with Kennedy's brain. But things have changed, or maybe it's just women."

Haney stared at the screen, where two women made love in a brass bed that hovered in empty space.

"They don't need us anymore," he said sadly. "They say they got more feelings than we do, but they only care about themselves. Pretty soon we'll all be divorced. They'll have our kids, and we'll be living alone and giving 'em money. It's already happened to the niggers."

Willie no longer walked: he didn't have the strength. He lay on the couch in the den, watching whatever was on—*The PTL Club, The Bugs Bunny Show.*

He was growing thinner, down to a hundred and thirty, and hardly touched his food. Doris had almost stopped eating herself. She lived, like Willie, on beef broth. Sometimes she scolded him for trying to do too much. At other times, she scolded him for not doing enough. His motionlessness frightened her: if he lay there too long, he might never get up again.

Doris decided to clean out the hall closet. Burl went over and found the contents scattered on the floor. There was a sepia photograph of little Willie, aged three, clinging to his mother and staring at the camera with huge eyes. There was a porcelain doll, a doughboy in uniform, that had been his favorite toy. "Hell," Willie said. "It's a wonder I didn't grow up to be a girl. I don't know why I loved it so." Burl did: the doll had red hair, like Willie's father Johnny Drennan, who had fought with the American Expeditionary Force in the Argonne Forest.

There were also booklets from the Rosicrucian Society and and several old copies of *Modern Photography,* with nude figure studies of smiling young women on California beaches.

"What did you keep these for?" Doris scolded him. "These are nothing but filth."

"They are *not* filth," Willie said. "The human body is beautiful. You never understood that. These are works of art."

They hardly spoke for the rest of the afternoon. Burl couldn't understand why his mother had to clean out the closet now. All she had to do was wait a few more weeks. But although his mother had waited most of her life, she could stand it no longer.

Bebe was doing well at the Rehab Center. Her teacher said when she got her GED, he would recommend her for the secretarial sciences program at Nortex Junior College. Burl was proud of her, and he asked his mother if he could bring her over to meet Willie. But his mother still said no—if you brought a girl home, that meant you were going to marry her. In fact, Willie saw no one. Friends from work and the Program called and asked if they could stop by, but he always refused them. His father suffered from the shame of cancer: it was the worst of his failures, worse than going broke. He had done something terribly wrong—he was going to die.

"But he must be lonely," Burl said to his mother, "just lying here day after day. What about George Staples? He's Dad's oldest friend."

"Your father hasn't spoken to George in years," his mother said. "Not since he stopped working for him."

"But isn't it time to forget all that? They won't be seeing each other again."

"That's how he feels, and he won't change his mind."

One night, Burl came back from Amarillo and found Bebe had fallen asleep studying at the kitchen table. There was nothing in the house, so he drove out to Food Emporium, the big new grocery store that was open all night. He walked the aisles, past bins of beef feet and buffalo burgers, looking for something he was hungry for. It was so big, it seemed deserted, but you might see anyone there: last week, Bebe had seen Waylon Jennings buying a six-pack of Bud and a Texas Lottery ticket. Sure enough, he ran into Nicky Staples. She was wearing a black leather jacket and had chopped off her hair so it stood up in stiff blond spikes, like Madonna's.

He told her about his father having cancer, and she said, "They found another spot on Daddy's liver. They think he's got it in his lungs too. It seems like everybody's getting it. They say it's something in the water."

"That's what my mother thinks," Burl said.

They stood in the parking lot under the American flag, which was said to be as big as any in the world. Nicky was having trouble with her marriage. "Jimbo's been taking too much cocaine. It makes him paranoid. He's like Elvis—he only trusts the people he went to high school with—and he's started carrying a gun. I need to talk to someone, Burl. Jimbo's in Oklahoma City tonight. Why don't you come over?"

She looked better than ever, but Burl thought of Bebe, asleep at the kitchen table. "I'm sorry, Nicky," he said, "but I've got someone waiting for me."

Did he really love Bebe? He had never felt so close to someone that he had no interest in other women. But she still refused to use the word. "Once you do," she said, "you start making promises." Burl himself wasn't sure what it meant. He did notice that when he was in Amarillo, he had trouble remembering her face. He could recollect the sound of her voice and most of all the light in her eyes, but her face was a shining blur. Someone had once told him, back in high school, that this was a proof of love.

In November, there was another sleet storm. For three days, the sky was sheet-iron gray. One afternoon, a lawyer came and Willie made out his will. He even agreed to talk to the minister of the Indian Heights Christian Church.

"But why, Mom?" Burl said when he heard about it. "Dad hasn't gone to church in forty years."

"Because he's going to preach the funeral sermon," his mother said. "And he wants to get to know your father."

The minister was too busy, but the associate minister came one afternoon and talked to Willie as he lay on the couch, watching the football game. Willie talked of reincarnation, Edgar Cayce, and the astral plane. The associate minister kept nodding, his looks getting cloudier and cloudier, sweat staining his polyester suit. He left in a hurry, telling Willie he hoped the Love of the Lord would shine on him.

The best thing that happened was John Arcement's visit. He came over one day to drop off a record that Willie Nelson, Johnny Cash, Waylon Jennings, and Kris Kristofferson had made about reincarnation, called "Again and Again and Again." Burl didn't think Willie would talk to him, but John stayed for three hours. "Your father's a very wise man," John told Burl when he left, "with a profound understanding of the law of karma. You shoulda listened to him more. I'm just sorry I never got to play golf with him. He must have been poetry in motion."

It was a time of sadness, but good things happened too. Sometimes he was overtaken by strong feelings that came out of nowhere. He felt he was seeing things clearly, as you did when things were coming to a conclusion.

He learned to appreciate the winter weather. A great cold high-pressure area moved in over the plains, and the clouds cleared away. Burl rode the train into incredible sunsets, when the air was so dry and clear, you could look off over the curve of the earth and see the molten contrails of airliners over New Mexico, a hundred miles away. Gradually the sky turned from gold to green to the icy blue of an Arctic lake. When he got back to Nortex, he was shocked at how much weight his father had lost. Even a day made a difference.

Doris wanted the family over for Thanksgiving, made turkey and dressing and pumpkin pie. Coy had to go to Dallas at the last minute on business. "I don't blame him," Doris said. "He's got a family to support." Burl didn't either: he dreaded his parents having a fight. But Thanksgiving was different. It was a cold, clear day, and after they ate, they noticed two small brown rabbits feeding in the backyard. "My bunnies are here," Doris said. Willie had found them under the back steps last spring, no bigger than grasshoppers. Burl had never expected them to survive. But the neighborhood had grown quieter since everyone's children had grown up and moved away, and there were dogs. They watched the rabbits for fifteen minutes.

"They'll make it through the winter," Willie said. "They're tougher than you think."

His father seemed stronger, his expressions clearer somehow. The cancer was burning away all his confusion, leaving something harder underneath—like erosion wearing away the soil, exposing granite. It seemed to Burl that his father might be right, that he could beat it after all, and on that day his parents were easier with each other than they had been for months.

The next night, his mother wanted to see the Festival of Lights, the Christmas decorations in the Country Club section. But when Burl came over, his father said, "I'm pretty tired. Why don't you two just go by yourselves?"

"I know why you want to stay here," Doris said. "You just want to watch *The Bitch*."

"I'll watch anything I please," Willie said, throwing his spoon onto his plate.

"What's *The Bitch*?" Burl asked his mother when they got in the car.

"It's this movie on cable starring Joan Collins," his mother said. "And that's just what she is. The moment we leave, he'll turn it on. He just loves that damned Joan Collins!"

Burl had to smile. It was hard to believe his mother could be jealous of Joan Collins—but didn't it also mean she still cared for him, wasn't it a sign of love?

They drove through the icy streets to Country Club, passing George Staples's house, a big Spanish-style home of pink adobe. Burl told his mother he had seen Nicky. "That's the girl you should have married," she said.

"Why does Dad hate George so much?" he asked her.

"George helped your father," she said. "And your father didn't want to be helped. George had money. They'd been close friends in high school, when it didn't matter, and that makes it harder later on. Then George got to fly. He was a spotter pilot, and your father was what they call a dogface. At parties, when all the men talked about the war, he used to kid your father. He said your father couldn't tell what was going on down there on the ground. Your father used to get angry—I knew what he was thinking, about his toes falling off and other things he could never tell me about."

Burl turned onto Brook Street, and ahead they saw the lights of the Blake house.

"But oh, those first years were wonderful," she said. "I didn't care for George's wife, but we had such a good time. The month after Coy was born, we flew down to the Cotton Bowl in George's airplane. I was the one who was scared. But when we took off, your father got airsick and started throwing up into a paper bag, and I felt so sorry for him, I forgot to be scared. And it was a wonderful weekend," she said, "except the night after the game, George took us to a nightclub in Fort Worth where a girl took all her clothes off."

Burl joined the long line of cars, most of them full of children. A policeman with a red flashlight directed traffic.

"The next day," she said, "we flew back into the sun, long after it was dark on the ground. I'd never known it could be that—still daylight up there, just for us, as if we were angels. Then I saw the lights of Nortex ahead, like little blue rhinestones scattered out there on the prairie. I thought: this is my town, my home. Then George brought us down into the dark, and my stomach came up in my throat. It was like falling in a dream, or jumping out of the hayloft when I was a little girl."

They moved slowly past the Blake house. New decorations had been added every year, so many that by now the house was almost completely concealed. There was a factory where elves made toys, a carousel, a Santa in a rocket ship. The Nortex Chamber of Commerce boasted that this was the largest display of Christmas decorations in the world.

"Is this the best place you've ever lived, Mom?" he asked her as they drove home.

"No," she said after a while, "I think the best place was Benjamin, way out in the Panhandle, when your father and I were first married. It was just a little town, but there was a wonderful feeling in the air right after the war. Everyone was glad to be alive. The doctor had told me he thought I couldn't have children, and we thought we'd be alone forever. But our loneliness brought us together. And we rented the nicest little house, with a bed of bird's-eye maple. Your father and I were very close then. There was this little mouse, and we used to watch him sit on the stove after supper and clean his face with his paws. But we didn't kill him because we were so lonesome."

Burl turned onto the block, and they saw the house ahead, its porch light burning. He pulled into the driveway. For a moment they stared at the house, its asbestos siding white as marble in the moonlight. "You know," his mother said, "you don't know anything when you're young." She looked at Burl, her face shining. "You can be the happiest you're going to be in your whole life, and you don't even know it."

Halley's comet failed to appear. It could be seen, but only faintly, when you were far out in the country and away from city lights. *Time* published another article: "Show of the Century Flops."

Burl wanted to drive out to Lake Caddo, but Doris was against it. "If your father got in the car," she said, "it could kill him." On the night the paper said their chances were best, Willie struggled into his clothes, and they set up the telescope in the backyard. But the streetlight on the corner was blinding, and after a while Burl had to admit he could see nothing.

"Well, that's a big disappointment," Willie said. "I sure thought we'd see more than that." He went to the fence and opened his fly. "What happened, anyway?"

"They've disappeared before," Burl said. "They're made of rock and ice. Every time they go by the sun, a little more ice burns off. Halley's has been seen for centuries. But maybe it's just about gone."

He joined his father, and they pissed together in the moonlight.

"It's incredible, when you think about it," Burl said.

"Why do you say that?"

"That it's been around for so long, for billions of years. And that we should be alive in the time when it finally disappears."

"Well, tough tittie for us," Willie said. "But I guess we've got one more chance, in the spring."

"Yeah, they say in April our chances will be better. It'll be higher in the sky then."

They stood there for another moment. "We had these nights, son," Willie said. "At least we had these nights."

The back door slammed. Burl stayed a little longer, looking at their backyard, the yards of the other houses on the block. The dead winter grass, dry as broomstraw, glowed in the moonlight, every blade distinct.

Then he went home to his apartment at the foot of the water tower. "It won't be long now," he told Bebe.

"Let's go to bed."

They took off their clothes and got in bed. "I wish you could meet him," he told her. "I know he'd like you."

"It's all right. It doesn't bother me."

"I don't know what I'm going to do when it happens. It's not going to be easy."

"Don't worry," she said. "I'll be with you."

Then they made love. As they finished, Pearl woke up and started crying. Bebe said she'd take her to the other room. "No," Burl said, "bring her over here."

Bebe brought her to the bed. But her milk was gone, and when Pearl kept crying, Burl sang her the song his grandmother had sung to him:

My dears, have you heard, how a long time ago
Two poor little babes, whose names I don't know
Were stolen away, on a fine summer's day
And left in the woods, or so I've heard say.

Now when it was night, so sad was their plight
The sun it went down, the moon gave no light
They sobbed and they sighed, and they bitterly cried.
Then the poor little things, they lay down and died.

At last, her tiny fist loosened on his finger, and she snored softly.

Bebe stared at him, her eyes black in the moonlight.

"I love you," she said.

"You don't have to say it if you don't mean it."

"We don't belong together," she said sleepily. "And I'll probably be sorry. But I do love you."

When she slept, Burl went out and sat on the back steps. He smoked a cigarette, staring at the red beacon atop the water tower and the dead grass glowing in the moonlight. He thought of Bebe and the kids, asleep in the house behind him. He put his hand to his chest, felt the slow, strong beating of his heart that seemed like it would never end.

Why, I'm happy, he thought. It seemed to him that he couldn't be any happier, not even if he lived in a log cabin.

6

Willie finally admitted he'd been having stomach pains for three days and told Doris she'd better call the doctor. An ambulance came and took him to the hospital. Dr. Young put him on glucose and told Doris and Burl his intestine was completely closed. "I can operate again," he said, "but in any event, it won't prolong his life more than a couple of months. What do you want me to do?"

"You'll have to ask him," Burl said.

Dr. Young went into Willie's room and came out a little while later. "He'd prefer not to have another operation," he told them. Burl asked him what would happen now. "He might get better,"

Dr. Young said. "Or he might drop into a coma and linger on for a month. It's impossible to say."

"I just don't want him to suffer," Doris said.

"Oh, he's not in any pain," Dr. Young told them. "I'm putting him on some pretty heavy medication. I'll see he gets it whenever he needs it."

When they went into the room, Willie was asleep. He woke up for dinner, then the nurse brought him another capsule of Nembutal in a paper cup.

The next day, Willie asked Burl to give him a shave. "That damned colored nurse scraped all the skin off my face when she tried it, and I can't do it myself," he admitted. "I hate to look at my face in the mirror. Could you do that for me, son?"

"Sure, Dad," Burl said.

That evening, he brought his father's straight razor. He heated some washcloths under the bathroom tap and soaked his father's beard. Then he lathered it with soap. He worked carefully, hearing the scrape of the bristles against the blade.

"I'm never leaving this hospital, am I?"

"The doctor said you might get better."

His father sighed. "Bring me my books, will you, son? I've made a list of which ones I want."

Burl told him he would.

"Now trim my hair for me. Take it off over the ears, before I start looking like a goddamned bum."

Burl was afraid to take off too much. He remembered how proud his father had been of his hair, the afternoons he'd gotten his hair cut at the Kemp Hotel barbershop—glaring at the mirror, telling Abner Spell to be careful, goddamnit. Burl finished, patted his father's cheeks with alcohol. "That's better," Willie said. His face was gray, but his hair was still copper bright, the only part of him that seemed alive.

When Burl came back the next day, bringing *The Collected Paintings of Maxfield Parrish,* his father was singing a little tune with his eyes closed.

"Dad?" he said.

" 'Stardust,' " Willie said. "Boy, that's a good old song. And old Hoagy Carmichael could sure sing it." He told Burl he'd had a good night's sleep for a change.

Jesus, he thought. Dad's stoned out of his mind.

In three days, Willie's personality began to disintegrate. Burl watched him float away on a tide of Nembutal. He lost all track of time. If Burl got there before he had his medication, he was coherent. Moments after he took it, he sounded as if he were talking in his sleep. He started sentences that turned into memories, snatches of music. Then his eyes closed, and he was gone for hours. He told Burl he kept forgetting the things he needed. He wanted a pad and pencil so he could take notes. Burl brought him one, but he kept losing it.

"Tell George I did it," he said once, his eyes closed.

"What's that?" Burl asked him.

"Found the Gunsight sand. And I did it with the jackknife. I couldn't punch a very deep hole in the ground with that old piece of tin, but I didn't have to. It was so shallow, I could have sucked it up with a soda straw." His eyes opened. "Where's George?"

Another time, he laughed quietly. "Thought he was God's right-hand man," he said. "The old sonofabitch."

Burl asked him who he was talking about.

"Colonel Blake. Thought he was the smartest man ever born. He was playing poker at the Petroleum Club one night. Asked me to come over to his house for a drink. He knew I hated him. Showed me a map of North Texas and said, 'The oil's right—

here—and here—and here. I got every location nailed down.' I said, 'Why are you showing me this?' He said, 'Willie, you won't remember it tomorrow.' Like he felt sorry for me." His father laughed again. "He was right."

"Be careful when you're throwing the chain, or you'll lose a finger," he said. "That's what that old jarhead told me. He was like me. Grew up in this red clay country, smelling oil from the day he was born."

Willie was getting injections of Demerol now. "I like this gal," he said of the black nurse who brought his bedpan. "We get along real good." And it was true—the huge black nurse liked him too. "He's a real joker," she said. "He's a character."

But when he hadn't had his pill, he cursed her when she rolled him over to change the sheets. "Goddamnit," he cried. "Take it easy!" A great yellow bruise appeared on one arm, then the other, where the needles went in every four hours. When his arms were so sore his father could stand it no longer, the nurses rolled him over and used his buttocks. Then he was off again: "That little German girl I met that day. Took me to her house. The roof was burned off, but the piano still worked. She had long blond hair, just like a collie dog's. And so, so thin—just skin and bones. We had ourselves a time that day. Drank some of that Rhine wine."

"Honey, do you remember that bird who came and sang on the kitchen windowsill every morning? He only had one foot, but he sure could sing. Stood on one foot and sang in the sunlight. To keep warm, I guess."

▼ ▼ ▼

Singing: " 'Roly poly, Daddy's little fatty, boy you're gonna be a man someday.' Don't you remember that, the way those cowboys used to sing to you, when I took you down to that location? They sure loved you. Told me when I left, they'd take you off my hands, and they were about half serious."

"When was that, Dad?" Burl said.

His father opened his eyes. "Oh," he said. "I thought you were Coy."

Now Burl sensed his father was involved in a great struggle. There was a frown of concentration on his face when he slept. Even his silences were full of effort. Sometimes Burl found him turning the pages of the Maxfield Parrish book, devouring it with his eyes. Sometimes he tried to say things, but the words would not come. The pencil had fallen and rolled under the bed.

Burl saw things with a new clarity. And what he saw was time. He began to be afraid he would miss the moment of death. His father came back to consciousness less and less often. Burl had to see the moment. Then he would know something. But he had to go to work too. He had already taken most of his days off.

It was all a matter of timing, like knowing when to take a day off so he could see a tornado. Burl began dreaming of tornadoes again. He was standing with his father on the front porch when one appeared over the Catholic cemetery. They hid in the bedroom. The house exploded around them, and he saw his father go flying up into the funnel, merging with blue rings. Another time, his father seemed to be caught in the grinding machinery of the power plant.

One night the phone rang, shocking him up out of sleep. He grabbed it, his heart pounding. "Who is it?" he cried.

"Son?"

THE STORM SEASON

189
▼

"Dad?"

He heard the phone being dropped, picked up, the sound of his father rolling around in the bed. Then trying to form a sentence, his tongue thick with Nembutal: "What—what—what time is it?"

Burl looked at his watch. "Four o'clock."

"In the morning? Or in the afternoon?"

"In the morning."

"They've got these—goddamned blinds closed, and I—can't tell if it's day or night."

"It's night, Dad. I'll be there first thing in the morning."

His father hung up.

All his father had ever wanted to do was *get out of time*. That was all anyone ever wanted to do, that was what religion was all about. The struggle to get out of time.

And now he had. He floated away on a tide of chemicals. If he had some important message—and sometimes Burl still thought he did—he forgot to give it to him.

On the first day of the new year, Burl went to Amarillo. They rolled up through an ice storm and worked another hour in the yard. When they got to the motel, there was a message saying his mother had called.

"He's in a coma," she said, "and it's getting harder for him to breathe. You'd better get back as soon as you can."

"Where's Coy?"

"Coy went to Houston. I've been calling his hotel, but he doesn't answer. I'm here all alone, and I'm going out of my mind."

Burl talked to the yardmaster, and they deadheaded him back. He lay on the bunk in the caboose, unable to sleep. The whole Panhandle was covered with an icy fog. He saw eight or ten semis that had slid off the road into the ditch. Just let him hold on until I get there, he thought.

They passed the power plant at dawn and rolled on into Nortex. When he called Bebe, she was just getting ready to take the kids to school. "Drop them off," he told her, "then pick me up at the yard office."

She came fifteen minutes later, and they drove to the hospital. "Come on," he said, taking her hand. When they walked into his father's room, his mother, sitting at the foot of the bed, looked up and stared at Bebe.

"Is he gone?" Burl asked his mother.

No, he was not gone, but he had not moved for hours. His breathing was horribly slow, his lips cracked.

He doesn't know a thing, Burl thought. He'll go out like this. But when he touched his father's arm, his eyes opened.

"Dad," he said, "this is Bebe."

To Burl's complete surprise, his father gave her a wink.

"I can see why he cares about you," he said.

Bebe was crying. "We just want you to know we love each other very much, Mr. Drennan."

Willie closed his eyes. "That's good," he said. "That's good. That's all you need. It's a pleasure to meet you. You should have come around here sooner."

When Bebe stepped outside, he told Burl, "She's a honey."

"She is, Dad," he said. "She loves me and she wants me to be happy, and that's the important thing."

"Love," his father said. "They've got to have it or they're no good."

Burl put Blistex on his father's lips. He had fallen asleep looking at *The Collected Paintings of Maxfield Parrish*. It was still on his lap.

"I'm hurting," his father said. "I'm glad you're here."

Burl kissed his hot forehead.

He stared at Burl for a long time. "You know," he said, "I used to think you were wrong."

"About what?"

"You were too soft, too easy on yourself. Not like Coy. But I'm beginning to think you had the right idea." He closed his eyes again. "Thanks for taking such good care of me."

"I love you, Dad," Burl said.

The black carbon smell of his father's breath was sickening. Burl tried to ignore it.

"Where's Coy?"

"I don't know, Dad."

"I'm going to sleep for a while."

The nurse came in, shook her head, and left. His father's breathing went on and on, like a telephone nobody would answer. Toward noon, Burl felt a gathering of energies. Let him go, he thought. He's struggled long enough.

"I can't take this any longer," Doris said. She went outside, to wait in the hall.

One minute Burl was staring out the window. Then something made him look at his father. His eyes were open, and as Burl watched, they filled with tears.

Burl took his hand. "Let it go, Dad," he said.

His father nodded.

The phone rang. Burl picked it up. "Hello?" he said, not taking his eyes from his father's.

It was Coy.

"I'm in Dallas," he said. "The flight's grounded, so I'm taking the bus home. But I just got this feeling I should call. How's Dad doing? Is he still holding on?"

"He's just going," Burl said. "I can't talk right now."

He replaced the phone. His father's eyes dropped to the book in his lap. He took another breath and let it go, staring at a sky of Maxfield Parrish blue.

The next breath never came. Burl watched as the light in his eyes faded. In another minute, he was sure. Something had left his father's body—a sense of light and motion.

Yes, he was gone now. Burl touched his eyelids, closed them. He had known. That was the important thing. Something about the moment had cut through the fog of drugs. Coy had known too—that had to mean something. The air was full of a tortured smell. It had been so hard for his father to die. The struggle was engraved on his face. Burl felt it was still going on. Willie had left his body, but Burl could still hear the echoes of the struggle going on, somewhere out of human sight.

There was much to do.

Dr. Young came, confirmed Willie was dead. "It was a blessing," his mother said, "it didn't last that long." But it had lasted long enough, Burl thought. It had been endless.

Bebe told his mother she was sorry. Then she drove home, and Burl took his mother to Barnett's Funeral Home, a few blocks away.

They sat in the waiting room. A man came and tendered his regrets. Then he gave them a brochure showing the different caskets. "They're all beautiful," he said, "but I think you'll be interested in this one. It costs five thousand dollars. The top of the line."

"This one will be fine," Burl said, indicating the six-hundred-dollar casket.

"That will be perfectly satisfactory," the man said. "But I think if you'll consider the others, you'll see—"

"This is the one," Burl said, and stood up. His mother signed the papers, and they went outside.

The day my father died, he thought. But there was nothing about it that stood out. The sky was gray and cold, and it had already started to get dark. He drove his mother home in the Lincoln. The neighbors had already heard somehow, and before long they started calling.

Coy and Margo showed up at six. "Oh, Mom," Coy said, tears streaming down his face. "Why did I ever go to Houston? I should have been here, and now you'll never forgive me."

"You couldn't help it," Doris said. "It was the weather."

Margo made coffee, and they all sat in the front room. Burl felt a need for light and walked through the house, turning on lamps. It was like the night after the tornado, except that nobody felt good, just that the worst was over. Before Burl left, Coy came up and hugged him. He smelled of travel: airplane seats and static electricity. "I was standing around waiting for the bus," he said, "when I got this feeling I should call, just like someone touched me on the shoulder. Did he say anything before he passed on?"

"Not then. He told me a while back that if he found the afterlife and there was any way to tell us, he'd let us know."

Coy wiped more tears from his eyes. Burl hadn't cried yet. When he left, he stopped at the stop sign on the corner and looked back at the house, every window lit and the porch light shining, the only lighted house on the block. Then he drove home and slept better than he had in weeks, dreaming of nothing.

The next morning the clouds were gone, and the forecast for the next three days was cold and clear. Bebe fixed him a big breakfast. There was an item in the morning paper about Willie's death. Burl called the yardmaster and took two personal days off.

In the afternoon he took his mother to the funeral home to view the body. The waiting room was empty, and he wondered if nobody had died the day before.

Doris didn't want to see the body. "But that's what we're here for," Burl said.

"You go," his mother said. "Tell me if his hair looks all right. I'm afraid they left it too long."

Burl opened the sliding doors and stepped into a windowless

room with a high ceiling that smelled of—formaldehyde, he supposed, thick as cleaning fluid. There were old horsehair sofas, purple drapes, lamps with red glass shades. The coffin, surrounded by floral arrangements, was gunmetal. He walked toward it, holding his breath. There was his father, sleeping in white cushions. Except it wasn't his father. It was the shell of his father, the cheeks rouged and the lips painted. Burl had expected this. But there was something to be learned from seeing it: the flesh had burned away, and he saw his father's true face. He looked more like his mother than he ever had in life.

He kissed his father's forehead. It felt like cardboard.

Burl sat down on the sofa by the coffin. Then he sobbed uncontrollably for two or three minutes, heard himself crying like a woman, gasping for air.

When he finished he took a Kleenex from the box thoughtfully provided by the management, blew his nose, and went back to the waiting room.

"How did his hair look?" his mother asked him.

"Fine, Mom," Burl said. He couldn't remember seeing it.

When they got home, he told his mother he was bringing Bebe to the funeral.

"All right," she said. "But she can't sit with the family. People might get the wrong idea. What are you wearing?"

Burl said he hadn't thought about it.

"You can wear one of your father's suits," she said. "I think it'll fit you."

Burl took the suit home and tried it on. It was bright blue polyester with gold threads—one of the suits his father had bought when he stopped drinking, to try to look young. That night, he and Bebe made love. He stood out in the backyard and saw a meteor roll down the sky, a droplet of molten metal. A dome of cold high pressure covered the whole United States. There were no clouds anywhere on the satellite photo.

▼ ▼ ▼

The service was held in the chapel of Barnett's Funeral Home. The associate minister of the Indian Heights Christian Church gave the sermon, sweating profusely. "I only knew William Drennan in his final days," he said, "but he made a profound impression on me. He was a man of many loyalties." A general murmur of agreement ran through the room, and even Burl found himself nodding. For once, the associate minister had said the right thing. The coffin was open, and the family stepped up first for a last look. This time, Burl noticed his father's hair—it was longer than he had worn it, but a beautiful, bright copper. He wore his mother's thick gold wedding band on his right hand.

An attendant helped Doris, Coy, and Margo into a Cadillac limousine. Burl found Bebe. They got in the Mustang and followed the hearse to Riverside Cemetery. He parked, and they walked uphill, past the mausoleums of the founding fathers, the wildcatters who had built Nortex, crowded together like a little Country Club section around the Reflecting Pool. Willie's plot was at the top of the hill—next to his mother's, beneath a twisted cedar. His nearest neighbors were Mexicans, their tombs decorated with bottlecaps and colored glass, and the Central Expressway was only a hundred yards away.

But so many people had come. Burl had never looked around at the funeral home. Now he did, and saw half the town was there. The Little Iron Men stood together—Garland Moffitt, Big Jim Naylor, Clint Yarborough, Sr.—old men now, wearing outdated suits, string ties, and cowboy boots. Some were millionaires, some just as broke as when they started. But they were all there.

Burl sat on a metal folding chair next to his mother. When he looked to the north, he could see for miles. It was so cold, he felt as if he were naked, sitting there in his father's blue summer suit.

▼ ▼ ▼

When they got home, the house was full of women who had brought food. Burl was hungry: he ate fried chicken, potato salad, chocolate cake. The doorbell kept ringing. "Your father would have been glad to have seen all these people here," his mother told him. At one point he met Coy in the hall. "Heard anything from the old man yet?" Coy said.

Burl shook his head. It seemed to him that his father had struggled so long, suffered so much pain, that the moment he left his body he had gotten out of here as fast as he could.

He told Bebe to drive home. He could walk, and he didn't want to leave the house yet, wasn't ready for it to be over. It was a long, silent, sunlit day.

When almost everyone had left, George Staples knocked at the door, his hair gray, wearing aviator sunglasses. Burl was shocked at how old and worn he looked. He sat beside Doris on the couch, saying things Burl couldn't hear. Coy stayed in the bedroom. He still thought of George as one of their father's enemies.

When Burl walked George to his car, he said, "Beautiful day. I think I'll go up and VFR around for a while. Feel like coming along?" Burl asked his mother, who guessed it would be all right. So they got in George's old white Cadillac and drove to Kickapoo Airport.

They rolled George's Cessna out of the hangar. It was so cold, George had to prime the engine three times before it would start. They took off and flew north, at two thousand feet, just above downtown Nortex. Then they turned west, toward Burkburnett. The sun was just touching the horizon. Below, Burl saw the storage tanks of the old Magnolia Refinery. George kept flying west along the Red River, over the Texas Wonder Pool. Burl thought he must be doing this on purpose. "Like to take it for a while?" he said.

Burl took the wheel. It trembled in his hand, so much more responsive than the steering wheel of a car. They were over Bradley's Corners, where his father had been born. Looking down, he saw for the first time how big the Boom had really been. The field went on for miles, one pool after another. It was dusk on the ground, but he could see the scars where each well had stood, little circles of red clay where nothing would ever grow again. The colors were the colors of the funeral home and his father's coffin—rose and gunmetal gray. Ahead, he made out the power plant at Okla-union, and in the remote distance, the Medicine Mounds. He felt they were flying back over his father's life, the history of Nortex, the story of the world.

"Now let's go home," George said. "Just give her a little left rudder." Burl did, and they circled back. God, he loved to fly. "That's right," George said. "Nice and easy."

George took the controls as they came in over the creek bed at the end of the runway. When they got closer to the ground, Burl felt the molecules of cold, dense air, which gave less lift, go out from under them. They dropped ten feet to the grass runway, bounced, and rolled to a stop. "Nothing like a little flying," George said, "to take your mind off your troubles." As they drove home, Burl asked him how Nicky and Jimbo were doing. "They're going to be fine," George said, "if Jimbo can hold on to his money."

When he got out, Burl thanked him, and George said, "Come see me sometime, and we'll do it again."

The house was empty and his mother was sleeping. Burl went to his father's room and lay down on the bed, still wearing his father's suit. His father's books, his belongings, were all around him. Burl closed his eyes. He found himself thinking how much he was like his father. When he was a child, his father had taken him to the movies. Burl always wanted to sit close to the screen, so he sat in the front row, and his father sat in the back. Every so often Burl had heard his father's cough in the darkness, the cough that was his alone, and knew he was still there. Now Burl coughed, and he sounded exactly like his father. Everything, even the air going in and out of his lungs, reminded him of his father.

He stood up, looked at the photograph that now stood on the dresser, of his father as a baby, clinging to his mother. There was something in people's eyes, Burl thought. It was there when they were born. When they got older and you saw them after a while, you noticed how they'd aged. But after a moment, the lines faded away and their eyes were all you could see again. Something in people's eyes never changed. Burl didn't know what to call it, but it was something like light.

DRYING OUT

1

Willie left him a thousand dollars and the Luger. There was a little trapdoor in the roof of the closet that opened into the attic of his apartment. He put the pistol up there, wrapped in a sheepskin saturated with Hoppe's Guncleaning Oil.

The closer his father had gotten to death, the more Burl had been aware of time. Time was real, and it had finally run out on his father. Now Burl looked at his own life and saw there was still time to change it, if he tried. His father had told him to leave Nortex and do what he wanted. The day after the funeral, Burl wrote off to the University of Oklahoma and Texas Tech, which had two of the best meteorology schools in the country, asking for applications.

"I've been telling you that's what you should do all along," Bebe said.

"If I get in," he said, "I want you to come with me."

"But we don't know how we'll feel about each other then."

"That's just it," he said. "We've got to think ahead."

He worked out a strict budget. By the summer, he would have enough to go to school for a year. And he stopped smoking pot. He couldn't afford to fail a drug test now—he needed all the money he could get. Something told him if he didn't do this now, he would never again have the strength.

February was cold and dry. He worked as often as he could. To his surprise, he found he didn't think about his father that much. To do so was to think of death, and he wanted to remember his father in better days. Sometimes he found he didn't think about his father at all.

One night as they neared Quanah, Burl noticed a yellow light flying along parallel to the train. At first he thought it was a Starlifter flying out of Altus. He'd seen them turn on their landing lights at night sometimes, signaling each other. But this was too low, and it was going too slow. He called John, who climbed up into the cupola, and asked him what he made of it. Once, the light flashed bright blue and seemed to shine right into the cupola for a moment, like a searchlight.

"What the hell was that all about?" John said.

Burl thought he had it figured out now. It was a McDonnell Douglas attack helicopter. He'd seen one patrolling the Pantex fence last week. They had a laser target designator atop the rotor, and the pilot must have shone it into the cupola.

John called the engine on his radio. "Haney," he said, "can you see that light to the south?"

Yeah, I see it, Haney said after a while. *Looks like an airplane in trouble.*

"It's a helicopter," Burl said. "It's playing games with us, that's all."

On the other side of Quanah, they pulled off of the siding to let the hotshot go by. Burl and John stood on the back porch of the caboose, watching the light. It made no sound, but Burl thought he felt pressure on his ears, like when he stood beneath a smoke detector—a faint ringing, not quite painful. Gradually, it turned the dim orange of characters on a computer screen and sank down into the field by the tracks, where it was hidden by a row of poplars. "Burl," John said, "that is a definite Unidentified Flying Object out there."

"John," he said, "there's no such thing."

"Maybe not," John said. "But I've always wanted to go for a ride on one of the damned things, and I'm going out there with you to throw that switch."

They started down the tracks. As they neared the switch, the light shining through the trees got brighter. "Here we go," John said.

Burl started laughing.

They were seeing the lights of an Allsup's Convenience Store shining through a thin fog that had collected down there in the bottom. Burl could see the open door, the lights of the video games, even hear a radio going inside, tuned to a Spanish-language station. "Well, I'll be damned," John said.

"See," Burl told him, throwing the switch, "there's no such thing as Unidentified Flying Objects. We were letting our imaginations run away with us."

"Hold on," John said.

"Now what?"

"There's no Allsup's here."

"There is so."

"No, it's a mile back," John said, "on the other side of the tracks. I've never seen this one before. There's no *town* here."

"John," Burl said, "you are so full of shit. I can see there's an Allsup's down there, and I'm going to get a Big Red."

He climbed through the barbed-wire fence and started across the field. "Wait up," John said, then started following him. As he crossed the field, Burl found himself wondering why he was doing this. But he was thirsty, and he was trying to make a point. For a fact, it wasn't the Allsup's he had thought it was. There were no gas pumps, and when he looked to the left and right for cars, there was no road. But he could see the open door, the video games, the little Mexican behind the cash register looking up with big dark eyes when he saw they were coming.

"*Whoa*," John said.

They stumbled backward into each other and fell down. The Allsup's was gone. In its place something hovered over the field. It looked like a big fat tire, made of smooth gray linoleum. There were lights around it that appeared to be portholes. The bottom was a glowing orange bell mouth that lit up the ground.

"What were we doing?" John said. "Weren't we going into an Allsup's? What are you seeing now?"

Burl could say nothing. He couldn't think. Everything had come to a dead stop. There was something out there in that field, something real, and it wasn't a helicopter or the planet Venus. His father had been right.

"I don't know," he said. "I think it's a flying saucer."

"But this is great," John said. "This is really happening." He thumbed his radio. "Haney?" he said. "You still got those lights?"

Can't hear you, Haney said. *You're breaking up*.

The pressure on Burl's ears deepened to a hum. The lights brightened, turned hot gold, and Burl felt a sickening surge of fear. It knows we're here, he thought.

He touched John's shoulder. "Maybe we should go."

Just then, the thing bobbed up into the air and right over their heads, blinding-orange light showing every detail of the ground at their feet. Burl felt electricity going through him and heard John's radio give a rip of static like a chain saw, before the light snapped out and was gone.

"Shit," John said hoarsely.

Burl stood there, feeling the tingle die away.

"You still with me?" John said.

"Yeah," Burl said. "I'm scareder than I've ever been in my whole life."

Sparks danced before his eyes, like sunlight reflecting off the water. But where was the UFO? It had completely disappeared.

The radio crackled. *You coming back or not?* Haney said.

"Right now?" John said.

We got a green block. Let's roll.

"We'd better go," Burl said. The whole thing had been like a dream, from the moment they'd seen the light. He couldn't collect his thoughts somehow.

When they climbed back onto the caboose, he caught sight of John's face. He looked frightened.

"We'll talk about this when we get to Amarillo," Burl said.

"You're damned right we will."

Nobody wanted to hear about it. They'd start talking, and the others would listen for a moment, then stare at the floor. "You must be the first guys in history," Royce said, "to see an Unidentified Flying Convenience Store."

They agreed it had been a solid object. The light had been orange, like heated metal, but the color of no heated metal they'd ever seen. Both had felt something when the light hit them. Burl thought it felt like electricity, John thought it felt like heat. Their eyes watered for three days.

An article in the paper said strange lights had been seen all over Texhoma that night. A Soviet satellite had fallen back into the atmosphere. That satisfied everyone, but it wasn't what they'd seen. "I've waited for this my whole life," John said, "and now that I've seen one, nobody believes me. It just goes to show nobody believes anything anymore, unless they see it on television."

Burl stopped trying to tell people about it after the first night. Now he had seen one, he thought, just like his father. But it was best not to talk about such things. It only got you into trouble. "There's just no proof," he told John.

That was the problem, when you got right down to it. There was no proof, and it had been so strange, more like a dream than anything else; he began to think it might have been one after all.

He had almost forgotten about it until the day two weeks later, when they stopped on the same siding and John walked off across the field, on a cold, gray afternoon. He stood there for a while, then motioned for Burl to join him.

"What is it?" Burl said, standing beside him.

John said nothing, just stared at the ground. Then Burl saw they stood on the edge of a circle of dead grass, flattened and scorched and somehow whorled around a central point, like iron filings clustering around the poles of a magnet.

2

Almost two years had gone by since the Big Tornado. Everyone said Nortex had completely recovered, that the town was bigger and better than ever. Still, you couldn't get over the feeling there was some sort of profound uneasiness, just under the surface.

Last year, the local drilling companies had begun to fold. Now the banks did, too, quietly at first. First Nortex was absorbed by the Metro Bank of Dallas. Metro was then absorbed by the Sunbelt Bank of Houston, which was in turn absorbed by Citicorp. Vernon Savings & Loan went down. The depositors had no warning, and no insurance.

Burl's mother said it reminded her of the Great Depression. She'd never thought she'd live to see the time when banks failed again. Still, she kept her money in Coy's bank, Prairie Savings & Loan, which had no depositor insurance but offered ten percent interest. There had been stories about it too. Coy said they were nonsense. "But don't you have a lot of investments in the oil business?" Burl asked him.

"Some," Coy admitted. "But most of our holdings are in real estate, and real estate is an investment that will never lose its value."

Maybe, but when Royce, Burl's engineer, tried to get a second mortgage, the appraiser told him his house was worth sixteen thousand dollars less than he'd paid for it. The chamber of commerce said everyone was working, but for a week a young man stood by an entrance ramp to the Central Expressway holding a sign that said I WILL WORK FOR FOOD.

Still most people agreed the town's number-one problem was drugs.

North Texas, the chief of police said, was "the amphetamine capital of the world." Several methedrine labs had been busted in the area. There was a lot of open country, and meth took only eight hours to refine. Sometimes the chemists just parked under a tree and worked out of the back of a pickup. To Burl, the reason was clear: meth was cheap, and people in Nortex were getting poorer. The Texas Employment Commission admitted record numbers of people were out of work. But nobody was interested in the reasons. Drugs were blamed for everything that had gone wrong.

Bumper stickers appeared: LET'S KEEP TEXHOMA DRUG FREE and LET'S SAY NO TO DRUGS. There were endless commercials for drug and alcohol clinics. The one for Faith City Hospital, where railroad employees went when they'd flunked their drug tests, began with a man sitting in the dark, saying to himself, *How can I tell them I've lost another job?* There were billboards showing husbands shouting at their wives and children, possessed by uncontrollable rage. There was a general feeling that anyone might become a wife beater or a child abuser, that everyone had a drug or alcohol problem, or both. That everyone needed help.

The number-two problem was Satanism.

At Christmas, a high school student had committed suicide by shooting himself in the head with his father's deer rifle. His friends said he had been into Dungeons and Dragons. The school board brought in Mormon experts on Satanic possession to speak to the students. There were rumors of Satanic rites, conducted in the storm drains under the shopping mall.

Channel Two did a special called *Satanism in Texhoma*. "Has Satanism crept into Nortex?" the announcer said. "The answer is yes. Cats have been killed, and blood has been shed." There were interviews with young people, their faces hidden by shifting dots, including a young girl who said, "Yeah, I used to be a witch. I've gotten people into trouble with my spells." The announcer asked her what kind of trouble. "Traffic tickets," she said. "Things like that."

This troubled Haney deeply. A Satanic lesbian had stolen his wife. Most of all, he was worried about his son. "What if he gets exposed to this sort of thing?" Haney said. "I'm not there to help him anymore. I should be taking him fishing, teaching him what's right and wrong."

Burl felt sorry for Haney—his son had been taken from him, and Haney clearly loved his son. But he was also a little afraid of Haney. Nobody had seen Haney sleep for months, and Burl suspected he was on crystal meth.

"Haney," John said, "this is nothing but mass hysteria. People got to find some reason for things going wrong, so they decide Satan's responsible."

Haney stood up. "I've had enough of you, John Arcement," he said. "You could have been a man of God. Instead, you're an atheist and a pot smoker who thinks he sees flying saucers. Satan's real, and he's after our kids. If you had a kid yourself, you wouldn't talk this way."

But John wouldn't let it go. "Thing I can't understand," he said, "is why you think Satan would be so interested in Nortex. I guess if he gets a foothold here, he can take Denton, Decatur,

Grapevine, and Jacksboro. It's the domino theory. He's got his eye on Dallas."

Haney looked like he was going to hit John, but instead he walked out of the room. Burl looked out the window and saw him disappear off down the highway into the dark.

The next time they got ready to take a train to Amarillo, the trainmaster told them they'd be taking a new brakeman. John asked Royce, "Where's Haney?"

"Ain't you heard?" Royce said. "Haney's on suspension."

"What for?"

Royce lowered his voice. "Well, I don't know if I should say this, but it's for sodomy."

Burl and John looked at each other.

"You know that new kid, Butch Huff?" Royce said. "Well, he says Haney got him out behind a boxcar and propositioned him. He complained, and they put Haney on suspension and sent him to the hospital for a drug test."

"Well, what do you know?" John said. "I guess Haney showed his dick to the wrong guy."

Burl wasn't surprised. He had figured out Haney's real problem a long time ago. But as much as he disliked Haney, he felt sorry for him. For one thing, it was the job that had put Haney in such a hard place, and for another, he found himself feeling sorry for anyone who was different. John felt the same way. Once they got rolling, he came up and sat in the cupola with Burl. "My heart goes out to Haney," he said. "The poor guy's had two people inside of him all these years, and one of them's a woman. Let this be a lesson to all of us: Everyone's life is full of secret pain."

Seeing the UFO had changed John. He'd always had the best disposition of anyone. But when people didn't believe him, his feelings were hurt. He became sullen and refused to talk to anyone. "They used to think I was the smartest guy on the Fort Worth & Denver," he told Burl. "Now they think I'm a fool."

Right now was a dangerous time for people to be thinking that. The Fort Worth & Denver was in a financial crisis. They were trying to get rid of as many employees as possible, and drug testing was the perfect way to do it. Hardesty, the new trainmaster, was a real company man. He started giving tests for every little infraction. Technically they weren't random tests, but they amounted to the same thing. Everything was "reasonable suspicion."

In February, a car derailed during switching. It happened all the time, but Hardesty sent the whole crew down for a drug test —he had a beef against one of the brakemen. The next week, he sent the same brakeman down for lying on the office porch at the end of the day—there was a clause in Rule G that said "assuming the attitude of sleep" was prohibited. John never smoked on the job, only at home. But he couldn't afford to take a drug test—pot stayed in your system for a month. Still, he refused to stop smoking. "They can tell me what to do at work, but not at home," he said.

Burl was glad he'd stopped smoking pot. Hardesty suspected every brakeman with long hair. Hardesty didn't much care for John either. One night they were sitting around waiting for their train, when Hardesty came walking through the office and asked John what he was reading. *"Aliens Among Us,"* John said. "It's probably over your head."

Hardesty blinked and said, "Get rid of it."

"Ain't I got a right to read what I want?"

"Not on company time," Hardesty said. "Rule E: 'Reading other than company literature while performing service is prohibited.'"

"But we ain't performing service," John said. "We're just sitting here on our asses."

"Get rid of it," Hardesty said, "or get ready to go pee in that little bottle."

At the next union meeting, there was a discussion of drug testing. John stood up and said, "Every time someone takes a urine test, they should write on the form that they're doing it under protest."

Some people applauded, but there were groans. The union rep said, "We can't come out against a measure that increases safety."

"First of all, safety's got nothing to do with it," John said. "Every day, I get cars with violations that I'm supposed to send to the shop. But I don't, because there's an understanding we got to keep things moving on schedule. If the railroad was really interested in safety, they'd upgrade their rolling stock and fix all that old track. What you guys don't see," he went on, "is that we're under a personal attack by Ronald Reagan and Elizabeth Dole. They fired the air controllers and got away with it, and now they're out to break the transportation workers, and they're doing it by portraying us as drug addicts."

John made what Burl thought was a pretty good speech. There was a definite class-warfare angle to this. Nobody wanted to give tests to Wall Street stockbrokers. Pot wasn't the problem. The problem was crack in the inner cities.

"But they can't do nothing about that," John said, "so instead they bust a few railroading men for smoking pot. They make it our problem, then say they're winning the war on drugs. The truth is, they're doing this for one reason: control. They're not trying to make the workplace safe, they're trying to get control over the working man, and I say we can't let 'em get away with it."

But nobody paid too much attention to John. Almost everyone in the room had voted for Reagan. "Shut up, you damned old hippie," someone said. "We know why you don't want to take a drug test."

Charlotte wouldn't look at John for the rest of the meeting. As they left, Royce told Burl that John was the best damned conductor on the Fort Worth & Denver, but he was turning into a real pain in the ass.

They pulled out at midnight. At sunrise, John came up and sat in the cupola.

"Still thinking about what they said?" Burl asked him.

"They called me an old hippie," John said. "It's an honorable thing. I'm proud to be one."

"They're assholes. There's no way you can fight them."

John stared back, into the rising sun. "I became a railroading man because I thought it would give me my freedom. It's turned out to be no better than a chain gang."

"Hell, John," Burl said. "Why don't you just quit?"

John looked at him. "You're right," he said finally. "I've put it off too long. This is my last year."

"You mean it?"

John offered his hand.

"I do," he said. "You've inspired me."

They shook on it.

"And you should stop smoking pot too," Burl said. "You don't want to get your ass in trouble."

"Oh, I will," John said. "But not yet. They may control my body, but they ain't got my mind." Five minutes later, he sighed and said, "It's hard to change when you've been doing what you're told for sixteen years."

Sometimes Burl thought that was why John kept on smoking. He wanted to get caught: then the decision would be made for him. But it was a dangerous game. If there was an accident involving loss of life, or a hundred thousand dollars worth of property damage, and he failed his drug test, John could go to prison. Two brakemen in Alabama had gotten three years for just that reason. And there could always be an accident. As they started up the grade on the other side of the Prairie Dog Fork of the Red, Burl could feel the old rails give.

Sometimes Burl went to see his mother. He did the chores, then she fixed him supper and they talked, the television going the whole time. She said it kept her from feeling lonely. He was proud of Bebe, told his mother how well Jason was doing in school, asked her why she couldn't show more interest. "They're not blood kin," his mother said. "And blood is thicker than water."

The last week in March, he painted the shutters. She heated him a frozen dinner in the little microwave she'd bought, which sat by the stove. When he asked her if she wasn't going to eat, she said she wasn't hungry.

"Mom," he told her, "you've got to eat."

"You go on. I'll eat something later, after you're gone."

When he looked through the kitchen cabinets for an ashtray, he found they were empty except for a box of Mr. Goodbars, his mother's favorite candy bar. So was the refrigerator. There were no groceries in the house, only candy bars, packets of cocktail almonds, a box of peanut brittle, and a carton of Saltines.

"Mom," he said, "is this what you're eating?"

"Sometimes it's too much trouble to make meals for myself," she admitted. "But don't bother about me, I'll be just fine."

For a while they watched another special on Satanism. The announcer spoke to Mayor Babbs. "Unfortunately," he said, "there is a very real danger of an outbreak of Satanism in this town. Federal agents have informed me of two Satanic cults operating in the area—one in Nortex, and one in Burkburnett."

"I have here some Satanic comic books," the announcer said, showing Babbs some copies of *Heavy Metal* magazine. "Are they evil?"

"Probably not," Babbs said. "But they open the way for hard-core Satanism down the line."

"Lord," Burl's mother said, "I'm glad your father didn't live long enough to see things like that going on in this town."

Burl stared out the windows, watching shadows lengthen in the backyard. He was glad the days were getting longer. He noticed two brown rabbits nibbling grass by the clothesline. So they had made it through the winter. Tears filled his eyes. Every time he came here, he got so emotional. He stood up and walked through the house, filled with a profound love for the rabbits and all living things. Gradually, he noticed some things were missing. He opened the door of his father's clothes closet, saw only empty hangers.

"Oh, I took them down to the Salvation Army," his mother said. "They depressed me, they made me think of death. Don't hold it against me. It made me feel better than I had for years. I'm going to clean out the attic next."

"And throw everything away?"

"No," she said. "I'm going to have a tag sale. Lum's wife had one, and she made almost five hundred dollars. Your father didn't leave me that much, you know."

"If you're worried about money," he said, "why do you keep yours in Prairie Savings & Loan?"

"Coy says it's safe."

"Coy works there," Burl said. "What if it folds? You'll lose everything."

The special ended, and a commercial came on for commemorative medals. "The American Heroes Collection," the announcer said. "Forged of solid silver and available for a limited time only. John Kennedy, thirty-fifth President of the United States. Neil Armstrong, first man on the moon. John Wayne as Rooster Cogburn. Collect them all. These medals will never lose their value."

"I have thought about doing that," his mother said. "Buying some of those medals."

"Mom," he pleaded.

"But I don't know what I'm supposed to *do*. Nobody does. I thought when I got to my age, I wouldn't have to worry about these things. But I'll be all right," she said, "as long as I take it one day at a time."

Before he left, they talked, as always, about his father. His mother hadn't felt him around that much. Burl agreed: It seemed to him that his father had not only wanted to escape the pain of death—he wanted to get out of Nortex as fast as possible.

"Don't worry, Mom," he said. "I'll take care of you."

He drove home, thinking that when the storm season started, he would feel better. It should begin in another week or so. The next morning, before sunrise, he took a train to Amarillo. Looking to the south, just above the horizon, he made out Halley's comet, a splash of cold blue among the stars.

3

On April third, the first cold front of the season came across the Rockies, pulling up plenty of moisture from the Gulf. A dryline formed out beyond Childress, then nothing happened for three days. The front couldn't push through.

Channel Two had a new weatherman. The old one had been fired after Mayor Babbs wrote a letter to the paper complaining he was "too negative." "I don't think we'll have any storms," the new weatherman said. "Just a good, long rain." The front finally pushed through at seven o'clock in the evening. There were no storms, but no rain either. The wind shifted around, the temperature fell, and the next day the sky was pink with blowing dust.

In another week there was another front. Burl took a day off, but the same thing happened. Some cumulus clouds built up, white popcorn puffs out beyond the Medicine Mounds. Then they evaporated, and Burl heard the dispatcher tell the Spotters, *Everybody come on home, it looks like we've dried out again.*

Burl sat at the kitchen table, staring at his college applications. He thought he would feel better when he stopped smoking pot, but somehow he couldn't seem to concentrate on anything. He had no energy, but sometimes stayed up half the night, drinking beer and watching television, before he fell asleep.

He put down the pen and listened to Bebe playing with Pearl in the front room. Even if he did get in, the only interesting course he could take his first year was Introduction to Meteorology. There were all those math requirements. Then the idea of taking Bebe and the kids along with him seemed impossible, but so did the idea of leaving them. He loved those kids as if they were his own.

Pearl was growing up. Bebe had cut her hair so it fit her head like a bowl. She could talk a lot now, and sometimes she called him "Daddy." When she smiled, her face lit up like a little candle. When she was at the daycare center, he sometimes walked through the apartment, picking up her toys and smiling—the monkey doll that sucked its thumb, the rubber mermaid with red Dynel hair.

Jason was turning into a normal kid. His passions were skateboarding, cars, and jet airplanes. Sometimes they went to the library to read *Aviation Week*, or out to the old Magnolia Refinery, where they sat atop the storage tank and watched the jets shoot landings at the air force base. They saw Thunderbolts, Eagles, Fighting Falcons. The week before, when American planes had bombed Libya, Jason had told Burl, "When I grow up, I'm going to be a fighter jock."

"I thought you were going to be a veterinarian," Burl said. "And take care of animals."

"That's kid stuff," Jason said. "I'm going to fly a Tomcat and shoot down MiG-29's."

For a moment Burl missed the old, secretive Jason who had talked to the neighborhood cats. But the bombing had excited him too: he loved airplanes, and America had the greatest airplanes in the world.

Bebe was changing, but in some way he could not understand. He no longer knew what she was thinking. At times, he sensed a sadness in her. On some nights, she studied. On others, she just got stoned, smoking out in the garage so Burl wouldn't get contaminated. The railroad had a zero-tolerance policy and didn't recognize passive inhalation. Then she wanted to make love. Burl insisted on wearing a condom, which she hated. So did he, but they couldn't afford to take chances.

Burl had been staring at the applications for an hour, and the bright yellow Formica tabletop had begun to hurt his eyes. The pen had gotten too heavy to hold. He let it drop from his fingers and went into the front room, where Jason was working on a plastic model of a Blackbird spyplane, which could fly higher and faster than any aircraft in the world. "Let me give you a hand," he said.

They worked for another hour, until he heard a motorcycle pull up outside, and a moment later someone knocked on the screen door.

It was Chaney.

"I'd like a word with you," he said to Burl.

Bebe was staring at Chaney with a look of disbelief. Jason didn't even look up, just kept working on the model. "All right," Burl said.

They stepped out into the front yard. The night smelled of new grass, and the lightning bugs were out.

"I'm in Nortex now," Chaney said. "Got a job out at the fiberglass plant. Thought I'd put some money away. I just wanted to get things clear between you and me. I got nothing against you.

If this is what she wants, that's fine." Chaney nodded toward the lighted house, his thumbs in his belt. The buckle was a chrome skull. "She says you're good with the kids, and that's the important thing. I'm going to leave you alone. I would like to see my kids now and then, but that's up to you. Oh, and I want you to know I've stopped taking drugs," Chaney said. "I'm seeing a doctor, this Chinese guy who does acupuncture. He's really helped me out." He offered his hand. "I'd like for us to be friends."

Chaney gave him the biker's clenched-fist handshake. His palm was warm, slightly moist.

"I'm glad we got that straight," Chaney said. "Feels good, doesn't it?"

Burl couldn't look at him. "When did Bebe tell you I was good with the kids?"

"Couple of days ago. I've known she was here for a long time. She called my sister, up in Lawton." He put a hand on Burl's shoulder. "We should get together sometime. Have a beer and get to know each other. If you want to get hold of me, just call the Rodeo Clown Saloon."

He gave Burl another handshake, got on his bike, and drove off. When Burl went back inside, he noticed his hands were trembling slightly. Bebe was getting a beer out of the icebox. "Did you know he was here?" he asked her.

"Shit, no," she said. "I thought he was up in Oklahoma, living in a tepee."

She was lying.

For the rest of the evening, he and Jason concentrated on the model of the Blackbird. It was the hardest airplane in the world to fly. There was no air up there, and if the pilot lost control, it went spinning end for end across the top of the atmosphere like a paper clip. Inertia coupling, it was called.

Bebe went to the garage and got stoned. At nine, they put the kids to sleep, then got in bed themselves. By unspoken consent they said nothing of Chaney, but Burl found he wanted her more than he had for weeks, and they made love. After a while, she said, "You go ahead."

"What about you?"

"I can't come when you're wearing that."

It was too hot to sleep. Burl stared into the darkness, wondering how his life had gotten to this joyless place. No pot, and no sex without a condom. But they couldn't afford to make a mistake.

"You didn't study tonight," he said.

"Don't start on me," she said. "You're just pissed off because you didn't finish your applications."

"If you don't get your GED, it'll all be for nothing."

"Oh, shit," she said. "I don't even know if I want to be a legal secretary. What for, so I can be like those other girls in my class? I hate those girls, all they ever talk about is getting a husband."

"What do you want, then?"

She was still for a long time.

"Sometimes," she said, "I want another baby."

"That's real smart," he said, "when you've got two kids now, and neither one of them knows who their father is."

"You son of a bitch," she said.

She pretended to sleep. Burl stared at the ceiling. If only the storm season would start, he thought.

On the second anniversary of the Big Tornado, John came over and they watched a special on Channel Two called *Day of Darkness, Day of Light*.

Burl was looking forward to the tornado footage, but they only showed a few seconds of the storm itself. There were several interviews with survivors. Burl was wondering why they had been chosen, when John pointed out that everyone had mentioned God or miracles.

"At first I didn't know why God let this happen," a young man standing in front of his house said, "but our new home is a lot nicer than our old one." An old woman in a rocker said, "I was on my way to Bible class when the sirens blew, so I went into Roy Rogers, where we had prayer and asked the Lord to look over us." "We credit three things with saving our lives," a woman wearing a tank top said. "The grace of God, TV warnings, and CB radio."

The balance of the program was about recovery. There was a long montage of carpenters hammering new homes together, with hymns playing in the background. "Two years later," the announcer said, "every church has been rebuilt." Not a word was said about the price of oil, the drug problem, or the rise of Satanic cults.

The program concluded with an interview with Mayor Babbs. In his first year in office, the mayor had dedicated himself to restoring the city's image. The worst part of that image was the weather. "It's time people got over the idea Nortex has a lot of tornadoes," Babbs said. "I think this idea was spread by a local weatherman. Fortunately, he's no longer with us. This town has one of the best climates in the world. We're developing a new pride in Nortex, working hard to make it the greatest town in Texas, and anyone who isn't for that can just move along. The tornado was our day of darkness," he added solemnly, "but we're entering a new day, a day of light."

"That was great," John said. "Makes me feel real good about living here, but I guess I'll just move along."

Another front came through, a dryline formed. The Spotters were put on alert. Burl took a day off and listened to the scanner.

What's going on? one of the Spotters asked.

Nothing, the dispatcher said. *The dryline's still out beyond Childress, but it's not moving. In fact, it's backing up.*

Think we'll get anything later on?

Negative. Fort Worth says there's a capping inversion forming on top of the moisture. Says there's no upper-level support, so nothing's going to happen.

Funny weather, the Spotter said.

It was funny weather. The atmosphere over the entire central United States was a stagnant pool. Articles appeared in the paper about what a dry spring it was. By the end of April, one blindingly hot day was like the next, and the temperature was hitting ninety.

Burl's hunger for storms drove him into the past into his memory. He could still see the towering golden thunderhead he had watched one evening from the front porch when he had been in the second grade.

Then he thought of the old newspapers on microfilm at the public library. The next time he took Jason down there to read *Aviation Week,* he checked out four spools, one for every year there had been a tornado in or near Nortex. The old weather maps were simpler than he remembered, but they showed the moisture flow. He scrolled them across the screen, following the progress of old seasons. At the end of two hours he sat up, feeling he had made a discovery.

Moisture was everything.

There were very moist years, and then there were very dry years, like this one. Three of the four tornadoes that had struck Nortex had come in moist years. "Let's hope we have plenty of rain and no tornadoes," the new weatherman said. But you couldn't have one without the other—they were part of the same thing. And there was something else about the moist years: you could remember everything about them. As Burl scrolled the weather maps across the screen, he started noticing the movie listings on the opposite page.

He realized he could remember not only every movie, but how it had *felt* to see them, to be himself and alive in that year. He found the spool for the year he had been in the second grade and seen the golden thunderhead from the front porch, and inserted it.

There were some periods in your life when you were more aware, more alive, and that year had been one of them: a moist year, when thunder woke him every morning and the classroom lights burned all day long. They had played new games, tramped up and down the alley in galoshes, played Exploring the Planet Venus, a world where it rained forever. That was the year he had discovered he could read, found his eyes sliding effortlessly down the pages of the *National Geographic*, while thunder rumbled through the screen door.

It was in the moist years that he had fallen in love, when Kiowa Creek flowed with water the color of beet juice and green vines coiled around the telephone poles. Something drew you to women in those years when the air smelled of growing things and the moonlight was the color of honey. He had first made love to Bebe on a rainy night.

Jason wanted a book on airplanes. Burl checked it out for him. When they walked outside, the air smelled like the air next to a light bulb, and the handle of the car door scalded his hand. The grass was already dead.

John told everyone his days with the railroad were numbered, but he was having a hard time making choices. Buying a vehicle, for instance. Jeeps were dependable, but used a lot of gas. Toyota Land Cruisers were the top of the line, but parts might be hard to get after the collapse. Then, when he wrote American Lincoln Log Homes, he found the company had folded and he would have to build his cabin himself. Every time Burl went over to John's, he found him sitting in front of the television, the floor covered with books on weapons, gardening, and carpentry.

"You're getting hung up on technicalities," Burl told him.

"I know," John said. "But I've got to know everything before I can make up my mind."

He lit a joint and opened a catalog of gravity-flow toilets and septic tanks. Another endless subject.

At the end of April, there were more special bulletins. The Soviet reactor at Chernobyl had exploded. Satellite photos showed the roof had blown off and a cloud of radioactive vapor was spreading.

John called him. "All right," he said. "What's going on?"

"You'd better get over here."

They watched for three hours. There had been a meltdown, and the core was exposed. Helicopters were dumping sand and boron, trying to smother it. John stared at the screen, his chin in his hand. Bebe smoked endless cigarettes. The Soviets were asking experts from France and Germany for help.

"They're in big trouble," Burl said.

He felt a strange excitement. Something had happened, even if it was a catastrophe. He had been waiting for this for years, ever since he'd done a science project on nuclear reactors.

"We got a day off tomorrow," John said. "Why don't we all drive up to the Wichita Mountains? We can get a Mears burger. They're the best in Oklahoma. And the kids might get a kick out of the buffalo."

Burl said it sounded good. They watched for another three hours. Contamination had been detected in other countries. A map showed the hot cloud curving down like a question mark over Finland, Poland, Rumania.

When John and Charlotte showed up the next morning, which was a Sunday, Akeem was not with them. Charlotte told Bebe, "His father's in town."

They all piled in the Mustang. Bebe held Pearl on her lap. Jason sat in back, with John and Charlotte. It was the first week of May, and it hadn't rained for thirty days. When they crossed the stateline bridge, Burl saw that the Red River was nearly dry.

They stopped at the Fort Sill Museum, so Jason could see Geronimo's grave. For a long time, John stared into a glass case containing Quanah Parker's peyote pouch. Then they drove to the park. The mountains were some of the oldest rock on earth—great heaps of yellow stones, like countless granite cannonballs. Buffalo cropped the roadside grass, their shaggy winter coats full of holes, like worn-out carpet. At the little town of Mears, they stopped and got hamburgers and cold beer to go. Bebe wanted to see the place where they'd seen the funnel and lightning had splintered the tree a hundred yards away. Nothing looked the same in broad daylight, but they finally found it.

They sat on the grass, eating their hamburgers, listening to the guns thumping at Fort Sill. John and Charlotte had little to say to each other. After a while John went off in the woods to smoke a joint.

Burl and Bebe walked up the road, looking for the tree. "I don't think they're getting along," Burl said.

"They're not," she said. "Charlotte told me he was getting too serious for her."

They found the tree, blackened and split. Bebe touched his face. "I think of this as the place where we fell in love."

He remembered how the base of the storm had pressed right down on their heads, how dark it had been. Now everything was exposed. There were no secrets.

"Let's go to the Holy City," John said when they came back. "I want to show Charlotte the scenes of my youth, when I was in the Easter pageant there."

They drove along, until they came to the empty parking lot and the buildings on a hill. Beyond the ramparts of Jerusalem, the naked granite domes rose up, reflecting heat down on them like mirrors. A sign said THE HOLY CITY IS OPEN 365 DAYS YEAR FOR WEDDING AND GROUP WORSHIP. YOU ARE WELCOMED TO "OKLAHOMA'S OBERAMMERGAU." Jason ran off into the rocks to explore. They followed John, who showed them Bethlehem, and the stable where the pageant began at sunrise. John had played a shepherd boy who brought a gift to the Baby Jesus. His father had played John the Baptist. "He was a great actor," John said. "And he just about stole the show. Then they found him with one of the Angels of the Lord, over there behind the gateway to Jerusalem."

They stood atop Golgotha, staring up at the three crosses. Then John led them back downhill to the Holy City Chapel, which, like everything else, was made of round yellow stones. John held the door open and they walked in. The interior smelled of heat, dust, and hymnals. A dead gold wasp lay on a windowsill. Christ smiled down from the dome ceiling, floating in a sky of robin's egg blue. "It's always been my idea of the ideal church," John said.

"Now what?" Charlotte said.

"Well," John said, "I thought I might be able to talk you into marrying me."

She laughed. "There's no preacher, fool."

"I'm an ordained minister of the Universal Life Church," John said. "I've got my license right here in my billfold. Burl and Bebe can be our witnesses."

Burl realized John was serious. His eyes were light, but there was a catch in his throat and his hands trembled. He thought if he took Charlotte by surprise, in this unexpected place, she might say yes.

"I told you, John, I'm not ready to get married."

"You think I'm too old."

"It's not that, but I can't take Akeem out of school and go live off in the middle of nowhere."

"Why not, when it's a far, far better life than he'll have here?"

"I worked hard to get that job. I'm not going to throw it away. Don't do this to me, John," she said sadly. "You know how I feel."

"But we love each other, don't we?" John said. "That's the important thing."

The floor cracked loudly in the silence. Pearl looked up at Bebe and whispered, "Momma, let's go."

They went back outside, Burl called to Jason, and the women started walking toward the car. John picked up a pebble and stared at the sky.

"My father died alone," he said.

"You never told me," Burl said.

"When he was sixty, he went blind. He ran off and left my

mother for a hippie girl. They lived in a trailer in the Ozarks and she read him the Bible. Then she left him, too, of course. Neighbor wrote and said there'd been no pain, but he died alone."

"I'm sorry."

John looked at the pebble. "Old stone," he said, tossing it away. "Old shit. Thing is, I don't want to die like my father. It never bothered me all those years I was thinking about having a log cabin. I thought I could be alone but never lonely, like Kit Carson living in the Shining Mountains. But now that I love Charlotte, I don't want to live alone any longer. And I don't want to die alone, and I don't know if I can leave or not."

Burl ranged far and wide, looking for storms. He met the dryline in Cottle, Foard, and Hardeman counties. Once, beyond Childress, he saw a little yellow Toyota by the side of the road and pulled over.

It seemed only natural that he and Webster would meet in the middle of this huge prairie, since they were both drawn by the same thing, the point of greatest probability. They watched a cell that looked promising, until it began evaporating before their very eyes. Webster's hair was turning gray, but they took up their last conversation as if it had taken place a few minutes ago. As before, he gave Burl the big picture, showed him things on a larger scale.

"This is already the driest year in decades," Webster said. "The jet stream is far to the north, as if it were already summer. All this has to do with solar radiation. The Pacific is very cold this year, and this pushes the jet stream up into Canada. Examination of the growth rings of bristlecone pines—the oldest trees on earth—shows this happens periodically. But is this year unusual, or is it the start of a trend? Perhaps this is the beginning of a dry cycle, or global warming. The polar caps may melt, producing a flood. On the other hand, this may be the beginning of another Ice Age. No one knows for sure."

"Whatever," Burl said. "I just wish there would be more storms."

"So do I," Webster said. "I drove eight hundred miles to see this front."

Burl mentioned he wanted to go to Texas Tech but had never sent in his applications.

"Well," Webster said, "if you would like, I'll write you a letter of recommendation. Mind you, I'm not sure it's the way to go for a serious student of the atmosphere, but my name might mean something."

Burl gave him his name, not at all sure Webster would do anything about it.

They watched the moon rise. The air smelled of dust, and to the west he could see the red cliffs of the Caprock. He was hundreds of miles from home, and in eight hours he had to be back at work.

"There are no firm answers," Webster said. "Only indications." Time moved slowly, but at some point it speeded up. Ice had covered the northern reaches of these plains for thousands of years, and mammoths had roamed almost where they stood. Now they were gone. "You have to ask yourself," Webster said, "are the changes always gradual, or do they sometimes happen overnight? Is this the end of one climatic era, and will another come in our lifetime? Against all odds," Webster said, "I think it will."

Burl made a tremendous effort and finished his applications, dropped them in the mail on his way to work. He went to Amarillo three times in one week and made almost a thousand dollars. When he got home, he drank six beers and fell asleep. He woke with Bebe pulling the covers off him, telling him he was on call, and found himself jumping up naked, shouting, "Leave me the fuck alone."

He raised his hand to hit her: then turned and put it through the closet door. There was a satisfying moment as he saw the hollow-core plywood door shatter in slow motion, like a karate demonstration, then pain shot up his arm.

"Shit," he said, staring at his bleeding knuckles. "What did I do that for?"

He sat on the toilet while she put iodine on his knuckles. He had never done anything like this before, not with any other woman he had ever known.

"I'm sorry," he said.

"Oh, honey," Bebe said. "What's happening to us?"

"Well, I'm working all the time," he said, "and it's hard for me to get enough sleep. It seems like every time I get home, the kids are getting up and you're going to school. And I wish you'd stop getting stoned around me. I want to get stoned, too, but I can't, and when you're stoned, you're just not . . . *there* for me somehow." He looked at her. "We've got to try harder."

"We will," she said, touching his face. "I promise."

The forgiveness was sweet—almost sweet enough to make it worth the crime.

He drove to work, past a billboard that showed a screaming husband and said IF YOU HAVE A PROBLEM THAT'S OUT OF YOUR CONTROL, CALL THIS TOLL-FREE NUMBER RIGHT NOW FOR THE WIFE ABUSE HOTLINE, SPONSORED BY THE CHURCH OF JESUS CHRIST OF THE LATTER-DAY SAINTS.

4

The neighbor woman stopped him when he came back from Amarillo one Saturday. "I don't know who your friend is," she said, "but would you ask him not to park in our driveway?" Burl said he wasn't sure who she meant. "The guy with the big hog. He was here all morning. I had to go to the store, but I was afraid to ask him to move it."

Burl told her he'd take care of it and went into the house. "Was Chaney here?" he said.

"No," Bebe said. But she wouldn't look at him.

"Goddamnit," he said, pulling her around so she had to look at him. "Tell me the truth."

"Just for a while," she said. "He wanted to see Jason."

Burl went outside and found Jason playing by the water tower. He asked him what Chaney had wanted. Jason slitted his eyes. "He wants me to live with him again. He says he knows a place up in Oklahoma where we could really have fun. It's out in the country."

"Do you want to do that?"

"He said he'd give me a rifle."

Burl went back in the house. Bebe was sitting at the kitchen table, smoking a cigarette.

"Where do things stand with you and Chaney?"

"He says he still loves me," she said. "I told him I didn't love him anymore. I love you, baby. But you should go to college, and I should get out of here. I should go on down to Houston."

"I'm not going to let him push us apart," Burl said.

"That sounds good," she said. "But everything sounds good to me." She put out the cigarette and covered her face with her hands. "Oh me," she said. "There's gonna be trouble."

He lay down for a while, but he was too angry to sleep. When it got dark, he drove to the Rodeo Clown. The guy at the door gave him a once-over with a metal detector. Inside, it was so dark that for a while all he could see were the glowing screens of video poker games. Then the chaser lights came on, and he saw Chaney sitting alone at a table, just as a girl who called herself the Mysterious Nicole started doing a strip to a Rod Stewart song.

"We've got to talk," Burl said, sitting down next to him.

"Hey, brother," Chaney said, his face breaking into a smile. "Good to see you."

"Stay away from Bebe and the kids," Burl said. "If you don't, I'll call the cops on you."

Chaney gave him a look of injured dignity. "Now that could be a bad idea for everybody," he said, leaning back and sticking his thumbs into his belt. "The cops might not like the way you're living over there. They might take those kids away from her."

"Just stay away from Bebe," Burl said, trying to hold his ground. "I know you're trying to get her back."

"You're wrong, man," Chaney said seriously. "I've got another girl now. Why should I want to do something like that?" He indicated the Mysterious Nicole. She looked Burl in the eye, licked her fingers, and touched her nipples so they stood up.

Chaney laughed and slapped Burl's leg. "Cool out, for shit's sake," he said. He signaled the waitress, who brought them two beers. "You know," he said, "you've got the wrong idea about me. Maybe it's because I belong to a motorcycle club. You should meet some of the Renegades. We're going on a run next month, out to the Quitaque. There's this guy who lets us use his ranch. Why don't you and Bebe drive out?"

Burl let him run on, watching the next girl perform, a brassy blonde with big breasts. Who were the girls who worked here, he wondered, and where did they come from?

Someone came up behind them and said, "Chaney, you got anything for me?"

"Talk to me later," Chaney said impatiently.

"Leroy?" Burl said.

Leroy stared at Burl a long time before recognition lit in his eyes.

"How you doing?" he said. "You know Chaney?"

Burl nodded. "Where's Tina?"

"Tina?" Leroy pointed to the stage. "She's right up there."

So those were Tina's breasts.

Chaney was delighted that they knew each other. "Ask Leroy what he thinks about the Renegades," he said. "He's a prospect. He's built himself a bike, and he's coming to the Quitaque."

Tina got off at midnight. They all went across the highway to the Sands. Burl told her she was looking good, and she told him she'd lost her baby, right after he'd moved away. Burl said he was sorry to hear it. Then Leroy showed Burl his bike, an old flathead with a sidecar for Tina. "Being into bikes is the ultimate adventure," he told Burl. "I think I've finally found my true calling."

People gave you room when they knew you were a biker. Leroy no longer took any shit from aliens. He showed Burl his tattoo, a skull with a rose growing out of its mouth, the old Grateful Dead logo.

Then Tina got out a green glass pipe and bought fifty dollars worth of crack from Chaney. She asked Burl if he wanted a hit, but he said no, thanks. He followed Chaney outside, and they sat by the pool.

"His wife's got the hots for you, doesn't she?" Chaney said. "I can tell."

Burl said nothing.

"If you want trouble," Chaney said softly, "I can give you trouble. But I don't think you do." A Buck knife appeared in Chaney's hand. Burl felt his chest tighten.

Chaney smiled at him, taking a Baggie out of his jacket pocket. "You're right not to smoke that shit," he said. "But I like to do a little crystal meth every so often. If you're careful, it can put you in just the right place. Want some?"

"No, thanks," Burl said. He was trying to figure out how to get the subject back to Bebe.

Chaney snorted meth off the blade of his Buck knife. "Leroy's right about one thing," he said. "Being a biker is the way to go."

"Not for me," Burl said. "No future in it."

"There's worse things. Like taking shit for the rest of your life."

"I guess I'll take the shit."

Chaney stared at the yellow moon, thin as a steel shaving. "Things look different," he said, "when you know you're not going to live forever."

"Bebe thinks you're in pretty good health," Burl said. "She says you made all that up about being contaminated."

"Bebe's a wonderful woman," Chaney said reflectively. "But I think all that was a little over her head. You know, I'm not an asshole. I've got above-average intelligence. They tested me when I was a kid, and my scores were right off the scale. When I was

fourteen, I'd already read everything. The Bible. *Mein Kampf.*
Atlas Shrugged. Stranger in a Strange Land. You ever read that
one?"

Burl shook his head.

"It's a great book," Chaney said. "You're intelligent too. I can
tell. But you're like me. You'd rather do things than think about
them."

"Tell me about Pantex," Burl said.

Chaney laughed. "I used to get high when I walked through
those blast-proof doors. It's strange, but I always felt safe there. I
always liked weapons. That's why I took the job. And there I was,
with the most powerful weapons in the world."

Chaney did more meth and talked about plutonium.

"Talk about your controlled substances," he said. "It's the
rarest, the most expensive, the most toxic element in the world.
And they had tons of it in there. Department of Energy pure. I
held a chunk of it in my hand once. It was warm to the touch."

Like all great drugs, it was a deadly poison. A grain no bigger
than a red blood cell settled in your bones, and you developed
acute leukemia. The whole place was hot, and any number of
workers had died. "But they kept right on making the shit,"
Chaney told him, "and it keeps right on getting loose. Nobody's
thought ahead, that's what I'm saying. Our kids are the ones who
are going to have to deal with it."

Listening, Burl felt sure that much of what Chaney was saying
was true. He might even be contaminated. It almost made him feel
sorry for Chaney. But he still didn't trust him.

"We should take Jason shooting sometime," Chaney said.
"I've got some really valuable weapons in a storage vault up in
Lawton, including a replica of a Sharps' buffalo gun. They're his
when I'm gone."

"You've probably got a few years left in you," Burl said.

"I'd rather think it could happen at any time. It doesn't pay to
be too careful."

"I'm a chickenshit myself," Burl said.

Chaney laughed.

"Oh, I know you," he said.

He stared at Burl, his eyes so dilated, they looked like black holes, all pupil.

"You're not like Leroy," he said affectionately. "Leroy's an all right dude, but there's a warrior in you."

"I've always thought so," Burl said, interested in spite of himself.

"I've seen guys like you before. Go along pretending they're anybody. Then one day they wake up and admit there's a hell of a lot more they want, and they're ready to break a few rules to get it. Someday," he said, "you're gonna stop being the everyday asshole people want you to be. I want to be there when it happens."

He smiled at Burl, nodding slowly. Burl found himself smiling and nodding back.

Leroy opened the door of their room. "Time to go to work," he said.

Chaney got up, gave Burl the biker's handshake. Then he and Leroy got on their bikes and drove off to the fiberglass plant. Burl went back inside to say good night to Tina. He told her he'd really enjoyed her performance. "Sure you don't want a hit before you go?" she said, loading the little glass pipe.

"I don't think so," he said.

She wore jeans, a denim shirt, unbuttoned halfway down, and smelled of baby powder. He kept thinking about the way she'd looked onstage, up in the lights.

"You got to try it. It's a real experience."

There had been an article in *Time* last week: "Crack, the New Scourge of America's Cities."

"Why the hell not?"

She took out a little propane torch. "Sit on the bed," she said. "Take deep breaths. Be sure to get it all."

The last thing he saw was the green flame in the glass tube. He inhaled a lungful of hot, sweet chemicals. Then the back of his head flew off, like Kennedy's, and he was gasping for air. His brain was full of molten metal, his thoughts had turned to light, he was coming in his pants. He fell back on the bed, hearing himself laughing because it was so good, so much better than anything he'd ever had, that it was a joke. For a moment he thought it would take him so far out, his heart would burst, then it began to fade. He stared at the ceiling. This was what it was like to be strapped in an electric chair and feel the voltage going through you.

Tina was smiling at him. "I love to watch people take their first hit," she said.

His head was empty. A few hot molecules bounced around, ricocheting off the inside of his skull.

"You want to do something now?" she said.

There was a look on her face that told him she meant: Did he want to do something to her? But he couldn't move, he was totally blown away.

"Let me feel your titties," he heard himself say.

She smiled and unbuttoned her shirt the rest of the way. Her nipples felt like rubber. She was so thin, he could see every one of her ribs.

He drove home and lay on the couch, so he wouldn't have to talk to Bebe. It was a betrayal, and he knew it. Somehow Chaney had tricked him into it. But after the rush, nothing was real. He stared into the darkness, his mind empty, thinking of the caves burned out of the earth by underground nuclear explosions. He'd seen pictures taken by remote cameras. Smooth, glassy bubbles of stone.

5

Burl had been worried about John when Charlotte turned him down, but he bounced right back. When Burl went over to see him, John said, "Don't worry about me, I'll be fine. I'm gonna get myself a Japanese or a Filipino mail-order bride. They advertise in the back pages of *Soldier of Fortune.*"

He was watching another special on Chernobyl, the family Bible open on his lap, the magnifying glass lying on the page. "Think you see a sign?" Burl asked him.

"Yeah, I do," John said. "There could be millions of acres of farmland contaminated by this thing. What if their wheat crop's gone for the next fifty years? The traditional Russian terror is famine. What if we won't sell 'em any, or our own wheat crop fails?" Burl was inclined to agree. The American wheat crop was in danger right now: this was the driest spring in fifty years, and it might only be the beginning. "Gorbachev seems like a good guy," John said, "but if there's trouble, he might get replaced by a real hard-liner." It was odd, too, John said, that birthmark on his forehead. It made you think of the Mark of the Beast. And didn't *Chernobyl,* in Russian, mean something like "Wormwood," the star of death in the Book of Revelation?

"If you can see the signs," Burl told him, "I'd say it's time you headed for the Guadalupe Mountains."

John agreed. But there were still a lot of choices to be made. He didn't know how much he'd have to pay for acreage. He didn't even know if land was available—a lot of the country out there was a national park. As he talked on, Burl realized John really knew nothing about the Guadalupe Mountains. They were just a name on a map. When he left, John was lighting another joint and staring through the magnifying glass at the bubble of thick block print floating up in the lens.

Burl got in the Mustang and drove down south of Mankins, along a dirt road, until he came to a place he had found when he was looking for storms—an acre of silver tubes, surrounded by a cyclone fence. It looked like a little refinery, but a plate on the fence said US NAVY SATELLITE TRACKING STATION—ENTRANCE RESTRICTED. Burl knew anything having to do with the navy and satellites also had to do with submarine communication, one of the hottest defense secrets there was. The Soviets undoubtedly had a missile targeted on it.

He got out of his car and stared off to the west, into the blinding sun. A dryline had formed near Childress, and the dispatcher had put everyone on standby, but nothing would happen. The jet stream was over North Dakota. All the factors were present, but there was nothing to turn them loose.

He turned on the scanner and listened to the Spotters.

Think we'll get some rain?

Don't think so. The dryline's just not moving.

Man, oh man. I sure thought we were gonna see some action today.

He could hear the longing in the voices of the Spotters. They were just like him. They loved storms, too—they just didn't know it.

There's nothing showing on the radar. You might as well come home.

Burl looked the other way, at the tracking station, wondering what it would be like to be standing here when a missile hit. Perhaps he would see it coming, a sudden shooting star, before the warhead detonated, heating the air to the temperature of the sun, fusing the red clay to glass.

He had always known it could happen: that was the Big Secret. When he was a boy, he had feared it. Now he longed for it. Because then the waiting would be over—and because knowing it could happen somehow made it harder instead of easier to change your life. Why even try, when it could happen anytime? It was easier to wait for the flash, to live for the moment.

He stared off into the glare for another hour until bright dots swarmed before his eyes. Sometimes he thought he saw the transparent domes of cumulonimbus, but he knew they weren't really there.

The wheat harvest had begun, the busiest time of the year, and Burl went to Amarillo several times a week. He stopped thinking ahead. Although they could work at any time, he seemed to spend more nights than days on the train. Sometimes he slept, but he never completely lost his awareness of the steel walls or the light bulb glaring overhead. It seemed he could see it even in his sleep. It was better up in the cupola, where he felt as if he were flying through space, while the green block signals shot by like meteors and the stars wheeled overhead. When John slept at his desk, Burl was all alone.

How many nights had he spent like this? He could remember the first time—on New Year's Eve, when he was in the second grade. The new year had come in, wearing a diaper, and the old one had gone out, carrying an hourglass and headed someplace Burl could not imagine. The hands of the clock had stood straight up, and he had stared at them, full of the light-headed, hollow sensation of being up after midnight, in adult time.

Now he had done it almost a thousand nights. You learned something from it—after you fought off sleep, there was an excitement to it, almost like fever—but you lost something by it too. One night, they had stopped out here and found the caboose surrounded by the yellow eyes of what seemed like hundreds of coyotes. For a moment he had felt closer to them than people, as if he were a nocturnal creature himself, something more than human and something less.

At first it was a presence, filling the air like dust. Then it was a hot glow. Burl leaned forward, peering through the dirty windows. The sun broke and ran, spilling across the horizon like a blob of mercury. Against it he saw the black smokestack of the power plant, towering at the end of the world.

Nobody thought Haney would come back, but he did, after spending a month in the Rehab program at Faith City Hospital—his drug test had come up positive for amphetamines. He'd lost his job in road freight and went to work in the yard, throwing switches and pulling coupler pins. Some of the men didn't try to hide their contempt. If Haney came into the bathroom, they'd button up and walk out. Burl felt pity for Haney.

In May, the kid who had replaced Haney quit, and Royce talked Hardesty into giving Haney back his turn on the Amarillo freight. He showed up ten minutes before they had to roll, and he looked as if he'd been drinking.

"Hello, Haney," Burl said. "Good to have you back."

Haney gave him such a strange look, it was Burl who finally looked away.

John had taken off a turn, and Burl was the conductor. They got to Amarillo after dark. The motel was full of harvesters, trying to get the wheat in before it burned up. Most of them were high school kids, away from home for the first time. They wore caps with Nebraska feedlot logos and drove fancy pickups with roll bars and halogen floods. "Oh, shit," Royce said. "Now we won't be able to get any sleep."

Royce took a shower. Haney sat down on the bed and turned on the television.

"I guess you heard that bullshit about me committing sodomy," Haney said.

"Yeah," Burl said. "I heard about it."

"I'm innocent," Haney said. "But you probably don't believe me, either. Royce won't even look me in the eye."

"Royce is still your friend," Burl said, unpacking his bag.

"No, he ain't," Haney said. He sat silently for a while. "My life has been destroyed. I thought it had been destroyed before, but this really put the nail in my coffin. Think I don't know everybody's laughing at me?"

"Why'd you come back?" Burl asked him.

"What am I supposed to do? Think it's easy to get another job when you've been busted for drugs and sodomy? The railroad's all I got left. They find out you failed a drug test, and you can't even get a job cleaning toilets. And I got to pay my child support, or I'll go to jail."

"I guess you're right."

"The thing is, it was all that kid's idea. I spotted him for a homo the day he came to work. You could see it in his eyes. Ever notice how when you look a homo in the eye, something deep down inside you goes off and you just know? They can't hide it."

Burl turned on The Weather Channel. There was a front moving down, and some echoes way out to the west. They would never work their way here, though.

"Now they're gonna try to cure me. That goddamned nigger," Haney said, meaning the railroad drug counselor, a black ex-cop. "He said he was going to get me drug free, alcohol free, nicotine free. Said I'd be happy for the first time in my life. That cocksucker. My life is over. When people look at me now, they don't think, There goes the guy with the biggest dick in town. They think, There goes the homo."

Burl felt profoundly sorry for Haney. He could see this had driven him into a terrible place. But they'd been on the road all day, and he was too tired to think.

"Give it a rest, Haney," he said.

He fell asleep. When he opened his eyes, Haney was watching television, drinking a six-pack, and gritting his teeth.

"Wake up, asshole," he said.

Haney was watching a gay porno movie. A college teacher told a student he had to stay after class. The minute they were alone, they started rubbing up against each other.

"It can happen to anyone," Haney said.

"What's that?"

"You get exposed to it when you're a kid, and you don't know any better. Say some older boy tells you he's discovered something called cornholing, where you don't need girls. You might say no, thanks, I think I'll just play with my toy soldiers. Or you might give it a try."

"I can see that," Burl said. He stepped to the door. The harvesters were still partying. To the west he could see lightning, a little convective thunderstorm way out in New Mexico. He thought about walking across the highway for a Big Red, but he was too tired.

"Or your wife turns out to be a lesbian," Haney said. "And some other lesbian puts a hex on you so you're impotent. You might be tempted to try it."

"You gay?" the teacher asked his student. "Sure," the student said, unbuttoning his pants.

"See," Haney said. "You can't escape the influences. They're everywhere. They come at you through television. This is one of the manifestations of Satanism, and people don't even realize it: satellite television."

Burl finally fell asleep with Haney talking to him, fell so deeply asleep, he never heard the commotion. The satellite fell below the horizon, and when Haney couldn't get his porno movie, he went to the manager's office and pounded on the door, yelling for him to tip the dish. When he didn't answer, Haney tried to tip it himself, and everyone's television went off. The harvesters came pouring out of their rooms. It wasn't clear what happened next, but there was an argument, and Haney broke the window of a pickup. Royce didn't get there until after the fight had started, and there wasn't a thing he could do. By the time the cops showed up, the harvesters had beaten Haney to a pulp, just destroyed him.

Burl got back to Nortex at eleven. When he left the yard, he stopped at a Seven-Eleven, bought a six-pack of beer, and drank one sitting in the parking lot. Even when he drank another one, he didn't feel sleepy. He decided to go out to the Magnolia Refinery.

On the way, he stopped at a package store and bought a bottle of tequila. He drank most of it sitting on top of the storage tank, chasing it with shots of beer. I've got to take a trip off, he thought. Maybe see a storm, get some sleep.

Instead of putting him to sleep, the tequila seemed to wake him up. He couldn't stop seeing Haney. Sometimes he also saw himself—a grown man sitting on top of a storage tank, looking for airplanes and getting drunk in the broiling sun.

There was no energy on the air, but he felt an anger building. He thought of the friction between cloud and ground, the potential building until it discharged in a bolt of lightning. He was in friction with the whole world: everything hurt.

When he came through the door, Bebe had just gotten out of the tub. She stood in the middle of the living room, wearing her old bathrobe and giving him an almost frightened look.

"What are you doing home?" he said.

"You got some mail," she said, picking up an envelope off the kitchen table.

It was from Texas Tech. He tore it open, read the mimeographed letter.

"What does it say?"

"I got in."

"Oh, honey, that's great."

But her face closed up, and a silence came in.

"Yeah, it's great," he said, letting it drop to the floor.

He would never go. He'd known for weeks now. He no longer had the strength. All those nights on the train had stolen it from him.

She put her arms around him, smelling of soap. Her mouth had that grassy taste it had when she was ripe. He couldn't fuck her without using a rubber, and that made him angrier.

"I'm so happy for you," she said into his ear.

He pushed her away.

"Why aren't you at school?"

Her face closed up again. "Oh, shit," she said tiredly. "I don't know."

Her eyes were red, her voice slow.

"You're stoned, too," he said.

She shook her head.

"Don't shit me, you're stoned out of your mind."

She pushed her hair out of her eyes. "All right," she said. "So I'm stoned. So what? Just don't lecture me, like I was your kid or something. I don't belong to you."

She went back into the bathroom. Burl took another drink of tequila and walked down the hall to the bedroom. In the ashtray by the bed, he found a roach, the end stained with resin and lipstick. She hadn't even tried to hide it.

Suddenly he knew he was going to smoke it. He found a book of matches on the floor, tore one out. As he did, he noticed the cover that said RODEO CLOWN SALOON.

Burl jumped off the bed. The sheets gave off a faint, stale odor of sleep in the sunlight that fell through the shade. He stared at them. The air in here was too thick to breathe.

He met her in the hall, brushing her hair. "Chaney was here, wasn't he?" he said, holding up the matchbook.

She wouldn't look at him.

"We had another talk," she said.

"What did you talk about?"

"He told me you had something going with another girl at the Sands Motel," she said slowly. "He said you smoked dope with her."

"You fucked him, didn't you?"

This time, she started to hit him. He blocked her hand, shoved her hard. She reeled across the room and fell. There was a wonderful release to it: now he was the asshole he'd always known he was.

"You'd do this to me?" he shouted. "Fuck this guy, when I've been pulling your weight?"

And why was there such sad sweetness to it, this moment of betrayal? Was it because he'd seen it coming for so long? Or was it because he'd wanted it? He didn't know. He only knew he had to *do* something. Worst of all, his cock was harder than he could ever remember.

He pulled her to her feet. "Nothing happened," she said. "But I'll tell you one thing. You'll never fuck me again."

"Oh, no?"

He put his hand inside her robe, felt hot slickness.

She closed her eyes and held on to him as he thrust again and again. He felt her contractions begin, tried to keep watching her face. Then he changed from flesh to metal as the current shot between their bodies and a storm of electricity raged through his head, melting down his brain.

They stared at the yellow ceiling. "We might have made a baby that time," she said.

"I know."

She reached down and touched herself between her legs. "What do we do now?"

"Make sure."

He rolled back over on her. This time it was longer, slower.

"If we have a baby, you'll never go to school," she said as he was falling asleep.

"I don't care," he said. "Anything's worth this."

He woke at sunset, to a mockingbird singing on the telephone line outside the window. A dryline was forming out in the Panhandle. When the yardmaster called, Burl told him he was taking a personal day off.

After the kids had been put to bed, John came over and he and Bebe got in an argument about abortion.

"But it's wrong to kill," she said. "It's a little life, and there must be some reason why it happened. And it makes it too easy for women who don't have any feelings."

"Your feelings are your own business," John said. "But you should have the right, don't you see?"

"All I know is, once you've had a baby, you can't kill anything," Bebe said, her voice breaking. "I couldn't even kill a mouse right now, I don't know why." She got up. "I'm too tired to talk about it. I'm going to bed."

"Sorry," John said when she had gone into the bedroom.

"What are you so pissed off about?" Burl said.

"I'm not pissed off," John said. "I'm a happy man. I've finally figured out what they've done to us."

THE STORM SEASON

249

▼

"What's that?"

"They've stolen our dreams."

Burl stared at the television, waiting for John to get to the point.

"I've been reading this book about sleep and dreaming," John said. "Seems like dreaming is one of the most important things we do. It allows us to sort through the things that happen to us during the day. Thing is, you can't just go to sleep and dream. Your body's got something like a clock, and it's set by exposure to sunlight. If it's off, you go to sleep, but you might not dream at all. See what I'm getting at? With our schedule, we might go days without dreaming. And you know what happens to people who don't dream?"

"I've got a feeling you're going to tell me," Burl said, getting another beer out of the icebox.

"Anxiety, depression, anger, and alcoholism," John said. "Why, it's a description of practically everyone who works for the railroad. And you know as well as I do that the minute you get off work, you have an uncontrollable urge to drink. That's to smooth out the anxieties produced by losing sleep. Thing is, alcohol stops you from dreaming, so you end up worse than before."

"I don't know about that," Burl said. "I have noticed I have an uncontrollable urge to watch television."

It was late, and he switched from one station to another, before he finally settled on The Weather Service radar, where the blue outline of Texas floated in a black void.

"I got a theory about that too," John said. "I think television is a substitute for dreaming. So is sex. Ever notice how when you get your rocks off, your mind spills over into all these strange thoughts? There's this sensation of heat or light, and later all your anger is gone."

He took out a joint. "If you're going to smoke that damned thing," Burl said, "get out of my house."

"I've got to have my dream for the day," John said, standing up. "We've all got to have them, or we'll go insane. I get mine by smoking pot. And you," he said, looking at Burl, "you get yours by chasing tornadoes."

Burl sat up long after John left, until four in the morning, watching the radar and drinking beer. Little blue echoes appeared along the dryline, but they weren't going anywhere. Every two minutes, the recorded summary repeated itself: *At three AM, skies were clear across Texas. A weak cold front had moved into Oklahoma, but was expected to become stationary. Outlook for Thursday, Friday, and Saturday: no rain is expected through the period.* He woke when Bebe got Jason up to go to school, his mouth dry and his neck sore, the blue outline of Texas still floating in the black void, empty except for bursts of screen static.

CONVERGENCE

1

Bebe took her GED exam on the last day of May. Afterward, she and some of the other girls in her class went to Luby's for lunch. When Burl picked her up, he thought how different she looked from the day when he'd brought her here a year ago. She no longer wore her white leather jacket and had taken to carefully doing her nails. No one would have taken her for a biker's ole lady now.

They went home and took a bath together, and she told him her period was a week late.

"Do you think how you feel when you make love has anything to do with what a baby's like?" she asked him when they got in bed.

"How do you mean?"

"Jason's so angry," she said. "And his father was angry at me the night we made him. Do you think that's the reason?"

"I don't know."

"Do you want to talk about what happens if I don't get my period?"

"No," he said, kissing her belly. "I don't want to talk."

"I'll probably get it," she said before they went to sleep. "I've been this late before."

That evening, Burl went over to see his mother. She had taken advantage of an offer at Camera World and had the old home movies transferred to videotape. Burl was looking forward to it. For the first time, he would be able to see them clearly.

After dinner, they put the cassette in the VCR and sat back. The difference was incredible. But as the tape ran on, Burl began to feel something was missing. The shifting grain and faded colors of the old film had given it a mystery that was no longer there. Now the images were bright and cold, like colored ice. When he saw his father lighting a Camel or his mother driving the old green Dodge, he felt he was seeing a made-for-TV movie. It looked even better than *The Winds of War,* but it was impossible to believe it had taken place in the past. The old jackknife rig spouting oil, Burl and Coy running over the backyard grass—all now took place in the present. The past had been absorbed by television.

When he got home, Bebe was sitting on the front porch. "Thank God you're here," she said.

"What's the trouble?"

"Chaney took Jason."

"Get a hold of yourself." She was shaking like she did when they made love. "Tell me what happened."

"Chaney came by. We talked for a while. He said he wanted to take Jason somewhere and raise him right. I went in the kitchen to make some coffee and heard his bike start up. When I looked out the window, I saw him going off with Jason on back."

Burl went to the telephone.

"What are you doing?" she asked him.

"Calling the cops."

"No," she said. "Don't do that. I'm scared of the cops. They'll just make things worse."

They argued about it for another twenty minutes, but he couldn't talk her into it.

Before he left, he opened the attic trapdoor, got down the Luger, and loaded it. Then he stopped. What was he thinking about? He couldn't go after Jason with a pistol.

But it made him feel better to have it. "Lock the front door," he told Bebe. He put the Luger in the glove compartment and drove to the Rodeo Clown Saloon.

Chaney wasn't there. He knocked on the stage door, asked for Tina. When she appeared, he asked her if she knew where Chaney lived.

"What do you want to know for?"

He told her.

"That's too bad," she said, popping her gum. "Stealing a kid, that's not right."

"Can you help me find him?"

"I could ask some people," she said. "Stick around until I get off work."

He waited, drinking beer after beer. At midnight Tina got off. They drove downtown, to a house in a Mexican neighborhood with a chopper parked in the yard. She asked for some money and told him to drive around for a while. Burl gave her a twenty-dollar bill, drove out to the air force base and back. She was waiting on the porch when he pulled up in front. "Let's go back to the Sands," she said.

Leroy was at work. Tina took out her glass crack pipe. "The Texas Rangers busted a meth lab down near Graham the day before yesterday," she said. "The guys they busted were Chaney's suppliers. He's laying low. A lot of people are."

"Will you keep asking people?"

"I guess I could." She sighed painfully. "But Burl, what's in it for me?"

"You want more money," he said.

"We could work out a trade. Burl, do you know I've been free-lancing?"

For a moment he didn't know what she meant. Then she unbuttoned her shirt and took it off.

"Just every so often, with guys I really like. Leroy's all for it, if that's what you're worried about." She put her arms around him. "For you, it'd only be fifty dollars."

But Burl thought of Bebe, waiting at home—Bebe, who might be carrying his child—and the thought of what he and Tina had done before filled him with shame. He stared into her eyes, which were dull as thumbtacks, wondering how he could have ever felt such hunger for her. All he felt now was pity.

"I like you, Tina," he told her. "But I wouldn't feel right about that."

"If that's how you feel," she said, picking up the pipe. "Sure you don't want a hit before you go?"

He dropped another twenty on the bed. "No, thanks."

"Come back anytime," she said as he left.

Burl got up at noon. Bebe sat in the front room all day long, staring out the screen door. They were both thinking of Jason but there was nothing to say. Burl watched The Weather Channel. A big Alaskan low, the most powerful he had seen all spring, was moving into California. This one looked promising. There was rain in Los Angeles, snow in the Cascades.

At six he got a call and drove to the yard. He hated to leave

Bebe alone still knowing nothing, but he had to go to work. He and John walked the train, checking brake hoses and measuring flanges with the wheel gauge. There were twenty propane cars up front, and in back, ten cars of anhydrous ammonia.

Halfway down the train was a flatcar with a large container on it, twelve feet high and covered with canvas. "Wonder what this is?" Burl said, folding back one corner of the canvas. Then he saw the red trefoils and the notice DANGER—RADIATION.

For a long moment, they just stared.

John looked through his waybills. "It's United States Navy property," he said, "and it's going to Arco, Idaho. Now you tell me—what does the navy do in Idaho? That's a hell of a long way from the ocean."

"It's a dumping ground for hot waste," Burl said. "Where did it come from?"

"Savannah, Georgia."

"There's a shipyard in Savannah."

"So what do you think it is?"

"I think it's a reactor core from a decommissioned nuclear submarine," Burl said. "And they're sending it up there to be buried."

"Are you sure of that?"

"No, I'm not sure. But whatever it is, it's hot."

John looked through his waybills again. "They didn't put out a bulletin on it or nothing. They can't do that to us. How do we know it's safe?"

Burl stared at the container. John was right, but there was also an excitement in standing so close to part of a nuclear submarine. Another piece of the Big Secret.

"I ain't sure I want to haul this thing tonight," John said.

"What can we do?"

"Refuse to take it." John spat into the cinders. "They're asking too much this time. Are you with me?"

"I'll go with you," Burl said, "and see what happens."

They walked to the yardmaster's office.

"Arcement," Hardesty said, "eight other crews hauled it this far. Now what makes you so special?"

"We got our health to think about," John said. "It might not be safe. And safety," he added, quoting the rule book, "is of first importance."

Hardesty smiled. "All right, then," he said. "Drennan, you'll be conductor on this trip. I'll start finding another brakeman. And you, Arcement, you're behaving unreasonably. Better get ready to pee into that little bottle."

John's face was white with anger. For a moment, Burl thought he was going to walk out. But he finally said, "All right. I'll take the train."

They walked back toward the caboose. "I should have quit this job long ago," John said.

Burl couldn't see why John had made such a big deal out of the reactor—if that was what it was. Over the long run, it made no difference. At night, when Burl stared at the light bulbs burning in the ceiling of the caboose, he could see hundreds of little motes of light dancing around them, some kind of metallic particles. The air of the caboose was full of them. He thought of the train ahead, with its two hundred pairs of steel brake shoes. He'd been breathing those particles for four years now. So far this year, three men had died of cancer—two of a rare type of lung cancer called mesothelioma. Nobody talked about it much. Burl had the feeling they were afraid to.

They pulled out at sundown, and the lights of Nortex faded behind them. At nine o'clock, they passed the flashing strobes of the power plant. They rolled on through Vernon, Chillecothe, and Quanah, the bells of crossing gates dopplering off behind them.

Beyond Goodlett, he climbed down and told John about Chaney taking Jason. "I knew he wasn't to be trusted," John said. "What are you gonna do?"

"Bebe's afraid to call the cops," Burl said. "I've got some people looking for him. When I find out where he is, I guess I'll have to go after him."

John filed another waybill. "You want to be careful with those bikers. I might have to give you a hand with that."

Burl started to say he'd appreciate it. Just then they heard it: a rolling, metallic boom of thunder, coming toward them down the train. For an instant they stared into each other's eyes. John reached for the conductor's valve above his desk, but before his fingers touched it the light flashed red, and they went into the Big Hole.

Burl heard the grinding of the hiss of the reservoirs emptying, the brake shoes closing on the wheels. He turned toward the wall to brace himself, but just then the shock hit, throwing him the length of the caboose. His shoulder struck the front door: as it did, the lights went off, and there was an orange flash outside that turned the night to day. He fell to the floor, tasting metal, tried to pick himself up. Another boom of thunder was rolling down the train toward him, the sound of couplers smashing together. This time, the caboose surged forward, throwing him toward John.

As he rolled across the floor, Burl found himself thinking as clearly as he had ever thought in his life. The train had derailed. Up ahead, cars were going off, one by one. Each time, the caboose was pulled forward. When the next shock hit, John fell on top of Burl. Then they were rolling on the floor together, trying to get up, but the toilet was splashing over and they kept slipping and falling down. The stove had come loose and was rolling around with them. They were screaming at each other, but all Burl could hear was the thunder of tons of metal as the train piled up like a chain, link by link. Burl saw it as a huge machine swallowing the whole train, the machine that had been trying to get him all along, and the question was, would it stop before the caboose was swallowed too? They were going right into the black throat of the noise, and the cars ahead were full of anhydrous ammonia.

Then it did stop, with a last jolt, and they were out the back door, jumping to the ground. There was an orange glare to his right. He didn't look, just kept running, trying to hold his breath—anhydrous ammonia was supercooled and heavier than air, and if you got a lungful, you died. He could see the ground in every detail except right ahead, where his shadow was thrown out in front of him.

He hit a fence wire, bounced back. John ran into him and they both fell down. When they looked back, they saw the prairie was lit up for miles. The whole train was burning. It sounded like a skillet full of hot cooking oil. Mushroom after mushroom of flame went up as propane cars exploded. The ground thudded each time, like a drum. They moved toward the front of the train, keeping well clear. Another propane car exploded, and Burl heard something go past his head. He saw a red-hot bolt lying on the ground. The sparkling orange cloud went up thousands of feet.

The derailment was right behind the engine, which had stopped automatically when the train went into emergency air, two hundred yards down the track. The shell was intact, but when they got closer they could see how it had sagged from the heat. The paint was burned off, and the windows melted.

"Royce bought it," John shouted.

Burl sat down on the ground. His throat was so dry, he thought he'd never be able to swallow again, and his lungs were full of chemical smoke. He coughed and coughed. "We've got to get out flares," he said.

John laughed. "Flares?" he said. They'd be able to see this for fifty miles. He looked in the other direction, toward the darkness. "I'm going on the run," he said.

Burl stood up. "What are you saying?"

"We got two men dead, and a major accident involving radioactive waste," John said. "I'm the conductor: I'm responsible for the safety of the train. And you know I can't afford to pee into that little bottle."

Burl stared at the blackened shell of the engine, streaming off white smoke all over like a piece of dry ice.

"It was a derailment," he said. "It wasn't your fault."

John laughed. "This is gonna cost the Fort Worth & Denver millions of dollars," he said. "Somebody's gonna pay for it, and it's gonna be me."

"If you run, it'll look worse."

"The whole world's gonna be here in fifteen minutes. If I stick around, I'll never get away. No," John said, staring into the darkness where his shadow pointed. "I'll take my chances out there."

John gripped Burl's hand. He sounded calm, but Burl saw he was terrified.

"Shit, John," Burl pleaded, "don't leave me like this."

"No, I got to," John said, laughing. "I'll call you."

"Where do you think you're going?" Burl cried.

But John was running, laughing. Burl saw him going off through the mesquite, dodging this way and that as he must have done in 'Nam, on the run.

Another tank car burned without exploding, like a giant match breathing out blue flames. Burl moved on, trying to stay out of the smoke.

He crossed the tracks and walked toward the highway, the sound of the fire fading behind him. When he got closer, he could see the flashers of a Highway Patrol car. Royce and the new brakeman were standing by it. They'd been able to jump from the engine just before the flames reached them. Burl told them he'd lost John in the darkness. Royce patched through to Amarillo on the car radio and told them there'd been a derailment and a toxic spill.

The fire department came from Childress, but there was nothing to do but let it burn. Burl sat on the ground, drinking a cup of coffee the firemen gave him. At sunrise, Foley, the assistant trainmaster, drove up in a company car and told them he was supposed to take them back to Nortex.

Burl was glad they were going back to Nortex instead of on to

Amarillo. He slept most of the way there. Foley drove right to the hospital.

"Well, you know what we're doing here," Foley said. "Let's get it over with."

The head nurse knew they were coming. She told Burl to disrobe. He did. Then she gave him the bottle and told him to use the bathroom down the hall. Foley stood right behind him, so he could see everything.

"Don't get too close," Burl told him. "It's only our first date."

He handed Foley the bottle of warm gold piss.

"You want to sign a paper or something," Foley said, "saying you're doing this under protest?"

"Fuck it," Burl said.

Foley gave the bottle to the nurse and drove him back to the yard. Then Burl drove home and took a long, cold shower. There were sticky black particles in his hair and nose, and his ribs were turning blue. He lay down on the bed and closed his eyes. He could still see flames.

Bebe woke him sliding into bed with him. He looked at the clock. It was eleven. "Shit, honey," she said. "Did you get in a fight?"

He told her what had happened.

"Poor John," she said. "What's going to happen to him?"

"I don't know. He shouldn't have done it."

"Your eyebrows are burned." She touched them, and Burl heard a dry crisping sound.

"I'm lucky. Real lucky. Have you heard anything from Chaney?"

She shook her head.

"I'll have to see to that," he said. "Soon as I get my shit together."

He ran his finger down her stomach. She'd taken her clothes off before she'd gotten into bed. She always knew what to do.

2

He was up and watching The Weather Channel at noon, when Hardesty called and asked him how he was feeling.

"Pretty good," he said.

"Burl, there's a fellow here from the board who'd like to talk to you. I think you'd better come down here right now."

Burl drove down to the yard and went to Hardesty's office. The man from the National Transportation Safety Board was sitting in the corner. Hardesty introduced him, then sat down behind his desk and cleared his throat. "Burl," he said softly, "tell us what happened out there."

"It was a broken rail," Burl said.

"How do you figure that?"

"I don't know what else it could be. That track hasn't been worked on for years."

"We found some split ties," the investigator said. "We figure it could have been a brake bar dragging."

"No, we would have felt it," Burl said. "And Arcement looked the train over carefully before we left. It wasn't that."

"Where is Arcement?" Hardesty said.

"He hasn't shown up?"

A silence came in. Then it got longer and longer. They were staring at him. Burl felt his face tingling and stared at the floor. He considered asking them if John was dead, but he knew he couldn't pull it off.

"No," Hardesty said slowly. "We thought you might know where he's gone to."

Burl told them he hadn't seen John since they'd jumped off the train.

They looked at each other. "Well, if you do hear from him," Hardesty said, "tell him we'd like to talk to him real bad." He made a note on a pad. "Take a day off," he said, "but don't leave town. We might want to talk to you again."

"I'm resigning," Burl said.

He hadn't known he was going to say it until the words were out of his mouth.

Hardesty made another note. "That's not gonna help you, Burl," he said sadly, "if you can't pass your drug test."

"I'm not worried about passing my drug test."

"Then why you want to quit all of a sudden? Looks a little suspicious."

"After last night?" Burl said, laughing. "Why do you think? I'm never getting on another train. They're too damned dangerous."

Hardesty looked at his fingernails. He smiled. "I think I know what's going through your head. I've known about you for a long time. You got a drug and alcohol problem. You fit the profile, right down the line. Of course, you're gonna have to go before the board. But Arcement's the one responsible here, not you. You get in the program, show me you're sincere, you'll probably be all right. You might not even have to go to jail. Anyway, it's just about the only chance you've got. I can't charge you until I get the results of that test. But I'll bet you a dollar it's positive, and if it is, your ass belongs to the Fort Worth & Denver."

"Not anymore," Burl said, and walked out.

He drove home, thinking he was free. He supposed he would feel it in a while. Right now, all he wanted to do was go to bed and sleep forever.

Five minutes after he walked through the door, he got a collect call from Ethan Edwards, the character John Wayne had played in *The Searchers.*

"Glad I got hold of you," John said. "They looking for me?"

"Well, they said they'd really like to talk to you."

John laughed. So did Burl. It felt good, cleared the air.

"You want me to call you a lawyer?"

"No, I'd like you to bring my car."

"I think they're going to be watching it."

"All right," John said. "Can you bring me some things?" Burl said he'd try. John told him what he wanted, and where he'd meet him. There was a key to his house, he said, under the back porch.

Burl drove back, told Bebe what he had to do.

"When will you be back?"

"Hard to say. I've got to see John's taken care of. Then I'll try to get Jason back."

He held her.

"Be careful," she said.

"Man, it's just one thing after another."

Before he left, he looked at The Weather Channel. The low was moving down through Utah, dragging the jet stream along with it. There was a thirty percent chance of thunderstorms for Thursday.

Burl drove back downtown. As he crossed the tracks, he looked over at the yard office just in time to see a police tow truck pulling John's pickup out of the parking lot.

He circled back to John's house and drove around the block twice, looking for cops. There were none in sight. He stopped in front, took a deep breath, and walked down the driveway to the back porch. Found the key. The house was hot, airless. As far as he could tell, no one had been there. He found John's tent in the closet, the metal footlocker under the bed. Then he carried them outside, put them in his trunk, and drove off.

On the way out of town, he stopped at the Food Emporium and bought some canned goods, a bottle of Herradura, a tin of tobacco, and a package of rolling papers. Then he had a thought and called Tina at the Sands Motel.

He listened to it ring. The world's largest American flag, faded and full of holes, rattled against its pole.

"Hello?" Tina said.

"It's Burl."

"You woke me up."

"Sorry," he said. "But I was wondering if you had anything more to tell me."

"No, honey," she said. "Not really."

"Look, if you know anything at all."

"All right," she said finally. "I shouldn't be telling you this, but Leroy said a lot of the Renegades have gone up to Oklahoma. There's a place they hang out up there, in Medicine Park. Do you know where that is?"

"Outside of Lawton."

"Yeah. That's probably where Chaney would be. But I wouldn't go looking for him, if I were you. Some real serious shit goes down up there. They don't like visitors."

"Thanks, Tina," he said.

"And don't ever say I told you anything," she said. "You'll get both our asses shot."

He drove out past Kickapoo Airport, turned off on a blacktop, and waited to see if anyone was following him. He waited five minutes, then drove on toward Seymour.

It took three hours to reach Lazare, where John had told Burl he'd meet him. There was no town, just a grocery store with a gas pump out in front and a sign that said LIAR'S CORNER.

Burl gassed up the car, then went into the grocery to pay. He bought a couple of August pies and a Big Red, then went back outside. Behind the grocery was a big mesquite patch. In five minutes John came walking out of it and got in the car. "Let's go," he said.

Burl pulled out. "You need breakfast?"

"I had a Mexican breakfast," John said. "A piss and a cigarette."

In the mirror Burl could see a faint blue pillar of smoke to the north, where the wreck was still burning.

"Well," John said, "what's the situation?"

Burl filled him in, told him Royce was still alive but that they'd towed John's car. He mentioned what the investigator had said about a broken brake bar.

"That's what I thought," John said. "They think they can prove negligence."

"Best thing to do is get a good lawyer."

"I called the American Civil Liberties Union, right before I talked to you." He laughed. "They said they didn't take drug cases."

"So what now?"

"Probably I disappear," John said. "But not right away. I'm gonna hang out and see if I can't get my money out of the bank somehow."

They hid out in Copper Breaks, back in the salt cedar behind the campground. Burl drove the Mustang down into a draw, where it couldn't be seen from the road. They carried the tent a little farther, along the top of a ridge where they could see for miles. It was an old green canvas army tent, heavy as hell, but once they got it up, it was invisible from ten feet away.

John built a fire of green sticks that didn't make any smoke, and sat a can of pork and beans into it to heat. His feet were covered with blisters. He cut them open and taped them up. By that time, the sun was going down. Twenty miles to the north, they could see the Medicine Mounds, and beyond them, the pillar of smoke. They ate sardines and crackers and spooned hot pork and beans out of the blackened can. Burl was hungrier than he'd ever been in his life.

When they finished, the moon was up. It was a cool night. John got an old combat jacket out of the footlocker and put it on. "That's how I found my way last night," he said. "The moon was bright enough to read a newspaper. When I got to that store, I lay down in the weeds and slept like a baby."

He opened the bottle of silver Herradura, clear as rainwater, and they passed it back and forth, listening to the night birds. Once every half hour, a car would go by. They could see the headlights coming for miles.

"You heading back to Nortex?" John said.

"It's too late. I'll spend the night with you, then go back in the morning."

"I'm glad Royce made it," John said. "If I'd known that, I might not have run. Of course, if I'd known this was gonna happen," he said, "I would have quit months ago."

"Me too," Burl said.

He told John he'd resigned.

"Congratulations," John said. "For a while there, I didn't think you had it in you." He leaned back and looked at the stars.

"How do you feel, John?" Burl asked him.

"I don't really know if I feel good or bad. It's more like I'm flying. It's like my feet ain't even touching the ground."

"Anyway, there's supposed to be storms, the day after tomorrow," Burl said.

John socked his arm. They laughed for a long time.

"I'm gonna miss you, partner," John said.

"I'm gonna miss you too."

John opened his sleeping bag on the floor of the tent so they could both lie on it. Burl went off in the cedars and took a piss. Then he started thinking about Chaney, wondering how he was going to get Jason back, and the whole crushing weight of his life fell on him again. He went back and told John what had happened, showed him the Luger in the glove compartment and the full clip.

"So you going to Medicine Park tomorrow?"

"I figure I've got to."

"I'll go with you," John said. "We've got to get your boy back."

Burl shook his head. "It's my business. And you want to keep your head down."

"I owe you one," John said. "And I ain't got anything better to do." He stuck the Luger in his belt. "Let me take care of this. I've got combat experience, and you don't."

3

The sandy ground was hard-packed, granular with fine pebbles he could feel right through the bag. He thought he'd never get to sleep.

When he opened his eyes, the sun was shining. He crawled outside, saw John walking down the ridge toward him, wearing his combat jacket.

"Get up off your knees, son," he said. "It's a fine morning, and we got places to go."

John ate cold beans out of the can. Burl had an August pie. "Nothing like waking up in the open country," John said. "Makes you feel like a kid again." He finished the beans, tossed the can away. "Come on," he said. "Let's get on the road. I'm not worth shit without my morning coffee."

The ground under the cedars was moist, Burl noticed. The humidity was coming up, a good sign for tomorrow. He backed the Mustang up out of the draw while John looked for cars. The road was clear in both directions. John got in, and they pulled out into the molten glare of the rising sun.

In Crowell, they got coffee to go at Allsup's and an Amarillo paper. There were photos of the wreck, but no mention of the reactor. The article said authorities were seeking the conductor, who was still missing. They drove on toward Vernon. The sun rose higher. When John finished his coffee he chewed tobacco, spitting the juice into the empty Styrofoam cup.

They reached Nortex in three hours. John told him to drive to the First Bank of Nortex branch in the shopping mall. He went in and came out five minutes later. "They told me it'd take three business days to get my money out," he said, "and I didn't like the way the officer was looking at me."

John went to the automated teller in the little glass booth in the parking lot and withdrew five hundred dollars before the sign floated up on the computer screen: SORRY, WE ARE UNABLE TO COMPLETE THIS TRANSACTION.

"I got a feeling this is the last I'm ever gonna see of my savings," John said. "But this should get me out of Texas anyway."

They drove out the Central Expressway. It was noon when they crossed the Red River bridge into Oklahoma and hit the tollgate of the Will Rogers Turnpike. Burl dropped in a quarter, waited for the light to turn green, and drove on under a sign that said LAWTON—45. In another mile, they met a Highway Patrol car. Burl felt his stomach go cold. John seemed unconcerned. As they drove along, he sang to himself in a toneless voice:

When you cross that ole Red River, hoss,
That name don't mean a thing.

No matter who's in Austin,
Bob Wills is still the king.

Burl turned on the scanner and watched his mirror all the way to Lawton.

Medicine Park was an old resort town in a narrow valley on the edge of the Wichita Mountains. Burl pulled off on the shoulder just before they got there. "What now?" he said.

"We got to be grunts today," John said. "Let's look over the terrain and choose our situation."

Burl pulled back on the road and drove slowly ahead. The town lay along either side of a crumbling blacktop that twisted this way and that, following the bends of Cache Creek. The houses, built of the same round yellowish stones that composed the Holy City, reminded Burl of gingerbread houses covered with gumdrops. In the past, it seemed, some collective urge for decoration had overtaken the population. Almost everyone had statues in the yard: of fawns, or rabbits, or elves sitting on toadstools. The road twisted again, and they passed a bar—another gumdrop building, painted white—with a chopper parked out front. The sign over the door said YO MOMMA'S.

On the far side of town, the road ran uphill, past an old thirties dam and power plant. Beyond it, Burl saw boats bobbing on Lake Elmer Thomas and the wooded slopes of Mount Scott. He pulled off on the shoulder again.

"Well, that's the town," John said. "Now all we got to do is find him."

"I would say a good place to start looking," Burl said, "would be Yo Momma's."

"I agree."

They parked in front and got out. Burl heard "Tough Enough" playing on a jukebox inside.

John stuck the Luger in his belt. "Don't hold back now," he said. "The only way to impress these guys is to show 'em you're not afraid of 'em. Pretend like you're the one who's got a gun in his pants. Let's go."

The record ended as they walked in. It was a long dark room with a poured concrete floor that reminded Burl of bars he'd seen in Mexico. There was no decor, just a long bar with wood-grain paneling, some tables and chairs, and a number of electric beer signs. He made out a heavyset biker and a fat girl sitting in the corner. The bartender looked at them, a matchstick in the corner of his mouth. Burl took him for an Indian.

John stepped up to the bar. "Give us a couple of beers."

The bartender took the matchstick out of his mouth and stared at it.

"I don't know you guys," he said.

"What is this?" John said. "A private club?"

"Yeah," the bartender said. "We don't serve assholes."

He laughed loudly at his own joke. The biker in the corner joined in.

John glanced at Burl. "He might know something."

Burl looked at the biker, not at all sure he could pull this off. "We're looking for Chaney," he said.

The biker stood up, his chair scraping the floor. "Well, who the fuck are *you*?"

Here's where I get my ass kicked, Burl thought.

Then he heard the smashing sound, and the chair John had kicked went flying past him across the room, hitting a table and knocking an ashtray to the floor. "I'll tell you who I am," John said, a ferocity in his voice Burl had never heard before. "I'm a Vietnam vet, and I wore this jacket when I was wasting bad guys in the I Drang Valley. We used to talk about what we'd do with your kind when we got back to the States. Now I'm here, and your ass is mine."

He took out the Luger and snapped back the slide, putting a shell into the chamber. The silence was absolute. The biker stared at John, then sat back down. His chair went out from under him, and he landed on the concrete floor.

The bartender cleared his throat. "Take it easy, buddy. What do you want, anyway?"

"Some common courtesy," John said. "And a free beer for all the shit I shoveled over there for the sake of assholes like you."

The bartender popped the tops off of two Pearls and shoved them across the bar.

"Horse piss," John said. "That the best you got?"

"Sorry," he said.

John handed a beer to Burl. "Now," he said to the biker. "Like my buddy told you, we want to know where Chaney is. We're friends of his, if it makes any difference."

"I won't tell you," the biker said after a strangled pause.

"I will," the fat girl said. "I'll take you to him—if you'll buy me a hit."

John pointed with his chin toward the door. "We're in the red Mustang."

They finished their beers. John tried to pay, but the bartender refused. "There's a certain style to these things," he said to Burl as they got in the car. "You got to make these guys feel guilty. My father always said that was the secret of a good sermon, original sin."

He turned to the fat girl, who was sitting in the backseat. She wore a tank top, cutoffs, and for the first time Burl noticed she had the fading impression of a black eye. "What's your name?" John asked her.

"Hand Job," she said.

She directed them to a house set back from the road, up a long driveway and hidden by a stand of live oaks. The house itself was up on a hillside and could be reached only by a long flight of steps, elaborately decorated with chunks of petrified wood, colored glass, and air force practice bombs covered with birdshit. Parked in front of it were a number of bikes, Camaros, and a black van painted with a pastel mural of sea serpents and Viking women.

"Leave that damned gun in the car this time," Burl said to John. "I don't want any guns."

They got out. Burl saw people on the porch looking down at them. One was wearing nothing but a German helmet. A girl seemed to be giving him a blow job.

"What is this?" he asked Hand Job.

"A crackhouse," she said.

He turned to John. "What do we do?"

"Show some cool," John said, a certain John Wayne gravel in his voice. Burl looked up at the crackhouse and wondered how this could be happening here. He'd always thought of Oklahoma as an innocent place, the home of Bob Wills and the Cowboy Hall of Fame. Now it seemed to have returned to the savagery of its early history, when it was the Indian Territory, a land of atrocities.

"Hey," the guy wearing the German helmet yelled. "What do you think you're doing?"

Burl turned and saw John was pissing on the grille of the nearest Camaro.

"That's my car," the guy said.

"Your radiator's about to boil over," John said calmly. "I was just trying to cool it off for you." He buttoned his fly with one hand, winking at Burl.

"We're looking for Chaney," Burl said.

"Up here."

Chaney had come out onto the porch and was looking down at them. He wore no shirt, and now Burl saw for the first time that his chest was tattooed with faded blue dragons that coiled around his nipples. His chest looked like a Chinese newspaper.

"Come on up," he said.

They climbed the hot granite steps. Burl heard flies in the silence and thought of the steps leading to the top of an Aztec pyramid. When they reached the top, he saw that Chaney's pants were covered with dried blood. He smiled at Burl.

"You come here for a hit?" he said.

"You know what I came for."

Chaney looked at the other bikers. "I know these guys," he said. "We're gonna have a little talk."

It was clear that Chaney, by knowing them, had to some extent fucked up. There were some grumbles and dirty looks, but the other bikers went back into the house. Hand Job was pulling at Burl's arm. "What about my hit?" she said.

He gave her a twenty-dollar bill, and they followed Chaney inside, through a room that smelled of ether. The floor was covered with brown shag carpeting. Two of the girls sitting around the coffee table were completely naked. Burl saw someone hold the propane torch to the green glass pipe, smelled hot chemicals. A girl wearing only red dime-store panties sat in the corner, picking lint out of her hair.

"Sure you don't want to sit down?" Chaney asked him.

Burl shook his head.

There were children playing in the dirt backyard, even a couple of babies. They walked uphill. Chaney had pitched his te-pee in the woods. A deer hung from the limb of a live oak, its body split open. Bluish entrails were piled on the ground beneath it.

Jason sat on a rock, playing with a skinning knife, not looking at them.

"He took that deer last night, with my Sharps'," Chaney said proudly.

Burl went to Jason. The dead deer gave off a sour metallic odor, like the body they had found in the hopper car.

"You shot this deer?"

"Yeah," Jason said. "We turned the headlight on him, and he just stood there. I think he was too scared to run."

Burl felt a hot, righteous anger at Chaney, an anger so strong, it cut through his fear. As he walked back toward him, he found he hated Chaney so much, he could hardly stand to look at him.

"What do you think you're doing with this kid?" he said. "He's coming back with me."

It was the wrong way to begin.

"You don't talk to me that way," Chaney said, his eyes going dead. "Not here."

John stepped between them. "Hold up," he said, taking a joint out of his shirt pocket. "We're talking honor here. Let's light up and move along. See if honor can't be withheld."

Burl wondered where John had gotten the joint. It must have been in the footlocker. Chaney looked at John, then back to Burl. "All right," he said. "Let's talk."

They walked a little distance away and sat down by a large granite boulder. They could still see Jason and beyond him, where the trees opened up, the lake and Mount Scott. John lit the joint. Burl let it go by. He hated Chaney for doing drugs around Jason, for bringing him to this horrible place, and most of all because he suspected Chaney had lured him here to humiliate him. Chaney took a couple of deep drags, coughed.

"This is foolishness," John said after a while. "You like each other—I can tell."

"Yeah," Chaney said, "but he stole my woman. It's a matter of honor, like you say."

"I didn't steal her," Burl said. "You lost her."

"There's something to that," John said.

"Maybe so," Chaney said. "But we've got to make things even. He gets my woman, I get my son."

"He's not your son," Burl said. "Neither one of those kids are yours."

Chaney gave Burl a hateful stare, charged with energy. He had his Buck knife out again. "You keep this up," he said, "and I just might kill your ass."

Burl met his stare, riding on the anger still pouring through him. "Oh, shit," he said. "I'm sick of guys like you. What do you want me to say, that I'm afraid of you? Hell yes, I'm afraid of you. Is that what you want to hear?"

Chaney nodded several times. "You'd better be," he said, taking out a Baggie and doing a little meth. In the silence, Burl was aware of the cicadas ringing.

"All right," Chaney said finally. "So he's not my blood. But I was there when he was born. We had things you'll never know. I taught him how to tie his shoes, took him out of school when they tried to give him drugs. See how he sits there?"

They watched Jason, who was still playing with his knife. He seemed to have forgotten they were there.

"I used to do that," Chaney said. "Just sit with a knife and listen. He's just like me." Chaney did more meth. "When he was a baby, I'd be watching him and get these little flashes of memory. I'd see him crawling around, and suddenly I could remember just what it was like, when the floor was hard and the chairs were higher than my head. That's how close we were."

Tears were running down his face. But whether they were tears of emotion or tears of pain as the meth burned his nose, Burl couldn't tell. "Let me have him," Chaney pleaded. "Let me have him for a year, and I can teach him things, I can make a warrior out of him. I got it coming."

Burl felt a great bitterness. "You won't teach him shit," he said. "When I got him, he thought people ran by electricity. He's starting to open up now, be a normal kid. What are you going to do, drag him all over Oklahoma with the cops after you?"

"But he'll forget me," Chaney cried. "I may not live long enough to see him grow up. He's mine."

"He doesn't belong to you," Burl said. "He belongs to himself. And he's got to learn to love, not hate. That's what'll make him strong. He loved animals. Why did you make him kill an animal? You won't teach him anything but guns and death." Burl stood up, feeling weightless. "When are guys like you going to learn there's only two ways to go. Find the things you love, or fight the things you hate. Strongest thing is to find the things you love. Either way, you got to let him go."

WILLIAM HAUPTMAN

Chaney was staring at him wonderingly. "You're just like Pearl's father," he said. "He had that long blond hair. Like Jesus Christ. He said the same things. That's why she likes you."

"What does it matter who he belongs to?" Burl said. "Kids don't belong to us anyway. We don't know where they come from, or where they're going, and we've got to stop trying to make them into what we want them to be. Life's hard enough without that. We just take care of them for a while," he said, looking at Jason, "and the sooner we learn that, the sooner they grow up, that's all I know."

Burl felt the time had come. He stood up and walked downhill. Jason still wouldn't look at him. He scratched the ground with his knife. "Did you bring my skateboard?" he said.

"No."

Jason touched a doodlebug with the point of his knife. It rolled up into a ball, a little black molecule. After a moment, it opened. He touched it again.

"Are you going home?" he asked finally.

"I am," Burl said. "Would you like to come with me?"

Jason said nothing, but Burl thought he saw the top of his head incline a few degrees. Tears flooded Burl's eyes. "Let's go," Burl said, taking his hand.

As they started for the house, Chaney stepped into their path. "If you want him," he said, "you got to walk over me."

Burl even liked Chaney for saying it, but he could think of only one thing: to get Jason out of there. He felt a profound sense of rightness and for a moment actually thought he could walk through Chaney, as if he were made of air, until he took another step and Chaney's hand came out and stopped him. Burl looked up. Saw crows high in the blue sky. He had known this was coming all day. He tried to think of himself as made of metal.

"If we got to fight," he said, "let's do it."

Then Jason was pulling at his hand. "Don't fight," he said. "Please don't fight." He hugged Burl's leg. "I can't stand it," he said. "I want to go home."

Chaney's face broke, went dull. He tried to swallow two or three times.

"All right," he said finally. "You can go home."

Chaney put his hands on Jason's head and pressed it to his stomach. He looked at Burl and John. "Get the fuck out of here for a minute, will you?"

They walked to the house and watched Chaney talking to Jason for a long time, saying things they couldn't hear. Chaney bent down, kissed him on the lips. Then they came walking toward them, Chaney's hand on Jason's shoulder. "You be strong now," he said to Jason. "Like I told you."

"You're doing the right thing," John said.

"You'd better hope so," Chaney said.

He gave them both the biker handshake. His palm was sticky with blood.

"You know," he said to Burl, looking away. "You'll never have kids."

Burl just wanted to get Jason out of there. "How do you mean?"

Chaney smiled a smile of infinite sadness. "I mean, you're the kind of guy who never has kids. You're just like me. You'll take care of somebody else's kids."

"You lost me there," Burl said, although he was afraid he understood.

"She don't really love you, you know," Chaney said, staring off toward the mountains. "She loves her kids. There's no room for you there. She don't believe in anything else. Someday you'll understand what I'm talking about."

"So be it," Burl said, and turned away.

▼　▼　▼

Jason fell asleep in the backseat before they even reached Lawton. Burl called Bebe from a pay phone and told her he was bringing him home. When they got back to Nortex, he lifted Jason out of the car and carried him inside. Bebe held him for a long time.

"I'm all right," Jason said indignantly. "Stop crying."

They had a beer. John read the article in the paper on the wreck, and Burl looked at The Weather Channel. The map showed the low moving into northwestern Oklahoma tomorrow. A dryline was already forming, out beyond Childress. "I'd appreciate it if you could get me to Amarillo," John said. "I ought to be able to leave from there without attracting attention."

"Could you come here a minute?" Bebe said.

Burl followed her out, and they sat on the back steps.

"I'm leaving town," she said.

"There's no need for that now."

"Baby, it's best. Chaney might change his mind. He might show up here again tomorrow."

"There's too many things up in the air," he insisted.

"Not anymore," she said. "I got my period. So we don't have to worry about that."

Burl stared at the grass, wondering why he didn't feel more relieved.

"I thought I was pregnant. When we made love that time, I thought it meant something. But I guess . . ."

She fell silent, and he knew what she was thinking: But I guess we didn't really love each other.

She was wrong. When you came right down to it, it just showed her ignorance. Although she'd answered all those test questions on human reproduction, she still had her own ideas about why people have children.

But he felt a great sadness, and he knew somehow he had failed her.

"Maybe all this trouble brought it on," she finished. "I don't know. Anyway, I'm going on to Houston, if you can loan me the money for the bus ticket."

"When?"

"There's a bus to Dallas at five-thirty. We can change there for Houston and be there in the morning."

"Can't you wait a day or so?"

"You've got to get John out of town," she said. "And I don't want to be here alone. Best for us to go now and get out of your way."

As long as she'd been there, she'd never collected any possessions. In thirty minutes, she had everything packed in his suitcase except for Pearl's toys, which Burl could send to them. John stayed at the apartment. He thought the bus station was a good place for him to avoid. They got there with fifteen minutes to spare.

"We had such a good thing going," he said.

"It's still going."

"I can probably come down in a week or two."

"Sure," she said. "And in a little while, when things calm down, I can always come back."

"Sure," he said. "You're right."

He bought Jason a copy of *War Birds* magazine and himself a cup of coffee. Then he and Bebe stood by the door. Here it was again, he thought, another one of those little corners when time was suddenly real, and every moment important. He wanted to say something, but all he could do was look into her eyes. Even then he kept glancing up at the clock. There were only ten minutes left, then five, and what was there to say after all? Nothing.

The bus started, and they stepped outside. Burl gave her bag to the driver, who put it in the luggage compartment. Pearl asked Bebe if Daddy was coming with them, and she said no. Burl shook Jason's warm, dirty hand and told him, "Take care of your mother." Jason nodded and got on the bus.

"I love you more than anyone I ever loved," Bebe told him. They kissed, and he drank in her breath. It smelled of blood. "I'll call you in a day or two," she said. "Just don't get yourself killed chasing a tornado."

The door closed with a hiss of air, and the driver backed out. Burl could see them dimly through the tinted windows. Jason stared straight ahead. Bebe smiled and lifted her hand. Pearl had already fallen asleep on her shoulder. Then the bus pulled out into traffic and the windows went gold with reflected sunlight, blinding him.

4

They got back to Copper Breaks just before sunset, pulled off the road, and hid the car. John looked over their provisions and announced they were down to coffee, three pies, a package of pork skins, and a bottle of Herradura.

They took a walk and found a ruin, a hundred yards up the ridge. There was a crumbling stone foundation, a few timbers, so weathered they looked like driftwood, and a storm cellar.

"Figure it was a settler's cabin?" Burl said.

"More likely a line camp. This was all ranch country."

"You'll notice they had a storm cellar," Burl said.

The door was still intact. There was a little cave beneath, full of spiderwebs and rabbit turds. The walls had softened and flowed together, almost filling it.

"Think they ever used it?"

"They must have thought it was worth going to the trouble to dig it," Burl said. He looked around the horizon, shivered. Tornado country. This was where the big ones were born, and you wouldn't have to sit around here long to see one.

They poked around, found fragments of stoneware, bits of glass turned to amethyst by fifty years of ultraviolet.

There was blowing dust out to the west. The sun, as it sank into it, turned pale heatless blue, then dull orange. Burl saw a big sunspot on the northwest limb, and pointed it out to John. "Looks like somebody took a bite out of it," John said.

Burl walked back to the car, turned on the radio. Through the static, he heard the voice of the meteorologist giving the Oklahoma thunderstorm forecast. An upper-level low was forming in New Mexico, and the jet stream had looped down to meet it. It was a big convergence: all the factors were present, and there was an eighty percent chance of severe thunderstorms in southwestern Oklahoma tomorrow afternoon.

"What do you think?" John asked him.

"They're saying all hell's going to break loose tomorrow. We're on the wrong side of the dryline right now, but it'll probably back up during the night."

They listened a little longer, trying to hear some news of the train wreck, then gave up and split the pork skins, chasing them with Herradura. The moon rose, a blurred yellow coin with two pale rings around it.

"You made up your mind yet where you're going?" Burl asked him.

"Probably Vermont," John said. "I got a sister there who's married to a guy who runs a ski lift. She says it's real fine country, with mountains and all. Sounds like a good place to get lost. It's cold, though. I'll have to get used to that."

John spread the sleeping bag, and they lay on the ground. The night was alive with insect sounds.

"I can't sleep," he told John.

"Why not?"

"I keep thinking about scorpions."

"How's one gonna find you in the middle of all this?" John said. "The odds are on your side."

"I know, but I can't stop thinking about it."

Burl found his flashlight, shone it on the ground by the bag. The moment he did, a big scorpion ran into it, like an actor coming onstage, stinger upraised.

"Look at this," he said.

But John was already asleep.

He poured insect repellent on the ground around the bag, tried to forget the scorpion. Later he opened his eyes and saw fast, low clouds hurrying across the stars. The dryline was on the move, backing up.

When he woke again, it was daybreak. The sleeping bag had a fine coating of dew. The wind was from the south, and he could smell the salt cedar. He opened the canteen, heard the air rush into it: The pressure had gotten lower.

John sat up and rolled a smoke. Burl built a fire and made coffee. Ants had gotten into the sugar. "I'm afraid you'll have to take it black," he told John.

"I don't mind a few pissants in my coffee."

While they were passing the cup back and forth, Burl saw a yellow German shepherd loping down the draw below, so starved its ribs showed.

"Stray dog," he observed.

"Dog, hell. That's a coyote," John said.

Burl looked again. "You're right."

They drank their coffee and split the last August pie for breakfast.

"Power food," John said.

He rolled another cigarette, and they sat on their heels like Indians, passing it back and forth. The sun rose higher, burning their necks.

"We're starting to look like we belong out here," John said, studying Burl's face.

"Shouldn't we be getting on to Amarillo?"

John smoked thoughtfully, staring off at the Medicine Mounds. An armadillo came out of the brush, stopped, and peered at them out of its almost invisible black eyes. Then it ran off on delicate little hooves, like a toy.

"You know," John said, "your father was right about the theory of reincarnation. Ever since we've been out here, I've thought of us as two of the early Texas heroes."

Burl stared at John, saw him as a cowboy. His face, eroded by the sun, looked like a western bronze.

"You're right," he said.

"I feel like we fought together at the Alamo."

"Especially after yesterday."

"It's this landscape."

They stared off at the Medicine Mounds, each one exactly like the other, but a slightly fainter gray than the one before. Multiple exposures, marching toward the horizon.

"If there's going to be storms today," John said, "let's stick around for a while. You been waiting for this for a long time, and it'd be nice to see one more with you. We can still get to Amarillo tonight."

"All right," Burl said. He had the feeling he might not be seeing John for a long time.

They struck the tent, put it in the trunk along with the gear. "You want to go somewhere else?" John said. "Move north or south of here?"

Burl looked toward the ruined cabin and the storm cellar.

They could see a long way from here, and there was something about that crumbling foundation. It reminded him of the melted foundations of the tower on which the Trinity shot had gone off, the first atomic bomb.

"This might be the right place," he said.

"If it's good enough for you, it's good enough for me," John said. "You're the expert."

They sat down under the biggest cedar, out of the sun. The shadows seemed to flow into the sandy ground like water and disappear.

"Thing we should do is purify ourselves," John said. "Clear our minds, so we can pick the right storm when it comes. We should build a sweat lodge, like the Indians did."

"I'm already sweating," Burl said. "And we're low on water."

"That's so," John said, taking a Baggie out of his pocket. "I guess we'll have to resort to this."

Burl stared at it, sweat stinging his eyes. The bag was full of dried blue-gray flakes.

"What's that?"

"Mushrooms."

"Where in the hell did you get those?"

"Ran around after it rained and picked 'em up off cow pies. That's where they grow," John explained.

"I know that, but how long have you had them?"

"They were in my footlocker." He poured some flakes into his palm and ate them. "Want some?"

John had no sense of the limits. In the last four days, they'd survived a train wreck and faced down a gang of bikers at a crack-house. John had become a fugitive from justice, and Burl his accomplice. So what did he propose they do now?

Take mushrooms, of course.

"What the hell," he said.

Just one would have little or no effect, and it was a way of staying close to John. He consumed a withered blue cap.

"You're the only one who could talk me into this," he said.

"It's what old Quanah Parker would have done," John said.

It was very still. The scratching of pebbles beneath his shoes, of his shirt against the trunk of the cedar as he shifted, trying to find shade, was loud enough to startle.

"I've wanted to do this for a long time," John said.

"What's that?"

"See a whole day pass, from sunrise to sunset. I'm starting to feel better already. This day is gonna set my internal clock. Maybe now I'll start dreaming again."

"I had a dream last night," Burl said. He had just remembered it. "I dreamed we saw a tornado."

"Then we probably will."

The sun climbed higher. Chills shot through Burl's body. He fought back a wave of nausea. When he closed his eyes, his thoughts were drawn down into a black hole.

"Christ," he said.

"What's the trouble?"

"I've lost Bebe."

"At least the cops ain't after you."

"I know, but what am I going to *do*?"

"You're going to go back to school and study tornadoes," John said. "You're a fool if you don't make this your life. You got a gift for finding storms. You're fortunate you've got such a gift, and you should follow it."

Burl watched a red ant trying to lift a large silicate pebble. It was so still he could hear its legs scratching on the sand.

"Shit," he said, "why did all this have to happen to me?"

"You ain't like other people," John said sternly. "Don't you know that by now? You're on your own now, just like me. Hell, you and I should be celebrating. We finally got out from under their control."

John smiled at him. White lines radiated from the corners of his eyes, where creases had hidden the flesh from the sun.

"You're right," Burl said.

"Damned straight," John said. "Anyway, there's no going back."

"I've learned a lot from you, John."

"Well, knowledge is where you find it," John said, eating another cap. "These grow on cowshit."

Burl stared off to the west, thinking of heat and moisture. He could feel the molecules of moist air growing lighter, starting to rise. The air was full of energy.

He stood up. "I've got to find out what time it is."

"You already know," John said.

He walked down to the car. John followed him. He turned on the radio and listened to the Oklahoma thunderstorm forecast. There was a high vertical lifting index, and the cap strength was eroding. Thunderstorms should break out in southwestern Oklahoma within the hour.

It was exactly the time he had thought it was: five minutes after twelve.

"See?" John said. "You don't need a clock out here. The mind. is a mirror, and once you get it clean, you can hear the sound of time going by."

Burl listened. Beneath the faint sound of the wind blowing grains of sand across the ground, he heard something else, like a chord that kept trying to resolve but never did. He couldn't tell if it came from the earth or sky.

"I can hear it," he said.

They walked back up the ridge. The sunlight strobed faintly, the sand crawled with hieroglyphics.

"That's how they got control of us," John said. "They destroyed our sense of time and trapped us in this damned continuous present."

"Who's they?" Burl said, falling into the spirit of the conversation.

"I think you know who I mean," John said. "The preachers. The railroad. The liberals, the conservatives. The President of the United States. Everyone in power. Only thing I can't figure out is how it all got started."

"I can," Burl said. "It started with the bomb. Everybody knows that. I remember first finding out about it when I was a kid. I stopped thinking there was ever going to be a future at all."

"Television didn't help," John said. "All those damned reruns. How you going to believe you're a day older, if Fred Flintstone ain't? Or that you'll ever die?"

Burl thought of his father in the hospital, floating away on a tide of Nembutal.

"But time's running out on us," he said. "They've got people thinking it'll go on like this forever, that things'll never change. Like after the tornado, everybody pretended things were going to get back to normal."

"It was already too late for that," John said. "Things are never gonna be normal again."

"People have forgotten how to change," he said. "That's how they got us under their control."

They walked along the ridge together, falling into step, going no place in particular.

"I'm as big a fool as anyone," John said. "I bought it, too, kept thinking there was always a little more time. Then the derailment came along, and when I heard those cars going off, I knew I'd fucked up in a big way."

They came to the ruin of the cabin and stopped.

"You were going to build a log cabin," Burl said.

John shoved his hands into his pockets, stared at the crumbling foundation.

"Yeah," he said sadly. "And now I see my log cabin was a dream of a place where time stopped. Where nothing changed, and I never got any older. That's why I thought I'd never be lonely there. But when the time came, I could no more make it come true than a dream, and now it's too late for me."

They stared off together, toward the western horizon: hot blue sky above, red clay and dark green cedar below, ridge after ridge rolling off until they shimmered and flowed together.

"Oh, I hate to leave this country," John said. "I hate to leave it behind. It's so beautiful."

To the west, where the horizon merged with the sky, clouds were appearing. Fast, bright little clouds that disappeared again almost the moment he saw them.

"Here we go," he said.

In minutes, a nickel-gray dome had shot up, building to twenty or thirty thousand feet. The dryline was breaking before his very eyes. There was so much instability—or maybe it was the mushrooms—that he could see it happening as clearly as if he were watching time-lapse photography.

"Lord, look at that," John said.

One dome after another exploded as the storm built towers, each one higher than the one before. Moisture was condensing into water vapor and ice crystals, releasing its heat. The towers were spouts of vapor from a great heat engine. They looked like great basins of soap bubbles, boiling higher and higher.

"Now that's what I call impressive convective activity," Burl said.

The whole sky was changing. He thought of something he had read in his astronomy textbook: of subatomic foam, bursting from a singularity and creating the universe. There were two other towers building to the north, but this was the biggest, and it was all alone.

"How does it look to you?"

"Like it's going to be a motherfucker."

"Want to head toward it?"

"No reason to," Burl said. "It looks to me like it's headed right for us."

"See if you can use your power to draw it to us," John said.

It should be easy, he thought. They were right in the middle of a tornado highway.

A lid of ice crystals appeared over the topmost tower. Then the storm grew an anvil. It flowed toward them like an alluvial fan, a great delta of cloud that hid the sun.

The temperature dropped, and the wind died. The Medicine Mounds, still in sunlight, looked pink. The open sky to the north, seen from under the anvil, was a soft, unearthly blue, a color never seen in broad daylight. Along the southern horizon, it was almost jade—a color Burl had seen only once before, on an airliner flying down to Austin as the sun set.

It was so beautiful, so sorrowful somehow, like a memory of a place seen long ago and forgotten. His eyes filled with tears. This was the world he loved.

"It's all gonna end, ain't it?" John said. "The world's going into the Big Hole."

Lightning flickered to the west, where falling rain hid everything from sight.

"Yeah," Burl said. "They're going to keep right on making bombs, keep right on poisoning the atmosphere. They're in love with power, and they think they can get away with it forever, but they can't. They're going to destroy it."

"Unless the flying saucer people step in and stop them."

"They're just here to watch the end," Burl said. "And it's almost here."

John stared at the oncoming storm. "Looks like this might be it right now."

"Let it happen," Burl said, his heart suddenly filled with joy. "I've known it was coming ever since I was a kid. I'm ready for it." He faced the rising wind, feeling his scalp prickle. "I was born to see the end of the world."

▼ ▼ ▼

Now a whole line of storms was moving down on them. But the last one, the southernmost one and the most powerful, would be the one to pass over them. It drew closer, and rain began falling. To the south, he could see the long yellow line of a rainfree base. Ahead, blackness swallowed everything.

Another bolt of lightning flowed across the anvil, licking the whole underside in a second, like a great flame. The thunder sounded like a steel ball rolling down an endless iron pipe. The wind started blowing hard, into the storm. There was sand in Burl's eyes.

"Best get to the car," he said.

They ran downhill to the Mustang. When they got in, he felt safe, ready to go. This was going to be a great storm. He could feel it. There were more moments of lightning, shocks of thunder. The rain shaft came closer, hiding ridge after ridge, a thick gust front rolling above it. He turned on the scanner, caught a fragment of Spotters talking on the Crowell net.

That one coming up in the west looks like a real booger.

Roger, I just talked to the Altus Doppler. They say it's so high, it's right off the scope.

Through a break in the rain he saw the whole side of the storm tower above them smoothed out, wrapped in laminar shells. "Look at that sucker rotate," he said. It was getting smaller, turning into one of those *little hot ones,* like the storm they had seen at the Holy City.

"Let's get on the road, in case we have to move," John said.

Burl started backing out of the draw. The clay had turned slippery, and the Mustang broke loose, slid sideways down the slope. John was yelling at him. The front end went into a gully, and he heard rocks scraping the bottom. He put the gas pedal to the floor, heard the wheels spin. They were bottomed out.

For the third time in three days, he had put himself in death's way. Here it was again, coming at him, and this time it was all his fault. But he was still laughing.

"Look at that," John said.

The storm was right on the ground, and had more *black energy* than any he had ever seen. The gust front rolled over them. Under the base, he could see a huge lowering with a curtain cloud going into it. It boiled like a lava lamp, great gobs of cloud going up and down.

A bolt of lightning hit the next ridge. He heard what sounded like the rattle of sash weights, an enormous window being thrown up. Blue balls rolled across the ground.

John took a big drink from the bottle of Herradura. "This is no place for us," he said.

"The storm cellar," Burl shouted.

They ran up the hill, their coats pulled over their heads. For a terrifying moment, he couldn't find it. Then John pointed it out. The old door broke like piecrust as he pulled it open. They fell into it, crawled as far back into the darkness as they could. The rain had stopped, but big hailstones were falling now, thudding into the mud.

John handed him the bottle, and he took a burning drink. "This is great," Burl said. "We've got ringside seats."

He crawled back to the mouth of the cellar, trying to keep under what was left of the door, and peered up. They were under the base. The air was black, the ground covered with glowing hailstones. The wind was really blowing now. On the next ridge, he saw vortices, little spindles of dust leap up, appearing and disappearing. The funnel built down. He closed his eyes, he couldn't look. It was as big as the big one, turning slowly, heading right at them.

How fortunate I am, he thought.

John was kicking him. "Get under cover," he shouted. Careless of the hailstones, Burl stood up. He never heard it. Just the wind blowing harder and harder until it was like a jet engine. A hailstone hit the ground in front of him. It was as big as a softball. The door flew off, the light was dying. He fell back and buried his face in the clay alongside John. It smelled like a grave.

Then all was silence, except for a thudding sound, the beating of his heart. Each time, he felt his forehead swell, as if his head were going to burst. He opened his eyes. Blue light fell on everything. He looked through the door and saw something outside that hadn't been there before. A brown curtain, just above the cedars, rippling smoothly up and down. With a shock he realized it was the rim of the funnel, shooting past at incredible speed, and they were inside of it. He looked up.

He looked up and up, into something huge and complicated and blue. Some kind of blue machinery in motion. The bottom of the funnel was smooth and brown as a ceramic pipe. Higher up, it was threaded, and looked like steel. There were rings atop rings, stacking up higher and higher, turning so fast they looked smooth. The light came from higher up. At the very top, there was a pointed cloud of blue light, like the pale blue flame at the heart of a gas flame. Lightning was playing up and down the walls, copper blue and green. The cloud jumped up and down with each flash. With the brightest one, it jumped down and touched him. He saw the flash behind his eyes, felt electricity on his tongue.

Then the topmost ring moved, slid over. The one below moved to stay underneath it. It was beautifully smooth and coherent. This ripple moved down the funnel until it reached the bottommost ring, the one surrounding him. Then it moved over, sending stones flying into the cellar. For a moment there was darkness, then daylight burst in, blinding him. They climbed out of the cellar and found themselves in another country. The car was gone and the cedars broken off. They walked around the hilltop, trying to talk to each other, but it was another twenty minutes before they could hear a thing.

5

In June, the National Transportation Safety Board held a hearing on the wreck. Burl made a written statement that the cause, as far as he was concerned, was a broken rail. Royce said the same thing. For a while he thought he was going to have to go to Fort Worth to testify, but he heard nothing more about it.

The accident had made the national news. There was mention of John, but nothing about the reactor. Burl watched all the follow-ups, but they never said anything about radioactive materials on the train. Still, he was sure he'd seen what he'd seen.

Charlotte wanted to know about John, and Burl told her all he knew. He had seen him get on the bus in Amarillo, but he wasn't sure where he had gone. In July, he got several phone calls from people who claimed they were friends of John, asking if he had any idea where he was. Burl told them he didn't. For a long time, he was sure his phone was tapped.

By then, he'd gone to the Texas Employment Commission and found another job. There were only a few openings for people who didn't have a college degree. He didn't want to be a food handler—they told him he'd have to cut his hair—so he settled for working on the loading dock at Atlas Industries, where they processed soybean paste, a useful ingredient in fast food.

In August, Prairie Savings & Loan failed without any warning. His mother lost three thousand dollars. Coy lost everything, including his job, and was worried about facing criminal charges when the bank examiners came. Buddy McAlester promised the depositors he would pay them all back somehow, if they would just not sue him.

At first, Bebe called Burl collect every Friday night. She'd moved in with her friend, a girl she had known in Oklahoma City, and was looking for work. She didn't like Houston: it was too hot, too big, and the people were unfriendly. But in another month, she got a job working as a secretary for the Department of Sanitation. She put Pearl in day care, and enrolled Jason in school. She stopped calling so often, and Burl began to feel somehow that she had a boyfriend.

One night she called at ten o'clock. "How are you doing?" he asked her.

"I'm fine," she said.

"How's Jason?"

"He still reads that book you gave him," she said. "The one about wild animals. And he's getting into baseball. I've got a friend who takes us to the Astros games sometimes."

"A boyfriend?"

"Not exactly," she said.

He was a real good guy, she told Burl, her boss at the Sanitation Department. They'd met when she and her girlfriend went to this Cajun place one night and drank a lot of beer. Then he'd showed up, just like he'd known she was going to be there. He told them they were too drunk to drive home, and when they said they weren't, he dropped a quarter into the breath-testing machines they had in the bars down there. Sure enough, she was legally intoxicated. "So he drove us home," she said. "He's a good friend, and I've been seeing him sometimes."

"I don't mind," Burl said after a while.

"I still love you, baby," she said. "If you were to come down here, it'd be just the same as it was before. I dream about you every night. You are coming down sometime, aren't you?"

"Before school starts."

"There's one more thing."

"What's that?"

"Pearl won't go to sleep, and I've got to get up early tomorrow, and I'm about to go out of my mind. She wants you to sing her that song about the Babes in the Woods."

So she put Pearl on, and he sang into the phone:

Now when it was night, so sad was their plight.
The sun it went down, the moon gave no light.
They sobbed and they sighed, and they bitterly cried.
And the poor little things, they lay down and died

He heard Bebe ask Pearl if she thought she could sleep now. Pearl said she could. "Thanks," Bebe told him.

"Tell her I love her too. And Jason."

"I will."

But somehow he never got it together to go down to Houston. In August, he drove to Lubbock to go to school.

▼ ▼ ▼

He looked around all one day for an apartment. The cheapest thing he could find was an old Airstream trailer in a vacant lot that looked like a big silver vitamin pill and rented for sixty a month. There was a used-car lot next door, and a titty bar across the highway. It reminded him of living at the Sands Motel. Later, he found out it was a part of town that had been hit by a big tornado back in the early sixties. He told himself he'd only stay there until he found something else, but he discovered he liked it, even though he had to drive five miles to school every day.

He didn't care for the other students that much. A lot of the meteorology majors were from the East. They'd come here because they couldn't get into the University of Illinois, which was another big meteorology school. He got to know a guy named Bruce, from upstate New York, and they studied together sometimes. Bruce told Burl he wanted to work for the Storms Lab, but if he couldn't do that, he'd be happy to work for The Weather Channel. He practiced giving forecasts in front of the mirror that were both entertaining and informative.

School was easier when you were older. He'd been afraid of the math, but he found the hardest subjects had a way of turning into the most interesting, if you just stuck with them. His favorite professor was Mr. Grimes, who'd grown up in Binger, Oklahoma, and made no attempt to clean up his act. He still talked like a redneck fishing from a bridge and looking up at the clouds. The other faculty thought he was a little low-rent, but he knew more about tornadoes than the rest of them put together. Burl wrote a paper on the dryline he liked, and Mr. Grimes asked him over for dinner.

It turned out Mr. Grimes was an old friend of Webster's, the one he'd written the recommendation letter to. They talked for a long time about what an interesting person Webster was. "I'm not sure if Dale Webster is a meteorologist or a prophet," Mr. Grimes said, "but the goal of both fields has always been the same: giving a correct forecast."

Burl told no one about seeing the rings, not even Mr. Grimes. Nobody would have believed him anyway. It was his secret. Sometimes he smiled when they showed tornado films in class, thinking no one had been as close as he had.

In November, his mother sent him a clipping from the Nortex paper saying Jimbo Naylor had shot himself. Friends blamed his money problems and recent divorce. His ex-wife had moved to San Diego and could not be reached for comment. At Christmas, everybody went home and it snowed. Burl thought he would go, too, but he stayed in the library for two days writing a paper on the structure of the tornado funnel.

When the library closed, he drove to Nortex. Coy had been unable to meet his mortgage and had lost his house, so they had moved in with Burl's mother. It was a good thing, in some ways. Their mother needed someone to take care of her, and now she wouldn't have to go to a rest home. On Christmas Eve, they all went to see the Festival of Lights.

Coy was still a little angry at Buddy. The day before the Prairie Savings & Loan went belly-up, he had taken all his money out but had not said a word to Coy, who was still waiting for the government to decide if they were going to prosecute him or not. "I still think he's basically a good man, but he sort of hung me out to dry," Coy said. "I guess you could call it a short adventure in being a high roller, and a good lesson in human nature." Coy had gone back to what he said he did best: selling used cars.

That semester, Burl made the dean's list. Mr. Grimes liked his paper on the structure of the tornado funnel and said if he kept doing good work, he would be able to get him financial aid for next year.

▼ ▼ ▼

In February, Burl's mother forwarded him a letter from John, on three sheets of ruled yellow paper. His handwriting was studied, careful. It looked as if it had been written with a quill pen.

Well, I finally got my log cabin. I can't tell you exactly where, but it's up near Stowe. My sister found it, she lives down the road with her husband, who's a worthless son of a bitch. It's just a little cabin with a gas heater and a cat for company. It was her cat until her husband made her get rid of it but I don't mind. I also got an alias which I can't tell you, even another driver's license. You can get anything in this country (except friendship) if you just talk to the right people.

Jesus it's cold here. Snowed 8 inches last night. You'd laugh if you could see me dolled up like an Eskimo or a Yukon explorer. You spit and it freezes, just like in *To Build a Fire* by Jack London. I'm reading all his books and the poems of Robert Service.

Her husband calls himself a liberal but he hasn't got the true spirit. When I go over he refuses to talk to me. He's too busy making money. Went down to the Big Apple last month and saw it for myself. Not sure I'd want to live there. Got lost in someplace called The Port Authority. You can't get a tattoo in Times Square. A disappointment.

My man Jesse's still looking good to me for the next election, but of course I can't vote. Might do some campaigning though.

There's a bunch of us old ones up here. Seems like this is where we fetched up. They talk about Woodstock and I tell them about shaking hands with Bob Dylan and going to 'Nam. There's one guy who was in the Central Highlands. He and I get along pretty good. I made nunc mam sauce for him one night, that's gook chow. It's made from rotten fish but you develop a taste for it. Every morning I drive 60 miles to work at Ben & Jerry's. That's an ice cream factory run by old hippies like me. Right now I'm pushing a broom. They do make the best ice cream on this coast. Important to feel like you make a good product.

Joined a computer dating service and got hooked up with this woman. She's ugly, like I said she'd be, but she's got a spiritual side too. She's gotten me to stop smoking (cigarettes) and even gotten me interested in astrology, which I always thought was bullshit. She can't compare with Charlotte, though. I lost a good thing there.

To tell the truth, amigo, I'm having a hard time. All those years of road freight destroyed my initiative. Remember what you said about change? Well I can't. Too easy to sit and stare at the wall, and there's always the thought of the cops on my ass. You never did hear any more about that, did you?

The whole country's in the same boat. The conservatives keep on trying to stamp out pot and abortion, and the liberals keep trying to protect us from cigarettes. And not a word about what's really going on. But if you don't change, things will catch up with you sooner or later. The trees on the mountaintops around here are all dead from acid rain.

When it snows, I sit and watch these woods fill up. They won't catch me if I can help it. I intend to be Lobo, the King of the Currumpaw, and live by my instinct and cunning. You may hear from me again. The woods of this country are full of old lobos like myself, and someday we may come back to play our part. In the meantime, I hope you're doing good things.

JOHN

For weeks after that, Burl had a dream in which he saw John walking through the black snowy woods, his footsteps making no sound.

In April, there were thunderstorms. Bebe sent him a Polaroid of her and Jason and Pearl at Astro World. One day when there was a tornado watch, the salesman at the used-car lot next door asked him if he wasn't nervous, living in a trailer. Tornadoes seemed to go right for them. Burl laughed and agreed. That night, the front moved through, and the aluminum walls of the trailer throbbed as the wind picked up to forty or fifty knots. White pills of hail shot through the streetlight. Burl stood naked in the doorway, staring at distant lightning. He was alone, and the future was unclear, but he felt happy. It might not be a log cabin, but it was as close to being the right place for him as any place could be.